Zen Face

Anthony Ginn

Talke Pits Development Company 2022

*Ease practice based
on intellectual understanding,
pursuing words and
following after speech.
Learn the backward
step that turns
your light inward
to illuminate within.
Body and mind of themselves
will drop away
and your original face will be manifest.*

Dogen

You cannot describe it or draw it.
You cannot praise it enough or perceive it.
No place can be found in which
to put the original face;
it will not disappear even
when the universe is destroyed.

Mumon

Tengus

IN 1810 a naked man found lying in the street in Asakusa, Japan, claimed he'd been dropped from the sky by a Tengu, who had abducted him two days previously when he was on a pilgrimage. A Tengu is a demon who can fly. The story was widely reported at the time and is still doing the rounds. You can read it on the internet. But I doubt if his wife believed it.

We like to think that as modern humans, we are free of superstition and no longer believe in demons and evil spirits like the Tengu. But this is not true. Humans all over the world fill their lives and the minds of their children with illogical beliefs and mythology. Nowhere is this more apparent than in our religions. How many modern Christians, for example, belief in the existence of Satan? Pick any religion and you'll find devils, demons and evil spirits hiding under the altar cloth. Our beliefs are infested with djins, gremlins and devils. And there's a demon that's found its way into this story too. It takes place in Japan, and contains a Tengu.

Tengu were originally bird-like, with wings and beaks, but over the centuries, like many demons, they evolved into creatures resembling people. Modern Tengu have long noses rather than beaks, and although they've lost their wings, they can still fly. There are two types of Tengu. Some have red faces and some black. Friendly Tengu are red, the more malicious are black. The black-faced Tengu, called KoTengu, amuse themselves by starting fires in temples, tying priests to trees, kidnapping children and, if they are feeling particularly malevolent, eating them. Some Tengu are particularly cunning, and switch their colour from black to red and back again.

Let's get on with the story. It's about a boy called Yosu who grew up to become a monk and an artist. He lived over two hundred years ago and lived in a small village in the countryside outside the

1

town of Nara, not far from Osaka. When our story begins, Yosu was eight years old. In those days there was no children's literature and no TV or cinema, no PlayStations and no computers. The most exciting pastime was listening to stories. This has entertained children and their parents for thousands of years. The appearance of a travelling storyteller in the village was a big occasion. From time to time, a storyteller appeared in the village and all activities stopped. When the travelling storyteller entered Yosu's village, all activity ceased. By the time he put his worn carpet down in the centre of the village, an audience was already sitting, waiting patiently for him to begin spinning his yarn. On this occasion his story was enhanced with a glove puppet.

Yosu, along with the rest of the children, sat in avid anticipation around the storyteller's mat. Most of them would remember the story for the rest of their lives and one day tell it to their own children.

"Are you sitting comfortably?"

Fifteen children enthusiastically replied in unison, like chicks in a nest, "Yes."

"Then I'll begin."

The adults behind them remained silent. They were all smiling because everybody enjoys a good story, as I hope you do too.

The storyteller took a deep breath.

"My story is about a little girl called Eshun. She lived in a village very much like this one. She was kind and happy, as most kind people are. But there was something different about her. She lived in a world where there were no colours. You and I can see that the sky is blue, and the leaves are green. Apples are red and rice is white. But Eshun had never seen any of these colours. She had never seen her mothers' eyes or her fathers' smile, the sun or the moon. She was blind. When she walked, she swung a stick before her so she wouldn't bump into anything.

The storytellers' left hand was covered with a small, well-worn silk cloth. "Now, I suppose you've all heard about the Tengu?" He whipped the cloth from his hand to reveal a small, black-faced Tengu sitting beneath the cloth.

The children shuddered. One or two gave out a small cry. A couple of the adults moaned in mock fear.

"Yes, when the Tengu is around, you must be on your best behaviour. Who knows what he might do to you if he catches you being naughty? So if you see one, hide away if you can. And if you can't hide, sit still and stay very quiet.

"Now, we all know that the Tengu is usually black. But sometimes he can be red." The storyteller waved the cloth over the puppet on his hand. When he removed it, the Tengu's face had changed from black to red.

"The red Tengu is a much nicer demon than the black one. Sometimes he even helps you if you're in trouble. If you fall in the lake, he might pull you out. Or if you fall out of a tree, he might catch you. If you get lost in the forest, maybe he'll show you the way home. You never know.

"Now there's another Tengu that not many people know about. It's a very clever demon, it can change colour from black to red, and then change back again."

The red puppet was cloaked in the cloth for a moment and reappeared black. It was covered again and emerged red. "Is it red or black? Nobody really knows. It depends what the Tengu feels like.

"Well, one day a black-faced Tengu was flying over Eshun's village, up to his usual mischief, looking for somebody to kidnap, tie to a tree or throw into the river, when it started to rain. The Tengu became angry. He was getting wet and the people he wanted to play tricks on were running indoors to take shelter, so he couldn't see anyone to swoop down on and capture.

"He called out to Raijin, the Thunder God, Raijin. What do you think you're doing? You big thundering fool. You've scared all the people away. And I'm soaking wet. You're the stupidest God in the Heavens. If you were here now, I'd take one of your stupid hammers and bang you on your stupid head."

"Well, the Tengu was a bit stupid himself. He didn't know that Raijin was standing on a cloud just above him, with his gigantic hammers and massive drums he used to make thunder. He had heard every word the Tengu said, and he wasn't at all pleased. He hammered

3

his drums and the thunder was the loudest you ever heard. The people below hid under their tables, in their cupboards, under their beds and in any hole or hiding place they could find. Raijin hopped on the clouds over to the Tengu. "The stupidest God in the Heavens am I? You'd bang me on my stupid head would you? The God of Thunder raised his hammer and banged the Tengu on his head. The Tengu was immediately knocked out. Raijin picked him up and dropped him into a sack. He looked over the edge of the cloud and threw the bag down to earth. The sack flew through the air and landed on the road, just outside a small village. The Tengu lay there inside the sack, unconscious as the rain fell on him.

"When Raijin, the Thunder God put the Tengu in a bag and threw him down to earth, Eshun was on her way to visit her grandmother. Her grandmother wasn't very well. She had fallen over in her garden, bruised her arm and bumped her head. Eshun was taking a basket of herbs called arnica that were good for bruises and headaches. When Eshun stepped outside her garden to walk to her grandmother's house, she heard a crash so loud she jumped with fright. The next minute the clouds opened and the rain began to pour down. Raijin continued to hammer his drums, frightening everyone down below. Eshun hurried back into her cottage so she wouldn't get wet."

The storyteller lay the Tengu puppet down on his knee, covered it with the silk cloth and moaned and groaned. The bag was tied tight. "The Tengu was hungry and thirsty and he couldn't escape. All he could do was wail and whine.

"Up in the clouds Raijin decided it was time for a cup of tea and a biscuit. He gathered his drums and floated up from his cloud to his house in the heavens and put the kettle on. The rain stopped and the sun came out again.

"Eshun heard the rain stop, so she picked up her basket of herbs and her stick and set off again down the road to her grandmothers'.

"As she walked, she heard a strange sound ahead. It sounded like someone who had been hurt. Somebody was moaning, Let me out. Let me out. Oh my head hurts. And my arm, and my shoulder, and my hand, and my leg, and my big toe, and my other toes, and especially my head. Oh my head.

4

"The further she walked, the louder the moans became. Then her stick tapped onto the sack. She crouched down and felt it. Something was moving inside.

"Who's that in the sack?"

"It's only me. Just a little birdie. I'm trapped. Could you let me out please?"

"Wait a minute." Eshun found the knot on the sack and untied it. The Tengu stuck his frightening black face out to scare her. ut of course she couldn't see it. Then the Tengu fell onto the floor and began moaning again. "What's the matter?"

"Everything. I was hit on the head with a hammer and thrown out the sky. I landed on everything and everything hurts."

"\Eshun said, "Well it just so happens I've some herbs that I'm taking to my grandmother. They might help you." She took a bunch of arnica from her basket, "Here, rub this on your head. In fact rub it on all your bruises."

"The Tengu was surprised that he hadn't frightened the girl. Then he saw she was blind. He rubbed his head with the arinica. Amazingly it started to get better straight away. So he rubbed it on all his bruises and in no time at all, he had recovered from his beating.

"Then it began to rain again. The raindrops were so big and heavy that the Tengu's black face began to go streaky and the black pigment was washed off by the rain.

"Eshun said, "I'd better get on to my grandmother's house. I'm getting wet."

"Well thank you for getting me out of the sack and thank you for the herbs to make me better. Is there anything I can do for you?"

"Oh, no thank you sir. Just glad to be of help."

"Well, I've got to fly up North to Asakusa. But before I go, maybe I can do something for you." The Tengu pulled a feather from the end of his wing. "Close your eyes."

Eshun closed her eyes. The red-faced Tengu gently stroked his feather across each of her eyelids. Her eyes began to itch. "Well, thank you for your help Eshun. I've got to fly to Asakusa now. There's a man up there on a pilgrimage waiting for me. It's his bath time. Say

"Hello," to your grandma, and thank your mother for the herbs. Have a good weekend."

"The Tengu flapped his wings and took off into the sky. Eshun slowly opened her eyes. Something magical had happened. The red-faced Tengu had cured her blindness. She could see. She thought she was dreaming. She sat in the road and didn't move. There were too many beautiful things to look at. She stayed there until a horse and cart came down the road and she had to move out of the way. She didn't reach her Grandmother's house until it was almost dark. She'd been too busy looking at flowers, trees, birds and clouds."

Everybody enjoyed the story. Little did Yosu know that soon his world would be visited by a real demon who would scare him so severely he would wet himself.

It happened a couple of days later. He was playing with his friend Ramon. They were evicting an imp from an old straw sandal, chasing it around the yard, beating it with sticks, shouting, "Go away Bakezori. Go home." Bakezori was the spirit who lived in straw sandals. If you annoyed him he might give you a verruca or break one of your toes out of spite.

Yosu looked over the fence and noticed a stranger walking down the lane towards their house. He was curious. He didn't recognise him. He crept out the yard and hid in the long grass not far from the path. He wanted to get a good look at the stranger without being noticed. He nestled into the grass and waited.

As the stranger approached, Yosu became uncomfortable. There was something amiss. The nearer the stranger was, the less like a human being and the more like a demon he appeared. Yosu became sure he was a Tengu; a demon who was once a black crow, but had gradually changed into a goblin creature, who could eat you if he so wished. The Tengu's face was black and his nose was long, still transforming from a beak. Ramon shrieked, "Tengu. Tengu. Black face Tengu."

The boys pressed their faces onto their arms and burrowed into the grass. Yosu burrowed deeper and squirmed backwards, away from the path. He was frightened. Tengus ate children, their pets, their friends and their parents. He wanted to run away, but knew that the demon

6

would see him. Then it would be all over. He was terrified. He had never been close to a devil before. It was worse than he could have imagined. He buried his face deeper and wished the earth would open and swallow him.

Ramon screamed and ran for home faster than a donkey with its tail on fire.

Things became worse. Yosu sweated and trembled and made quiet whimpering noises. He tried to raise his head to look at the Tengu, but he was frozen with fear. His body had quit, and wouldn't move a fraction.

Then the demon spoke to him. "Yosu. Is that you?" Yosu gave an involuntary yelp and emptied his bladder. The demon knew his name. There was no escape. He squeezed his eyes tight shut. His sweat had gone cold. He had stopped trembling, but he still couldn't move. The black-faced goblin would soon eat him. He forced his breath in and out and waited. Nothing happened. He could move again. He raised his head slowly and squinted through the grass. The demon was gone. He was probably hiding somewhere, waiting to bite his limbs off. He pushed his face down into the grass again, and waited for his life to end. He tried to remember what he'd done that caused the demon to come for him. Whatever it was it must have been terrible. And whatever it was, he was truly sorry.

Then a spark of light entered his dark, hopeless world. He heard his father's voice, "Yosu. Where are you?" He had come to rescue him. He raised his head up from the grass and let out an involuntary bleat. His father noticed him, picked him up and put him over his shoulder. "What's the matter Yosu? What are you frightened of? What's the matter? What happened?"

Yosu sniffled and blew a bubble of snot from his nose. His jaw trembled, he spluttered, and glanced towards the doorway. "The black Tengu."

His father carried him into their house, "Yosu. Come in and meet someone."

The stranger turned to look at the small boy peering over his father's shoulder. Yosu shrieked and froze. It was the demon who had recently crawled out of hell. His face was completely black. He raised a

7

hand to calm the terrified toddler. The demon's hand was black too. Yosu shrieked again, He was sure the black demon was there to bundle him off to Hell, and he didn't want to go. He was trembling and sniffling, muttering, "Tengu. The black Tengu has come."

His father laughed. "Yosu. That's not a demon. It's your Uncle Toshio. That's ink on his face. Uncle Toshio. My little brother. He makes ink. That's why his face is black. How could your uncle be a demon?"

His father lowered him to the floor. Yosu was puzzled. Uncle Toshio came forward to pick him up, but he scurried behind his father.

Yosu eventually realized there was a human behind the black face. In fact it was his uncle. By the time Toshio was ready to leave a few days later, Yosu didn't want him to go. He'd become used to his black face and loved the gentle attention he gave him.

Painting

Toshio unrolled a woven bamboo mat. He brought a cup of water from the rain barrel outside, placed it on the mat and beckoned to Yosu to sit with him. He placed his cloth bag on the mat, and looked at Yosu like a magician about to perform some magic. By now Yosu was spellbound. Toshio removed a small black brick from his bag. He showed it to Yosu, then gave it to him to hold and examine. Yosu turned it around in his hands. There was some writing engraved on one side.

Toshio explained, "That's a sumi. It's an ink stick for painting pictures." He put his hand into his bag again and removed an oblong black stone, about as long as his hand. There was an oblong hollow on one side. The floor of the dent sloped gradually toward a shallow well at one end. Toshio handed the stone to Yosu and let him examine it.

"That's an ink-stone. It's where you make the ink for your pictures. I'll show you. First a little water. Just enough for a frog to wash his face." He dropped a couple of pearls of water onto the ink-stone from the cup. "Then you take the sumi and get to work." Toshio slowly slid the sumi down the slope towards the well at the bottom. He reversed the direction just before it went over the edge. Gently moving the ink stick backwards and forwards, he intoned in time, "Wave comes up the beach. Wave goes back to the sea. Wave comes up the beach. Wave goes back to the sea." Yosu smiled. He was enjoying this game. Toshio handed the sumi and ink-stone to Yosu. "Here. You try." He held his hand and guided him through the first couple of waves. "Wave comes up the beach. Wave goes back to the sea."

He added a couple more drops of water. Yosu continued pushing the ink-stone back and forth, muttering, "Wave comes up the beach." A small pool of black ink began to form in the well at the end of the stone. Yosu was absorbed in the new game. "Wave comes up the beach. Wave goes back to the sea."

Toshio added more drops of water, and the well began to fill with shining black ink. He dipped his finger in the ink, and touched the tip of Yosu's nose. "Now you are a kawauso."

A kawauso is a magical otter spirit who lives in the river.

"Now let's see what your ink can do."

Toshio reached into his bag again and produced a brush. The handle was bamboo, and the brush, inserted at one end, was white goat's hair, shaped like a candle flame.

He pointed at the tip. "This part of the brush draws the picture." He touched the centre of the brush, "This is where the ink lives." He touched the top of the brush, where it entered the bamboo handle. "And here is where the brush does all the work, delivering the ink to the picture. You don't have to do anything. The brush already knows where to go."

Toshio reached into his bag again, and withdrew a small roll of white rice paper. "Let the magic begin."

He unrolled the paper onto the mat, put a piece of wood on each end, to hold it flat and smoothed it with his palms. "Because this is your first lesson, we will use good paper. But when you paint again, you must paint on old rice paper. All the masters practice with paper that has been used to wrap food, or parcels. Sometimes they use paper with something already printed on it. Even an old newspaper if ever you find one. The ink can't tell the difference, and the best paper is reserved for their best work. Now, the first thing to learn is how to hold the brush. And before you hold the brush, you have to learn to breath. Like this." Toshio closed his eyes and slowly took a deep breath. He held it in for a couple of seconds, then let it out slowly. He breathed in again, "Wave comes up the beach." He slowly released the air. "Wave goes back to the sea. You try. Close your eyes. Breathe in slowly. Wave comes up the beach. And, let it out. Wave goes back to the sea. Very good Yosu. I can hear the waves. Are you ready to hold the brush?"

Yosu nodded.

"Have you ever seen a flag flying at the top of a flagpole?" Yosu nodded. Toshio held the brush vertically, then slanted it in different directions and angles. "Like this? Like this? Like this?" Yosu

10

shook his head at each suggestion. "Show me." Yosu took the brush and held it vertically.

"Perfect. That's how you hold the brush when you're painting a picture. And if you hold it like this," he said bending it at an angle, "or like this, do you know what will happen?" Yosu shook his head. "The sky will fall down, your picture will fall in the river and a hungry kawauso will gobble it up for breakfast. So always hold the brush like a flagpole. Straight up to the sky. Now all we need is the ink and we'll be ready to paint a picture."

Yosu was so excited, anticipating what was about to happen, that he almost forgot to breathe. Toshio gently adjusted Yosu's hand so his fingers were further up the flagpole and the thumb at the back. He moved the hand over the ink-well at the end of the ink-stone, lowered the brush into the ink then lifted it out. He pointed at the paper. "Now you can make your picture." Yosu was confused for a moment. "Remember your breathing. 'Wave comes up the beach', and when the wave goes back to the sea, then you move the brush on the paper and let it paint your picture. It's alright. You can open your eyes. Move the brush when the wave goes back to the sea."

Yosu's hand trembled as he held the brush. Wave goes back to the sea. The brush moved slowly over the white paper. Yosu watched in awe. The brush was moving by itself, leaving a shining black line so he would know exactly where it had been. As the brush neared the edge of the paper, it turned around and went back the way it came. Yosu was filled with pleasure and wonder, watching it. It moved to the top of the shape it had created and took off for the upper edge of the paper, like the shoot of a plant scrambling up towards the light.

Yosu leaned back and looked at the picture. He recognised it. The brush had sucked up the ink and painted a turnip. He was overwhelmed. The brush had done it on its own. It had created a picture before his eyes. He took a deep breath and the wave went back to the sea. He would treasure the turnip for the rest of his life. It was the first picture he ever painted. Wherever he lived, the turnip would sit on the wall to remind him of the day he discovered Zen. Although at that time he'd never heard the word, he had watched the brush paint the turnip, and that was enough.

11

After a few days Uncle Toshio departed for home. Before he left, he gave Yosu the brush, ink-stone and ink-stick, and ripped a couple of old paper bags into squares, so could practise painting whenever he felt like it. Then he took his black face back to his black house and his black workshop in the village of Kobaien, outside Osaka. He went into his black kitchen and with his black hands made some green tea in his black teapot.

Ink

When Yosu was five years old, growing up in a rural village south of Edo, his world was filled with magic, demons, gods and mystical creatures. They inhabited the stories his parents told, the games the children in the village, played and the paintings on the walls of the temple. And as the children were often reminded, they lived in the dark forest at the end of the village.

After Uncle Toshio's visit, Yosu continued painting with his new ink-stick and ink-stone, but it was never as spectacular as the first time when he'd watched the turnip appear. He'd run out of scraps of paper and didn't have his uncle there to guide him. It wasn't long before he stopped painting altogether. The season had changed and the magic had gone back into hibernation.

It was several years before Yosu saw Uncle Toshio again. The next time he appeared, Yosu was thirteen, and was one of the "big boys" of the village. This was the age when boys began to turn into men and earn their keep. Some stayed at home and became farmers. Some left the village to learn a trade with a mentor in another town. Some went to a monastery and trained to become monks. Yosu's first steps into the big wide world were destined to be along the way of the dirty face.

Uncle Toshio had come to see Yosu's family because he needed an apprentice ink- maker, and he wanted to see if Yosu was willing and able to move to Kobaien, enter a black hole and learn the art of making ink. Making sumi ink was an ancient, skilled art and there was a lot to learn. Yosu would live with his uncle and learn a trade and an art. It was an opportunity that seldom walked through your door more than once.

After discussing the business with Yosu's parents, Toshio called him into the discussion and offered him the opportunity to learn the skills of an ink-maker. There was a lot to learn and his apprenticeship would take three or four years, depending on how hard he worked and how capable he was.

Yosu looked at his parents. They said nothing, but both hoped he would accept the offer from his uncle.

He felt a butterfly in his stomach and knew this was one of those moments in life where his decision would determine the rest of his life. He remembered when Toshio had shown him how to paint.

"Wave comes up the beach. Wave goes back to the sea."

Wave flows through the village up to the door.

Wave leaves the village and goes back through the fields and the sunshine to the dark studio in Kobaien.

The Tengu had opened the door and invited Yosu to come and see what was happening in the big wide world. He stood on the edge of the nest and stretched his wings. It was time to fly. Yosu looked into the black crow face of the demon and said, "Yes Uncle. Thank you for asking me. I'll be glad to come and learn. I still have the turnip we made."

"There'll be plenty of time to grow more vegetables when we get to Kobaien. I've enough ink to fill Japan with carrots, turnips and rutabagas."

Toshio did indeed have plenty of ink. As well as having it all over his face, hands and feet, his clothes were black, his furniture was ebony, the walls were negroid, the floor was pitch dark and the ceiling was sooty. You could say he lived in a black hole, a fitting abode for a demon with the face of a black crow and the hands of a blackamoor.

Yosu threw himself into his new life. Much to Toshio's pleasure, he was eager to learn and his uncle enjoyed teaching him.

Toshio didn't only teach Yosu how to make ink. He was a keen Go player. He taught Yosu to play the ancient board game so he would have a partner. Playing Yosu would allow Toshio some practice time before Ryokan's next visit. The monk Ryokan was Toshio's arch-rival on the Go board. Maybe he'd surprise the old monk and beat him for once.

14

Go is sometimes called Japanese or Chinese chess, although the only resemblance to chess is that it's played on a board with black and white pieces called stones. The black stones are made from black slate and the white stones from clamshells. The board is a grid of nineteen lines by nineteen, and the pieces, or stones, are plain. Once played, the stones don't move unless they are surrounded and taken. The aim is to surround territory. At the end of the game the player with the most territory, minus the captured stones, is the winner.

In Japanese, the word for 'four' (*shi*) sounds very much like the word for "death". This means four is the most unlucky number in the world. Thirteen, eat your heart out.

All cultures have superstitions associated with death. In China it is taboo to stand your chopsticks upright in your bowl of rice, because this resembles sticks of incense burning on a grave. When I was growing up, if you saw a hearse, you had to hold your collar until you saw a four-legged animal. Seeing the animal would break the spell and disperse the bad luck caused by seeing the hearse. Once this was done you could let go of your collar.

"Are you superstitious, Yosu?" asked his uncle

"No, Uncle. Not at all."

"Good. Then I'll tell you about the four treasures that came to Japan from China with the Zen monks hundreds of years ago.

"Many wonderful things came from China: tofu, tea, paper, silk, soya beans, fireworks, pottery, and two of my personal favourites, rice and soy-sauce. But the four treasures the monks brought us are: the brush, paper, the inkstone and sumi-ink. That is good luck for us who make the ink, the artists who use it and the folk who love Art and calligraphy, which is just about everyone. Art allows us to find ourselves and lose ourselves at the same time. We are very fortunate to have this force in our lives Yosu. If we hold on to Art firmly, it will guide us through life and, nothing will really harm us. If we take a step backwards, we can turn even out worst moments into Art. "

And so began Yosu's life in the black house of Sumi.

The secret is soot. To make ink you first have to collect the soot. Two kinds of soot were used to make sumi ink: soot from lamp oil and soot from pine wood. The soot was collected and then mixed with *nikawa*, the glue that binds the soot. A shelf held several bottles and jars of oils, such as sesame oil, rapeseed oil and soya oil, that could be burned as alternatives to lamp oil. Toshio had several small vessels for burning various oils and pine, to produce black gunk. The ovens were sealed to capture as much smoke as possible without allowing the contents to stop burning.

Nikawa is made by boiling down bone and skin from fish and animals. Sometimes perfume, spice, such as ginger, or other aromatic plant extracts are added. Every year, Yosu went out with his uncle, to collect sunflowers, daisies, sand ginger, sambong and mugwort to include in his homemade *nikawa*.

Yosu loved the smell of camphor in the studio, when they were cooking up a fresh batch of *nikawa*.

Once they harvested the soot, it was mixed with the glue. This is done by hand and is similar to kneading dough to make bread.

Yosu's first jobs were gathering the pine wood and oil needed to make the soot. He learned which parts of the wood made the best soot when burned. The soot needed to be smooth and consistent. The pine should be neither too young nor too old. Yosu learned how to extract the most suitable sections of the timber and prepare them for incineration.

There was always something to learn, and no sooner had Yosu mastered one technique, than there was something new to discover.

One morning Yosu was collecting soot. He prepared several ceramic vessels with oil he'd distilled from the sambong flowers. He poured oil into each pot, added a wick with a ceramic weight, to prevent the wick from tipping over in the oil. He then ignited the wick and placed a lid on the pot. The lid would accumulate soot from the flame, and when the oil was gone, he would scrape the soot for the next batch of oil.

The lamps filled the studio with the rich menthol aroma of camphor. Yosu breathed deep.

From a Buddhist Perspective

Many years later, after Yosu had finished his apprenticeship he never forgot how he had watched the brush paint the turnip when his uncle had first visited, and given him first painting lesson. That magical experience had beguiled him and lured him into a monastery.

However, the life of a renunciate wasn't always as easily as he'd hoped. Not for the first time, he was having second thoughts about his new career. Early one morning he stumbled and plodded along the path towards the river. The wet stones peeping up from the mud were slippery, waiting to tip him onto his bottom when he slipped. His toes were sore, as if something had been chewing them when he wasn't looking. They were numb and tingling, as if they'd been stung by nettles. He was wondering if a life of renunciation really was for him.

It was too early in the morning and too cold. Life in the monastery was shit. He didn't like it. When he'd decided to take his life by the throat and commit to a spiritual existence the scriptures had promised a breath-essence would rise to the top of his head and shower him with light. The only thing showering this morning was snot from his cold nose, forced out onto his top lip by the headache emanating from the space between the eyes.

The Zen master Sekiso once asked, "How do you proceed from the top of a one-hundred-foot pole?" His advice was "Move on from there and appear with your whole body in the ten parts of the world."

Yosu thought the more obvious solution was to fall off the pole, crash down onto the floor, land on your head and die. His third eye of insight was obviously closed for the day.

He'd been having second thoughts about living in the monastery for some time. After being handed a map of the road to Nirvana, along with the promise of realization and knowledge of his true nature, he'd ended up in a damp bedroom surrounded by miserable ignorant judgmental monks, lousy food and a map showing the way from the monastery down to the freezing cold river, then the route back up the hill to a bowl of watery rice porridge in the dining room.

He was sick of it. Sick of getting up early. Sick of sitting on his arse in the lotus position shivering for hours, trying to concentrate on "nothingness" while falling asleep. Sick of eating rice gruel. Sick of miso soup. Most of all he was sick of Abbot Nami, the head of their monastery. Yosu longed for a piece of fish, a glass of saki and a soft warm bed. He hated the fake humility and phoney wisdom that pervaded the community of monks, like an abbots fart that everyone pretended they couldn't smell. Most of the brothers were in serious competition to demonstrate who was the most spiritual, detached and unworldly. Yosu felt like punching them in the face. Maybe that was what was meant by 'the sound of one hand clapping'.

Abbot Nami slept on a soft mattress (his ailing back), had his own cook and special diet (his delicate stomach). His robes were made of expensive wool, brought from Kyoto (his sensitive skin) not the coarse hemp that made you itch like a dog with fleas. And he was always attended by a pretty young nun.

The trouble with Abbot Nami was that he was a total prick. He was shallow, insincere, greedy, superficial, patronising, lazy, sanctimonious, sycophantic, self-serving and self-righteous. He attracted a group of acolytes with similar qualities, like flies round the arse of a donkey on a hot day. They followed him around whenever they got the chance, eager to ingratiate themselves with him, laughing at his pathetic jokes and exalting the glib Zen wisdom that dribbled from the hole at the bottom of his head in a squeaky voice.

Yosu usually avoided Abbot Nami but sometimes it was impossible. Monks were encouraged to pursue art and crafts. These activities were seen as encouraging Buddhist in their spiritual practices, but to Abbot Nami, more important was the money they brought into the monastery. After all, monks and nuns have to eat.

Many magnificent paintings, known as mandalas, were created to help focus the attention in mediation. Their beautiful, intricate patterns represent the universe and symbolise the idea that life is never ending and everything is connected. Many mandalas are cosmic mazes.

18

You stumble around the monks, fauna, waves, temples floating on clouds, demons burning in Hell and magical creatures cavorting over mountain tops, until you arrive at the centre, where the Buddha has been sitting since breakfast, waiting for you to solve the puzzle.

Many monks and nuns were excellent painters, poets, musicians, carpenters and calligraphers. Art was seen as a tool to help guide followers in their daily practice.

In Gisu monastery there was a secular aspect to Art, and in Yosu's case, calligraphy. Yosu was responsible for a large part of the monastery's income. He had become well-know, and his calligraphy and drawings were in great demand. The abbot was a pragmatist, and didn't want to bite the paintbrush that was feeding him. So he mostly left Yosu to his own devices. As long as there was a regular supply of ink drawings to sell, Yosu was left undisturbed.

Painting and calligraphy were the only things that kept him sane and made life in the monastery bearable. It gave him peace of mind and was the only part of existence that was connected to the reality of Buddhism and the living consciousness of Zen. Sometimes he felt like a fish searching for the sea, or a child trying to peel his shadow from the floor. But on rare occasions he felt life trying to teach him, and demonstrate its magic, just as it had many years ago, when he had watched his brush paint a turnip. On those days the porridge tasted good Abbot Nami and Polo, his ambitious, loyal sycophant, were nothing more than clowns making children laugh. His memory of the moments he had seen clearly and his desire to return to those moments of realization kept him sane. The internal politics of the monastery were a constant irritation. Polo was filled with his own importance, and mistakenly believed he was fast approaching enlightenment. Yosu loathed the sight of him and hated the sound of his sickly, sanctimonious voice. He found it difficult to talk without preaching.

Yosu had his own room inside the monastery, which served both as his studio and bedroom. He began his daily journey down to the river to bathe. In the monastery garden on his left the cherry blossoms were straining, in a hurry to burst into springtime. On the end of a few branches, beautiful pink blossoms were already prising open the green bars keeping them from the spring sunshine. Observing the arrival of the cherry blossom was such a significant event that it had its own word- *hatami*. Around the end of March the trees began to wake up. When the blossom first appeared in the South along with the warm weather, it was greeted with picnics, parties and street festivals. The blossom only lasted one or two weeks. When it disappeared, it was the signal to begin planting rice.

Yosu set out past the cherry trees, down the slope towards the river. Today, however, was not a day for picnics. It was cold, dull and raining.

Jo was a monk who was a bit of a dreamer. He often had his feet in a puddle and his head floating in the clouds. He was standing by a cherry tree, intensely examining the buds. He noticed Yosu making his way towards the river and smiled. "Brother. The *sakura* (cherry blossom) has arrived. *Praise Lord Buddha of the Three Worlds.*"

Yosu was cold and miserable and he knew the river water was going to make him colder still.

He muttered, "You can shove your *sakura* where the sun doesn't shine. I'm cold and want to go back to bed."

"Sorry, brother. I didn't get all that. What did you say about the sunshine?"

"I said, 'Shove the *sakura* where the sun don't shine. ' "

Jo thought Yosu was testing him with a koan, a type of illogical riddle monks were given by a teacher to push their minds away from rational thought towards enlightenment. It had hit him between the eyes and he froze, contemplating the answer to the koan, asking himself, "Where did the blossom go? Where is the place where the sun never shines?"

Yosu continued down to the river. Spring felt like a gigantic stone wheel on a massive cart, turning slowly through the year, crushing anything in its path. It was relentless, rolling on through the centuries, leaving destruction in its wake. A ruthless, invisible tsunami. Yosu thought eventually all life would be crushed beneath its metal rim. He felt small and hopeless, like an ant beneath a descending boot. Even the end of the Earth would not stop the wheel rolling. The future looked grim. He wandered down towards the river. Although the spring sunshine was coaxing the *sakura* out into the world, it had done

20

nothing to the icy river water, which was still cold enough to frighten the chipmunks back down their holes and turn a monks' prayer wheel numb. Yosu arrived at the riverbank.

There were already three monks bathing, up to their knees in the river. One was Polo, a slightly older monk who considered himself wise and almost enlightened. With him were two younger monks, who were attracted by Polo's aura of self-con. They followed him around the monastery like flies behind a buffalo, hoping to glean drops of wisdom from the stench of his pontificating. Polo was preaching about subjectivity. He glanced towards Yosu, and raised his voice slightly as he addressed his two companions. "If the water, along with the rest of the material world, is an illusion, from a Buddhist perspective, does this river only exist in the mind?"

There was nothing Polo loved more than an audience.

The two young monks were mystified. They remained silent. Yosu stared at the water hurrying over the stones holding the river up. It spun and sang as it cavorted around the rocks, changing every moment like the flames around a cooking pot. He leaned forwards. He could hear it giggling sadistically as he lowered his bare foot into the stream. He shuddered with the cold. He removed his robe and slowly lowered himself into the freezing current. He gritted his teeth and washed with unnatural haste. He couldn't wait to get back into the monastery for breakfast. Suddenly thin rice porridge didn't seem so bad. He dried himself and put his robe back on.

Polo was eager to parade his superior class and education. Yosu hadn't even been to school. He turned, eager to flaunt his realization before his dozy acolytes. "Yosu, what does the cartoonist think? Is the river only in the mind? From a Buddhist perspective?"

Yosu turned and stared at Polo for a moment. The three monks held their breath in anticipation of his reply. He squinted at Polo, took a deep breath and spoke, "Polo. Fuck off you idiot." He paused, "From a Buddhist perspective of course."

Polo's face contorted. His ego had been hit below the belt. The acolytes waited for a reply, but none came. Polo coughed nervously to hide his confusion. Yosu climbed the bank and set off back towards the monastery for his long-awaited rice porridge.

Polo composed himself and said, "His understanding is less than that of a beetle, pushing a ball of dung along the monastery floor."

The two young monks forced out a couple of skinny laughs.

"You are wise Polo."

"You see wisdom when others are blind."

"A beetle. Ha ha. Very good".

"Pushing dung. Brilliant."

Polo added, "The dung is Yosu's Zen." He grinned sanctimoniously.

They laughed. They had recovered their wisdom. Polo looked serious for a moment. "He really is straying too far from the path. I must mention this to Abbot Nami at our next meeting."

Yosu walked slowly back to the monastery. He passed the cherry orchard and noticed brother Jo, who had announced the arrival of the blossom, still standing perplexed beneath the emerging sakura, his mind still gnawed by the "koan", wondering where it was that the sun didn't shine.

Yosu nodded to him, smiled and said, "Don't worry about it, Jo," and continued up to the monastery.

Jo said to himself, "Don't worry about it." His face relaxed.

"Don't worry about it. Yes. Brilliant. Such wisdom."

Takamori

Abbot Nami sat on the veranda of the *hojo*. Life was good. All was as it should be. He was being served. The small bamboo table before him held a tray with his breakfast. There were several small dishes and plates, containing food cooked especially for the Abbot. He picked up a cube of tofu coated in sesame seeds (goma tofu) and popped it into his mouth. He groaned with pleasure. He looked over his shoulder to the young nun, serving his breakfast, "Ohara, this goma tofu is delicious. Go to the kitchen and get another plate."

Ohara bowed her shaved head and went to the cookhouse.

Abbot Nami was overweight. He ate much and did little. The most active part of his anatomy was his mouth, and unfortunately chewing and talking weren't very conducive to losing weight. Although he was a monk, and had supposedly renounced worldly pleasures, he used the monastery's wealth to ensure that his personal cook had no shortage of fine food for his meals. He did, after all, have a delicate, sensitive stomach and needed a special diet. He also had delicate, sensitive skin, which was why his habits needed to be woven from exclusive, expensive wool. And because of his ailing back, his mattress had to be excessively thick and filled with the finest down feathers. And because he was detached from worldly pleasures, it didn't matter that he was attended on by the most attractive young nuns. And of course the massages he demanded were for medical reasons only. After all, some said he had attained Buddhahood and transcended earthly pleasures many years ago.

He burped and farted simultaneously. If he'd sneezed and had an orgasm at the same time, he would have entered to seventh level of Heaven and been free of earthly chains forever. Such is the strength of gas-powered Zen.

The nun carefully placed the extra dish of tofu before Abbot Nami, who strained to get a glimpse of her breasts as she leaned

23

forward to put it on the table. She stood up and the Abbot put on his "enlightened smile". He'd cultivated this "I am a Buddha in bliss" face for decades, along with his gentle "I know everything" Buddha voice.

The Abbot was nervous. An important visitor was arriving later that day. Gisu monastery thrived on donations from rich citizens. The main supporter of the monastery at Gisu were the aristocratic Takamori family. The current head of the family, Saigo, was also a supporter of the arts. He was an avid collector of calligraphy and ink drawings. He loved the pictures, but also enjoyed the status that the ownership of important works of Art gave him.

To own an expensive picture not only displayed your wealth, but also your sophistication, learning and cultural awareness. No wonder that the rich yearn to own them, even if they are worth so much money they have to keep them locked away where nobody can see them. Saigo Takamori wasn't like this. His paintings were on display in his palace, and he enjoyed showing visitors around his art gallery.

Abbot Nami's appreciation of Art went no further than the answer to the question "How much is it worth?"

Yosu made his way back up from the river to the monastery. His room came into view. There was already a line of people standing outside, most of them holding sheets of paper. They were supervised by a young monk, acting as a steward.

Yosu muttered, "Looks like a queue for the toilet."

He spun around on his heel and headed for the refectory, a warm bowl of rice porridge and a hot cup of tea.

He hummed with pleasure and swallowed the first spoonful of his breakfast. The rest of the day could only go downhill after such an appetizing start.

He felt a hand on his shoulder "Yosu, Abbot Nami wants to see you."

"Tell Abbot Nami that I'm eating my breakfast."

"But he's with Lord Takamori. And they're waiting."

"Lord Buddha taught health is the greatest gift, contentment the greatest wealth, faithfulness the best relationship and rice porridge is the finest breakfast. So go and wait over there until I've finished."

"But Abbot Nami said I was to tell you…"

24

The monk, thinking he wielded the authority of an Abbot, had pushed Yosu a little too far. "Brother, from a Buddhist perspective, fuck off until I've finished my porridge."

Yosu smiled and continued eating. He hadn't expected things to start going downhill so quickly. He finished his porridge and poured himself a small cup of green tea, much to the frustration of the monk waiting in the wings, who was moving from foot to foot, like someone about to burst if they didn't get to the toilet. Yosu finished his tea and carried his bowl and cup to the table at the end of the refectory, rinsed them in the wooden barrel, lay them to dry and turned to the messenger."Shall we go?" They left the refectory and walked around to the Abbot's *hojo*.

Lord Takamori was seated on the balcony drinking tea. He was surrounded by flunkeys from the monastery, including Abbot Nami, bowing and scraping, eager to gain his favour.

As the Shinto monk Bundo Daishu once said, 'Money doesn't talk, it swears.' (On second thoughts maybe it was Bob Dylan who said it).

Abbot Nami saw Yosu approaching and burst into action. "Ah, here he comes Takamori sama. So sorry to keep you waiting. Ohara, bring some more tea and snacks for *no tono*."

Lord Saigo Takamori was famous throughout Japan. He was the oldest of seven children, born into a humble family in the district of Satsuma. His father was an unimportant tax official. With seven children and his father's meagre wages, the family were always struggling to make ends meet.

Takamori lived at a time in Japan's history when great changes were taking place in society. The Samurai class had been in existence for almost seven hundred years, but by the time of Takamori their days were coming to an end. Takamori is known in Japan as 'the Last Samurai'.

At the age of six, he started at the local samurai school, known as a *goju*, where he was given his first short sword. He was very intelligent, and was successful in his studies. When he left school he got a job in local government. He was rapidly promoted and became a confidant of the local feudal lord, known as a *daimyo*. Soon he was the

25

daimyo's closest advisor. They moved to Edo, where there were two political groups. One party supported the Samurai and their opponents thought that the samurai had become too powerful and that this authority should be restored to the Emperor. The conflict between the Emperor and the Samurai would continue for many years. The conflict eventually took the life of the daimyo, who was poisoned. Takamori was well liked and trusted. Along with his wisdom and experience, this made him a prime candidate to replace Daimyo Shimazu. It was a wise choice. Takamori understood that when there is harmony between the government and the population, and the people are treated fairly, they are loyal and more willing to support the government in times of trouble.

Yosu approached the group on Abbot Nami's balcony. "Here's the artist Lord Takamori." said the Abbot. "So sorry to keep you waiting. Allow me to send for some more snacks."

Takamori was sick of simpering sycophants. He dismissed Abbot Nami's request with a wave of his hand. "Please. I'm here to see some of brother Yosu's fine calligraphy, not to eat tofu."

Abbot Nami smiled nervously. "Of course, Lord. "

Yosu bowed to Lord Takamori,

"Please. Sit down Brother Yosu. I've come to see if you've any new work to show me. As you know, I'm a great admirer of your art."

"Lord Takamori, you're too kind."

Abbot Nami nodded enthusiastically, "Yes, too kind Lord."

Takamori glanced at him for moment, then turned back to Yosu. "So, Brother Yosu, what has flowed from the tip of your brush since we last met? Perhaps we could walk round to your studio and have a look?"

"Of course Lord."

Yosu stood up ready to leave. The abbot motioned to join them.

"There's no need for you to trouble yourself Nami." Takamori nodded towards Polo and his cronies, lingering in the shadows. "Perhaps someone could bring us some tea, if they're not too busy. We'll be in Yosu's studio. See we're not disturbed."

Takamori and Yosu left, accompanied by his two armed retainers. When they reached Yosu's room, they stood outside, one on each side of the door, hands resting gently on their sword hilts, while the monk and the aristocrat went inside.

The room was sparse and simple. Takamori and Yosu went through his pictures and discussed them. Takamori was impressed by Yosu's attitude of detachment and the possibility that inaction was sometimes the best course of action. "I wish I could use your ideas in government and administration, Yosu."

"But you can, Lord. The principles of Zen may be applied on many levels, be it war, peace, business or even your personal life. Who can deny that in war, victory without fighting is the most advantageous way to win?"

Yosu was giving Takamori plenty to think about. The *daimyo* was getting an insight that he rarely got from his assistants and advisors in government, who were usually obsessed with their position and status in the daimyo's palace. It was refreshing to have advice from outside court politics. He would have to consider getting Brother Yosu to move to court. It would be useful to have him around all the time.

Ryoken

Then he heard a strange voice coming from the room next to the studio, He couldn't see the owner. Whoever it was was making his uncle laugh. The most noticeable thing about the voice was its accent. It was from snow country, in the far north.

Yosu strained to see through a crack in the door, to discover the identity of the mysterious stranger with a strange accent. It was to no avail. He was out of view. Yosu went back into the studio, took another breath of menthol and lit another wick.

The door opened and Uncle Toshio came in with a couple of *mon*. *Mon* are round coins with square holes. He handed them to Yosu, "Yosu, go down to the village and buy two bottles of saki."

A voice came from next door, "And don't drink any of it on your way home."

Toshio pressed a couple of silver coins into Yosu's hand.

"Ask for two bottles of the good stuff. No cheap rubbish."

Yosu took the money and turned to leave. Just behind his uncle, in the next room, he glimpsed the black, threadbare robe of a Buddhist monk. He was shocked. What he'd been overhearing from next door hadn't sounded like a monk. And drinking saki didn't seem like the sort of thing a monk should be doing.

"Well, get going. Haven't you seen a monk before?" Toshio asked.

Yosu held the *mon* tight and hurried down to the village. When he reached the house of the saki seller,

he asked for two bottles.

"Two bottles. Your uncle must be thirsty."

"No, he's got a guest."

28

People in the village loved to know everyone else's business. There were no TVs, newspapers or internet in those days. Only mouths and ears.

"Anyone special?"

"I don't know. I think it's a monk."

"A monk who likes saki. That's interesting. Tell me, is he tall and thin, and does he have straggly hair and speak in a northern accent?"

"Well, I haven't seen his hair. But he speaks funny."

The saki seller thought for a moment, "Yes. It's probably him. He must have run out of ink."

"Who?"

"The monk. It must be Ryokan. He's one of the greatest artists and poets in Japan. Even the emperor wants Ryokan's calligraphy on his wall. He rarely leaves his mountain home these days. He's probably come to stock up on ink. You're very lucky to meet him. He usually keeps himself to himself."

Yosu wandered through the village back to Toshio's home. His conversation with the saki seller had made him more curious about the enigmatic monk.

All he thought about was the mysterious monk. If he was an artist, it made sense he came to Toshio to buy ink. And if he was indeed a famous artist, Yosu wanted to know more. The turnip that grew itself was still pinned to the wall next to his bed, reaching up for the sky. The magical moment when the brush had taken control was still there in the picture. Maybe Ryokan could make it happen again. He held a bottle of saki in each hand, gripped a little tighter and increased his pace.

When he reached his uncle's house, Toshio and the monk were standing in the middle of Toshio's vegetable patch discussing his leeks. The monk indeed had straggly long hair. A bird could have been nesting in it. The saki seller was right. It was Ryokan.

"They have shallow roots, so they need plenty of water. They also like plenty of sun, so this is a good spot for them. Ah, here's the wee lad with the soup."

"Yosu, this is my dear old friend Ryokan. He's an artist. His calligraphy is a wonder to behold."

29

"Don't believe that, lad. All you do is slap the ink on the paper. Your uncle's ink does the rest."

"I told him you like painting. Maybe he'll show you a few tricks before he leaves."

"Ah. You're a wee artist. I'd like to have a look at what you've done. But first a wee drop of soup eh Tosh?"

Toshio took the bottles from Yosu and went into his kitchen. He put one of the bottles into a pan and poured water halfway up the saki bottle. He then removed the bottle and lit the stove. After a couple of minutes the water was boiling. He removed the pan, stood the bottle of saki in it and produced two small saki cups from a cluttered shelf.

After a couple of cups of saki, Ryokan suggested that Toshio bring out his Go set.

Yosu went back into the workshop and continued preparing lamps with various oils, ready to make soot. He could hear Toshio and Ryokan in laughing conversation through the door. The lower the level of saki in the bottle, the more raucous the laughter became. The crack of the stones as the players slapped them down onto the board became louder.

Saki makes you happy. At first.

By the time they were halfway down the second bottle, the laughs had evolved into shrieks and the stones had started to slide around of their own accord, so they abandoned the game, and agreed to try again tomorrow.

They reached the bottom of the second bottle and kept forgetting whose turn it was, so they decided to abandon the game and inspect the leeks again, and see what progress they'd made since their previous visit, an hour ago. Under the weight of the two bottles of saki they sank to their knees, and then rolled onto their backs. Yosu peeked around the door enjoying the performance of the artist monk and his friend Blackface the ink-maker.

"They seem to be coming along well." Toshio observed

"Aye, it's a lovely sunny spot."

"Green. Green."

"Green as leeks."

"My eyes are green." Toshio effused.

"Green as leeks."

The monk rolled onto his back and gazed into the sky, "My eyes are green as leeks."

"I love leeks." Toshio leaned over and bit the top off a leek.

"You idiot. You have to cook them first."

"Green. Green. Green as leeks."

The monk turned and looked at Toshio. The top of the leek were sticking out of his mouth, growing upwards as if he were a plant pot. Ryoken shrieked with laughter, looked at the clouds. He looked back at Toshio and shrieked again."Do you want me to water it for you?"

More shrieks.

"Only if you use saki."

Toshio snorted and giggled.

"I need a piss, Tosh. Thought best not to waste it. Maybe it would wash that black crap off your face."

They both groaned and laughed in saki-fuelled insanity.

Yosu thought this would be a good time to tidy the workshop and then go to bed. He would collect more soot tomorrow.

Next morning Toshio and Ryoken both declined breakfast and drank copious amounts of green tea. They spoke in grunts and groans for the first hour and earnestly agreed that last night was the final time they would drink so much.

Yosu overheard their conversation and resolutions to moderate their drinking through the doorway. Finally Ryokan said, "Let's see what inks you've got for me. Then see what your young apprentice is up to. Bring the tea pot."

Yosu felt a slight pulse in his chest when he heard Ryokan refer to him. The monk nodded to Yosu then turned his gaze to the shelves behind him. They were stacked a large variety of black ink blocks stacked in neat piles.

"Tosh, my old pal. How many shades of black have ye got here?"

"Last count, sixty-six." Toshio smiled proudly.

"Sixty-six shades of black. You could write a book about that many."

Ryokan took down a block and examined it closely. Toshio explained, "That's charcoal ink. Wood charcoal. Doesn't have so much glue and spreads easily."

"Aye, that's good for calligraphy. Let's the brush run free, like a wee hairy dog let off its leash."

Toshio reached up to the shelf and removed another block. "This is pine soot ink. It's made with a new type of glue I'm trying out, a mixture of ox-glue and deer-glue. It dries with a blue tinge."

"Yes, I'd like to try that one."

Toshio handed him the block. "Test it for me. Next time you're down, let me know how you got on. It's got lemon oil and peppermint oil in it. So it's good for sore throats."

"It won't turn my face black will it?"

"No. A saki cup full will sort out your sore throat. The charcoal cleans the poisons from your blood and will make you fart for a while."

"That's alright. Farts only bother you when they're not your own. Now I've sorted out the calligraphy. What about the painting?"

"Well, oil soot ink give warm black colours, and it doesn't spread around the paper as much as pine and charcoal. He took another block of ink down from the shelf. "This is oil soot ink. Mainly from burnt tung oil, with a bit of sesame oil and a few drops of soya oil."

Ryokan sniffed the ink block. "Mmmn. Smells good. It's the sesame. If you put some sugar in, you could sell it as sweets."

"Well it wouldn't do you any harm to eat it. There's a bit more glue in this one than usual. It dries a lovely warm black, and if you need it, it's good for calligraphy too. The glue in it is the best you can get. Made from bits of fish, deer and who knows what other creatures. They boil it for days, strain it, clean it, then start all over again. You end up with a little orange cube."

"Should make a good stock for soup. Last time I came, you gave me some lacquer soot ink. That was good for painting. Have ye got some more of that?"

It wasn't long before Ryokan had a pile of ink blocks for both painting and calligraphy. "Well that lot should keep me going until New Year."

"If you don't eat them all before you get home."

"Shall we go next door and try a couple of them out now?" He nodded towards Yosu. "We'll see what the wee laddie can do?"

Toshio cleared the kitchen table, wiped it clean with a damp cloth, put a small bottle of water in the middle and brought in a sheaf of virgin white rice paper.

Toshio and Ryokan had a mutually advantageous business relationship. Toshio gave him whatever ink he wanted, fed him and bought his saki. In return, Ryokan always left at least one picture or piece of calligraphy with Toshio. Money was never discussed, although Toshio could have sold one of Ryokan's pieces of Art for a small fortune. He loved Art and calligraphy and preferred to see his friend's work hanging on the wall.

Toshio understood that people who spent their lives accumulating money were missing the point. Nobody could own a jewel brighter or more beautiful than the moon. And it cost nothing to enjoy it. The beauty of life was free for all. Ryokan's pictures somehow captured that magic. The force moving his brush and delicately easing out the words of his poems was the same modest, silent energy that opened the petals of a flower in the morning and gently coaxed the silver moon into the sky at night. Pretentious, snobbish nincompoops who evaluated Art by its price were completely missing the point.

There was a famous story about Ryokan. He'd chosen the life of a hermit, living in a small hut outside the village, on the slopes of Mount Kugami. He was out on the mountain one day. When he returned home there was a thief inside the hut. Unfortunately for the thief, because Ryokan had no use for "stuff" there was nothing to steal. Ryokan took pity on him.

"Well ye can't leave empty handed. Here, take my robe." He removed his robe and handed it to the thief. It was old and tatty. As the thief was leaving, Ryokan called him back, "Hey, do you no say thank you when somebody gives you a gift?"
Embarrassed and confused, the thief said, "Thank you sir." And quickly left.

That evening Ryokan sat naked, staring at the moon.
"That poor fella'. I wish I could have given him this beautiful moon."

A couple of weeks later, two constables from the prefectural police department arrived at Ryokan's hut. Someone in the village had heard about his loss and given him a new robe, so he wasn't naked. Knowing his reputation as a great artist and poet, the constables were polite and respectful. They told him the local magistrate had requested his presence at the trial of a thief. It was the man who had left with his robe.

At the trial, Ryoken was asked if he recognized the thief.
"Yes".
"Did he take anything from you?"
"Yes. I gave him my robe."
"You gave it to him?"
"Yes. He thanked me for it."
"He didn't steal it?"
"No. It was a gift."
The thief's other victims weren't so generous and he was sentenced to a public flogging for his misdemeanours. The thief was so impressed by the monk that after his back healed up, he went to visit him. Ryokan made him welcome and he spent a few days as a guest in his hut. The thief liked the taste of Ryokans' miso soup almost as much as he liked Ryokan's company. He looked out from the side of the mountain and for the first time, glimpsed life clearly. Ryokan's calm prescence affected him in the same way it affected Yosu. He was glad he'd tried to rob the curious, skinny monk with the wild hair and tatty old robe. He'd left with a tatty old robe and been given a new outlook on life. Ryokan remembered the thief in a haiku:

The thief left it behind:
the moon
at my window.

Back in Toshio's studio Ryokan was putting his pile of ink-stones into a small bag. "I might even have enough for a couple of pots of stew. Shall we try some of the ink out now?" Toshio looked at Yosu and nodded towards the kitchen, where he'd laid out the painting materials. There were three cushions around the table and in front of each chair a sheet of rice paper, an ink stone, brush, ink-stick, an ink-well and pot of water. Ryokan poured a little water into the well of the ink-stone and smiled. The saki hangover was in retreat. He was enjoying himself. He slowly slid the ink-stick up and down the slope. He looked at Toshio and intoned, in time with the moving ink-stick, "Wave comes up the beach. Wave goes back to the sea." Yosu smiled. So that was where Toshio learned the technique. He dropped some water onto the stone and began sliding the ink-stick up and down the slope, "Wave comes up the beach. Wave goes back to the sea." Ryokan looked at Toshio in surprise for a moment, realising that his ink-stick mantra had taken on a life of its own. He joined in the chorus with Yosu.

Occasionally life changing incidents happen owing to forces of nature, accidents, wars and a variety of dramatically different reasons. Spending time with Ryokan was one of the most life-changing experiences of Yosu's life. If you'd asked Yosu about it, he wouldn't have been able to explain it. Some things can't be explained. What exactly happens when you fall in love, or laugh at a joke, or are silenced by a sunset? The calm feeling Yosu got from being with Ryoken attracted him like nectar attracted a bee. What was it about him that had such an effect whoever he was with? He wasn't speaking wise words, or giving sagacious advice on 'liberation' and the meaning of life. He seemed more like a child enjoying himself.

For the first time in his life, Yosu began thinking about the future. Up until the time of Ryokan's visit, he'd been rolling along a track that went from his village to the ink-makers. But the monk from the north was prompting him to re-examine his journey. His perspective was usually fixed in the present but Ryoken had nudged him enough to see that the future wasn't unchangeable. For the first time since he'd been invited to become Toshio's apprentice, he felt he had some control over where his life was heading.

The three scribes had made enough ink for their first piece of work.

"Ah think we'll start at the beginning. That's what my old master Kokusen taught me. What d'ye think Yosu?" asked Ryoken.

"A good place to start, sir."

35

"Oh, don't call me that laddie. It makes me feel like a tax inspector or a jumped up, fat, bloody abbot. "Nami"will do. That's what folk who know me call me. Call me Nami. It's my nickname. It means "great fool". It describes me well enough. It means I have nothing to live up to. I can relax. And when ye paint a picture or do some calligraphy, that's the most important thing. If you don't relax, the brush can't do its work. It never hurts to do a little za-zen before ye start. Meditation calms your mind and opens the door into the artist's workshop where you go to collect your picture."

Ryokan closed his eyes and lowered his head for a moment. He took a deep breath. He poured the ink into the well, added some water, dipped his brush into it and swirled the ink around. He added more water until he was happy with the consistency. Not too thin, not too thick. He wiped the excess ink on the edge of the inkwell, took another deep breath and said, "Number one."

He painted a horizontal line on the paper. It was effortless. There was something hypnotic about the way the line emerged from Ryokan's brush. At first it was as if Yosu was watching a magician perform a trick, manifesting something from nothing. He realized that Ryokan was enjoying the show along with the rest of the audience.

The air in the kitchen, colourless, weightless and invisible had become solid. Without moving, it was pulling, pushing and moving everything.. Yosu was spellbound. He told himself that it was all in his head. But it didn't matter. Wherever it was, he liked it.

Toshio had the contented look on his face of somebody enjoying a warm bath.

"Nami, why did you become a monk?"

"Well young Yosu, it isn't a very nice story. Are ye sure you want to hear it?"

Yosu nodded.

"Well, my father was the head man of our village. I was his eldest son and I was due to be the next head man after him. Well, one hot summer afternoon, I was working in the fields outside the village and I felt a wee bit sick. I think I must have had too much sun. I decided to go home and have a lie down. When I got there I heard somebody moving around inside. We'd had a lot of burglaries in the village

36

recently, so I was careful. I went in quietly, and sure enough, there was the thief, filling his bag with our valuable stuff. I knocked him out and tied him up. A week later, the Daimyo was in the village, and he judged all the criminals and decided on their punishment. Unfortunately the thief couldn't keep his bloody big mouth shut and when he was hauled in front of the Daimyo, he was shouting stuff about Daimyos being no different from anybody else and having no right to judge other folk."

"What happened?"

"Two of the Daimyo's men dragged him to his knees and held him still. Then the Daimyo cut his head off with his sword. It was an awful mess. The blood shot out his neck like a fountain."

"Why did that make you want to become a monk?"

"Well, I suppose a couple of reasons. When you see death, you realize how precious life is, and you don't want to piss it away for nothing. All the hopes and dreams of that poor thief soaked away in the grass. He'd never see his children grow up. Never see the beautiful moon again. Never laugh, never cry. Never love. All because some bloody high and mighty Daimyo didn't like what he said about him. And if I started saying what I thought about those privileged bastards, my head would be rolling in the dust too."

"And another thing that bothered me was, I was the one who'd caught him. And he ended up dead. The few trinkets he'd stolen weren't worth one of his fingers, let alone his whole life. After that I wasn't interested in following my father and becoming the head of the village. I was confused. My life didn't seem to be going in the right direction. I was being pushed to a place I didn't really want to go. I needed to find out what it life was really about. Why was I alive? Was there anything to do in life besides eat, drink, shit and fuck? And if there was, how would I find out what it was?

"So I decided I'd forget about being the headman. My little brother could do that. I'd go away and be a monk. And see if I could work it out.

"I messed about in Kosho-ji monastery for a while, but it wasn't until Zen Master Kokusen came along that things started to work out for me. Kokusen gave off a real feeling of peace wherever he went. Like the scent from a gardenia. Nothing bothered him. He was like a bright lotus flower floating on top of a muddy pool, peeping out between the leaves from Nirvana. I knew there and then that wherever he was, I wanted to visit, and maybe stay a while. So I left Kosho-ji with Kokusan when he left the monastery. I followed him to Soto temple where I stayed with him for twelve years."

"So what do you do nowadays?"

"I'm happy living in my little hut on the side of Mount Kugami, I paint pictures, write calligraphy, knock out the odd poem. Sometimes I take a break and wander around the country with my begging bowl. It's not a bad life. Beats having to work for a living, being bossed around every day by some dickhead who doesn't know his arse from his elbow."

Ryokan looked at Toshio, then at Yosu. "Don't worry Tosh', I'm not talking about you. You know where your arse is. And from what I see, you treat young Yos' pretty well. And all the ink he can eat, right?"

Yosu smiled. When Ryokan was describing his encounter with Kokusen, he might well have been talking about the impression he was making on Yosu. Something was tugging inside him, and for the first time, Yosu thought maybe he wouldn't spend the rest of his life making ink after all. He could hear a distant call coming from the big wide world outside his Uncle's house.

Ryokan picked up the brush and said, "Well, let's get on with our calligraphy. Starting at the beginning. "A very good place to start," as you said Young Yos'. And what's at the beginning? The number one."

Ryokan dipped his brush in the pot, wiped off the surplus ink, closed his eyes for a moment, then dragged his brush across the paper in a simple, horizontal line, narrow, leaning down at the start, broad and glancing upwards at the end.

Yosu's line was broad at the start, where he'd paused nervously for half a second, before launching into the stroke. It tapered at the end where he'd finished it in a hurry. Toshio's line looked more like Ryokan's.

"Try a few more. And relax. It's only a bloody line."

Toshio and Yosu watched Ryokan paint a column of figure 'ones'. There was something happening before their eyes, but it was impossible to comprehend what it was. How could such a simple, straight forward act as painting the simplest number, a short horizontal line, become so profound? And what made it more significant and mysterious was that somehow it seemed connected to their breathing. The air filling the room had become a massive invisible hand, gently pushing itself in and out of their lungs. Wave comes up the beach. Wave goes back to the sea. It wasn't only breathing them, but it was clear that it was guiding Ryokan's brush. The invisible hand was reaching out from behind the curtain and signing its work.

"Well come on, you two. Let's see them numbers. And don't try to be clever. Just do it."

Yosu watched Toshio close his eyes, take a deep breath, open them and dip his brush in the ink. He did the same.

Where was the invisible hand?

It was deep in Yosu's stomach, tickling his heart, forming a question. But at the moment it was only scrambled tofu. Like the patterns formed on freezing ice, it evolved into something recognizable. It solidified into a sentence and slowly climbed from his stomach into his throat, then into his mouth and stepped out into freedom. "Nami, could I become your disciple and you could teach me how to paint?"

Toshio's eyebrows jumped up in surprise.

"Why do you want to be a disciple? Why can't you just learn to paint? Your Uncle Toshio here is a good painter. I've been teaching him for years and he's not bad. You could do much worse than learn from him."

The words tumbled out from Yosu's mouth, "It's not just the painting, Nami. It's about other things too. I think you could teach me about living. About the mystery of a happy life. The secrets of the Buddha."

"Well, as far as I can tell, the Buddha doesn't have any secrets. The problem is most folk have their ears blocked with wee frogs and spiders, and can't hear what he's saying.

"I've had a few followers, and they all started out eager and sincere and finished up a pain in the arse. I learned long ago not to take disciples. There's only one Master, and his physical form left us centuries ago. You won't find him in a temple or a monastery. If you think you could be my disciple, you're looking in the wrong place. I'm just another pilgrim on the path, like yourself. So you need to figure out exactly where you're heading, and what it is you really want. And in the end you realize we're not going anywhere, and you've had everything since the day we were born."

Ryokan glanced at Toshio, who was enthralled as if watching the final climax of a Noh play.

"And what's your poor Uncle going to do if his best apprentice runs off to draw pictures?"

Yosu's face crumbled. He hadn't thought about that. He felt like a dog that was deserting his benevolent master.

"You'd probably hate the life of a novice. Because that's what you'd be. Freezing cold, sleeping out in all weathers. Begging for your dinner. Eaten by mosquitos. Getting pissed on by dogs when ye were asleep. It's not all happy smiles and drawing pictures ye know?

"And if you have a master, well then you've got to do what you're told. Can you do that, Yosu? This is serious."

Yosu nodded.

"Really?"

He nodded again.

"All right. I'll give you something to do, and we'll see how you get on. Toshio, how long has he got to finish his apprenticeship?"

"About a year."

"Finish your apprenticeship with your Uncle here. He can teach you how to paint the basic characters. Master making your own ink. You're almost there. When Toshio thinks you're ready, he can find someone to replace you. By then, you'll have had plenty of time to think it over. And if you still want to follow the footsteps of Lord Buddha, sleeping in the rain, with freezing cold feet, scratching flea bites with a grumbling stomach, come and visit me in my hut on Mount Kugami and we'll talk about it again. No promises though. The best I'll be able to do is recommend you to a monastery that will accept you as a novice. If you think you'll walk into my hut and I'll teach you how to paint you're mistaken. Becoming a monk is much more than learning to

40

paint, or living in a monastery and not going to work. But if that's what you want, give it everything and see what happens. "

That wasn't the answer Yosu had expected, but there were no other doors open. If he was serious about following the path Ryokan had taken, he had no choice. There was only one set of footprints.

Yosu spent the next year learning the calligraphy alphabet, completing his ink making education and preparing himself to take the biggest step in his life and commit himself to the life of a renunciate.

Yosu took Ryokan's advice and stayed with his uncle until he finished his training as an ink-maker.

His desire to live the life of a monk didn't diminish. A year and a half later he said goodbye to his Uncle and, remembering the invitation from Ryokan, made his way to Mount Kugami. He enjoyed seeing the world, visiting different towns and areas of the countryside. After sleeping in guest houses, barns, the odd monastery and the occasional field, he eventually made his way to Ryokan's hut on the side of the mountain where the old monk was happily living the quiet life, enjoying nature, painting, writing poetry and practising za-zen. He spent a week with him, playing Go and picking up tips in calligraphy. At the end of the week, Ryokan discussed Yosu's desire to become a monk.

Ryoken pointed out the disadvantages; the main one seemed to be dealing with monks and abbots who were living for their own material benefit, power or simply a life of ease. He also warned him about the other problems: lice, cold, mosquitoes, hunger, illness, gruelling, repetitive work, obeying orders from idiots, sleeping in the rain, and so on. Yosu convinced him he would overcome such problems. After a day, he realized that Yosu was sincere and committed.

Ryoken accompanied Yosu to the Zen temple at Koshu-Ji, where Ryoken had spent time as a novice. On his recommendation, Yosu was accepted into the temple. He spent six years as a novice, studying under Ryokan's old teacher, Kokusan who was then over eighty years old.

When Kokusan died, he was replaced by the new abbot Gento Sokochu. Yosu didn't get on with Gento, and he wasn't the first abbot Yosu would fall out with. Gento was strict and changed lots of the teaching methods. He forbade calligraphy, artwork and writing poetry.

Yosu began to feel fenced in. The spirit of independence and liberty that had attracted him seemed to be leaking away.

It wasn't long before Yosu decided he would be better off leading the path of a wandering monk, or *ensui*. So he took his brushes, inkpad and roll of paper, along with his begging bowl, blanket, razor and staff, and stepped out the monastery onto the path of the unknown.

Something Artistic

Years later Yosu entered the monastery at Gisu, where his painting and calligraphy were encouraged. This was because he had become well known as an artist, and his work earned a good income for the monastery. The most famous collector of his work was the Daimyo Lord Takamori, who was a great lover and sponsor of the arts.

The last time Lord Takamori visited Yosu at Gisu monastery, he infuriated Abbot Nami. Takamori told him to wait while he went to see Yosu alone. Nami felt snubbed and publicly humiliated. He'd had enough of the troublesome cartoonist. Nami had been fuming for months. This wasn't the first time Yosu had caused him open embarrassment in front of the other monks. Nami only tolerated Yosu because of the wealth he brought into Gisu. But he'd had enough of the arrogant little shit. He began thinking of a way to take care of him once and for all. But first he had to make sure he had enough of his pictures to keep him in the manner to which he was accustomed for the rest of his life. He hadn't become abbot by sitting on top of a hundred foot pole waiting to appear on the other side of the world.

Yosu had made a lifelong enemy of Abbot Nami. The Abbot hated him with a vengeance. On the few occasions Takamori visited Gisu, he made it plain that he'd come to see Yosu, not the abbot. Like many powerful men, Nami had an incredibly sensitive ego. Lord Takamori invariably bruised it when he visited Gisu.

Takamori was due to visit the monastery, and Nami knew he had to be on his best behaviour. The Daimyo liked to check things were running smoothly, and make a donation in the form of buying one of Yosu's pieces of calligraphy. The Abbot wanted a new, expensive robe from Kyoto. This meant that he had to keep both Yosu and Takamori happy and hide his true feelings of indignation and rage which rose when he was inevitably snubbed by the Daimyo. Nami was skilled in hiding his true feelings and intentions. He was a master in the art of duplicity. He knew Lord Takamori was expected and Yosu hadn't produced many cartoons or pieces of calligraphy recently. He had been harassing him for days, trying to force him to produce more work. The Abbot's veiled threats may have worked on monks like Polo, but with Yosu they were counter-productive.

The morning of Takamori's visit arrived. The Abbot, accompanied by Polo and his acolytes, went round to Yosu's studio. "What have you got to show Lord Takamori?"

Yosu pointed to a piece of rice paper on his table, "An *enso*." The *enso* was the ultimate subject in Zen calligraphy. It was circle, completed with a single stroke. It symbolised everything: the void, and the moment of enlightenment, when the world of duality falls away and the monk enters Nirvana and transcends the cycle of birth and death that is reincarnation.

Nami picked the paper up. "It's just a circle. How can I sell this to Lord Takamori? He'll laugh in my face. Probably use it to wipe his arse."

Polo and his two followers laughed. Polo picked up the *enso*, threw it back onto the table and echoed Abbot Nami, "Wipe his arse. That's brilliant, Holy Father. Brilliant."

Polo's acolytes nodded in harmony, "Yes, brilliant, Master. Brilliant."

Abbot Nami clenched his teeth, "Yosu. I've had enough of your crap. You've been on a free ride here since I became abbot. And it's not going to last much longer. You're going to pay your way like every other monk. If you don't, you'll get a taste of good old-fashioned Buddhist discipline. Your privileges will be removed. I'll personally shove your paintbrushes up your arse, and you'll be working in the fields in the snow unto springtime and sleeping in the novices' dormitory. Lord Takamori will be here this afternoon, and I want you to have a masterpiece ready for him. Not this crappy little circle that took you two seconds to do. Don't take the piss Yosu. It doesn't work with me. Geddit?"

Nami snatched a sheet of rice paper from the pile on the shelf and banged it down hard on the table.

"Something artistic., Tasteful. With some people and nature stuff before Takamori gets here. You know the sort of thing. Something a bit Zen, like flower in the void or something."

The abbot and his entourage swanned out the room. Polo paused in the doorway and turned to Yosu, "Get yourself sorted out, Yosu. Or you'll be out of here."

"Fuck off, Polo."

Yosu placed his brush, ink-stone, and pot of water along the edge of his table. He poured a few drops of water into the well of the inkstone. He took a sheet of rice paper down from the shelf, placed it on the table and smoothed it out. He then shut his eyes and took a deep breath and began mixing some ink.

Wave comes up the beach. Wave goes back to the sea.

When he was happy with the consistency and the amount, he closed his eyes again and breathed deep. He smiled.

A haiku Ryokan once told him came into his mind,

> **"A fool holds the brush**
> **Makes a mess on the paper**
> **wastes another day."**

"Something artistic. People and nature stuff."

Abbot Nami certainly wasn't going to get his fat fingers on Yosu's brush and waste another day.

He took another deep breath. He dipped his brush into the ink and it set out on its path .

When he'd finished, there was a fat monk sprawled across the paper. He was surrounded by half eaten plates of food and spilled cups of saki. His expensive robe was stained with wine and food. He was, attended by three attractive young nuns. One of the nun's robes had slipped from her shoulder and the fat monk was ogling her. The monk was slouched on a throne with what looked like a fart emitting from his posterior. He was holding a copy of the *Tripitaka*, a sacred Buddhist text. Unfortunately, he was grasping it upside down. He wrote, "The Wise Abbot" in large characters, down the left side of the picture. It was a Masterpiece.

45

There was a knock on the door. Lord Takamori had arrived. Yosu opened the door. "Lord Takamori. Please come in. I'm sorry the place is in a bit of a mess."

Takamori beckoned to his two samurai bodyguards to stand outside."Don't let anyone else in."

Takamori said, "No work, no mess. Please don't bother with it. I'm here to see if you've done any more paintings."

Takamori stepped into Yosu's room. Nami moved to follow him in but the two samurai simultaneously drew their swords a few centimetres from their scabbards and stepped across the doorway. Nami got the idea and stepped back. He gritted his teeth and smiled. He hated Yosu even more when Takamori took him aside and he was barred from the proceedings. He hated him. If he could have seen the picture he'd painted he would have hated him even more.

There was an old aphorism that said you should never insult an artist or a poet, because if they responded with picture or poem, it would still exist long after you were dead, and when you were gone it would be the only thing about you anybody remembered.

If Nami had seen the 'The Wise Abbot', he would have wanted to kill Yosu there and then.

"I've two pieces to show you, Lord." He handed the circle to Takamori.

Takamori studied the circle, The *Enso*. This is beautiful Yosu. You've done it with two brushstrokes instead of one. And yet it works. It gives a new meaning to the form. It is almost yin-yang. The two forces that make up life. Your two strokes embrace each other. Emptiness and completion. It is brilliant, Yosu. You've broken the rules, but it's magnificent. I've never seen anything like it before."

Takamori stared at the *enso* in silence, then asked, "Do you have anything else?"

"Well. This is a little embarrassing." He handed his cartoon " The Wise Abbot" to Takamori. Takamori studied it for a minute, then began to laugh. The more he looked at it, the louder he laughed. Soon tears were streaming down his cheeks.

"Brilliant, Yosu. Absolutely brilliant. You've captured him perfectly. This one will take pride of place on my wall."

46

Takamori lowered his voice and asked Yosu, " Has he been making life difficult for you here?"

Yosu thought for a moment before he spoke. "When Abbot Kokusen was alive, we had a good relationship. He was tolerant, kind and taught me calligraphy. But since he died, things haven't been going so well. Nami is…"

"Takamori finished the sentence for him, "An idiot."

"That's the least of his faults. A real idiot can't be blamed for his condition. No Lord, Nami is such an irritant that I'm contemplating taking the path of an *Ensui* (wandering monk). My master Ryokan followed this path for some years. Sleeping beneath the stars, living from the contents of his begging bowl. In the world but not of the world."

Yosu quoted one of Ryokan's haikus, referring to starting life as an *Ensui*:

> *New pond*
> *no sound of a frog*
> *jumping in.*

Takamori surprised Yosu by responding with another of Ryokan's poems on the same subject.

> *Mountain storm*
> *Don't blow so hard*
> *at night on my journey*
> *I sleep on one sleeve*
> *of my white robe*

So Lord Takamori was familiar with Ryokan's poetry too. This Daimyo was full of surprises.

"Yosu. If things get really bad with Nami, and you get in trouble, send me a message and I'll send someone round to help you out. I know Nami's a master of duplicity and can be a real bastard. I fear for my favourite artist."

47

Yosu put his hands together, bowed and said, "Thank you Lord Takamori. But I hope that won't be necessary."

"Now, can you wrap these two sheets up for me? I don't want Nami looking at them before I go. Try to keep him sweet."

"That crab apple can never taste sweet, Lord. If it's boiled in honey for a year, it will still taste bitter."

"Well, he's already as sour as a donkey chewing an unripe lemon. Don't make him more sour than he already is."

Yosu carefully rolled up the two sheets of his work, then rolled them in another sheet of rice paper and neatly tucked each end in. Rolling and folding paper was a national pastime. He handed the parcel to Takamori, bowed his head and said, "Thank you, Lord."

"No, Yosu. Thank you. "The Wise Abbot" is pure genius. And your two-stroke 'Enso' will keep me thinking for months, if not years."

Yosu bowed again. "You're too kind, my Lord."

Takamori stood up and left.

He called in to say "Good-bye." to Abbot Nami. The abbot was agitated, telling Polo what he'd do if Yosu hadn't produced the required quota of artwork. "Lord Takamori. I trust my monk delivered the required product?"

"Yes, thank you, Abbot Nami. He produced two works of art that I'm very happy with."

"Two?"

"Yes, he did a beautiful, original enzo, and a deeply meaningful cartoon."

Nami was surprised. Why would anyone want to pay good money for a simple circle? "Oh. You liked the circle?"

"Yes. I've never seen an *enzo* like it before. *Enzos* are always painted with a single brush stroke. But Yosu broke with convention and used two, opening the subject to a host of interpretations. Yin-yang and so on. He really is an original artist."

Nami thought, "He's talking complete bullshit." But he said, "Yes. Brother Yosu explained the significance of the *enzo* to me. It was an education. What could be mistaken for a simple circle embodies both the roots of Art and the spirit of Zen. Truly fundamental. And what was the other picture?"

48

"Again a splendid piece of work. A picture of a monk studying the *Tripitaka*. Quite spiritual."

"Oh, may I see it Lord? I'm in love with the spiritual."

"Alas, Abbot Nami. Both pictures have been packaged, stored with the baggage and are probably already on the way back to my palace. But remind me next time you visit and I'll show you. Oh, I almost forgot, I should make a donation towards the running of the monastery.

"*Next time you visit.*" Echoed in Nami's ears. Nami had never set a foot inside the Daimyo's palace.

Takamori nodded to his servant who carried the purse. The servant removed two *mon*, a generous price for the pictures. Takamori nodded to indicate an extra coin. The servant added a third *mon* and handed them to the abbot. Nami couldn't keep the grasping grin from his face. One new robe, twenty sacks of rice. Yosu was worth his weight in gold. Nami was already thinking about his new cashmere robe.

The Wise Abbot

Yosu's life improved after Takamori's visit. His wants were satisfied and Polo kept his distance. He was even having second thoughts about returning to the life of an ensui. Maybe life in Gisu wan't so bad after all. Everything was going well until Abbot Nami heard about the new portrait hanging on the Daimyo's wall. "The Wise Abbot" had become famous.

Abbot Saigyo was well respected and well loved by clergy and laypersons alike. Unlike Abbot Nami, who spent his time in Gisu Monastery, Abbot Saigyo spent his time travelling around the country, staying as a guest in monasteries and in mansions. He made a couple of visits every year to Lord Takamori. He enjoyed his time with the Daimyo. They were both keen players of the board-game Go. They both loved art, poetry and culture so Takamori was naturally eager to show the abbot his new pictures from Yosu.

Abbot Saigyo had already heard about 'The Wise Abbot' and was keen to see it. He wasn't disappointed. Like Takamori, he was captivated by Yosu's painting, and like Takamori, he split his sides laughing at it.

"The *fude* (calligraphy brush) is indeed mightier than the *katana* (samurai sword)", he said.

"Yes. Yosu has slain Abbot Nami with one stroke of his brush."Takamori replied.

"Death by Siberian weasel hair."

A couple of weeks later, Abbot Saigyo and his entourage arrived at Gisu. It wasn't long before one of the monks accompanying Nami was talking to Polo, and let slip that Abbot Nami was becoming a celebrity thanks to Yosu's hilarious cartoon. Polo sensed blood and began to question the monk. He realized he'd struck gold. He dragged out every bit of information about the picture he could from the monk.

As soon as he had found out all he could, he hurried around to see Abbot Nami and tell him. He told the Abbot how Yosu's cartoon had made him a celebrity,"Everybody is talking about it. The picture is famous. People are coming to Takamori's palace all the way from Edo just to see it. " Polo drew the dagger with which he hoped to stab Yosu, "Lord Nami, I fear that rat Yosu has made you into a laughing stock."

Nami spluttered with anger, but he had learned not to display such feelings. Revenge was best served cold and quietly. He swallowed his rage, "Well Polo, he is an artist and artists are often eccentric. We all know they need space and freedom to express themselves. Time will smooth things out. Patience Brother Polo. Patience."

Beneath his tolerant veneer, Nami was thinking, "You will pay Brother Yosu. How you will pay. You will wish you were burning in Hell by the time I've done with you."

Polo bowed his head, "Lord you are so forgiving. Your tolerance and compassion rival that of the Lord Buddha himself".

Nami smiled modestly, wondering if he could get away with killing Yosu.

Meanwhile, Yosu was on his way down to the river. As he passed an entrance to a small courtyard, he heard somebody sobbing. He looked through the doorway. Taishin, one of the young nuns who Nami had recruited as a personal attendant was standing by a pile of firewood. Yosu looked at her. Taishin had been married to a doctor. When he died prematurely, she took the vows to become a nun. She wrote poetry, practised calligraphy and played a small bamboo flute. Although quiet and apparently shy, during her 29 years she had become a strong woman. The burden she carried through life was that most men were attracted to her. Many fell in love with her. She envied women with plain looks.

Abbot Nami was disturbing her peace. She was in turmoil, torn between obedience to the Abbot, which she understood was her duty as a nun, and listening to what her heart and common sense agreed on. The more time she spent with him, the more her suspicion grew that he was an obnoxious, lecherous prick. Tears had made tracks down her cheeks, bars to her prison cell. This realization confused her and became a burden she carried every day.

When Yosu saw her tears, he felt an invisible cloud rise in his chest and flood his brain, Like anyone finding a beautiful bird locked in a cage, he wanted to set her free. She was standing next to a bucket of water, holding a fairly large brush. Taishin had been practising calligraphy, painting the characters on the stone floor with water. This was a common method of practising brush technique. Water was free and your mistakes evaporated soon after you finished.

Yosu was confused. He couldn't deny the alien feeling inside when he looked at Taishin, yet he was monk. He'd renounced worldly pleasure. Women who were more than sisters were off limits. They were signposts to Hell. Chastity was one of the pillars of a monk's life. The attraction of women to men was a path leading to the edge of a cliff. The floor at the bottom was littered with skeletons.

The feelings rising inside Yosu were frightening him. He thought they would all disappear when he shaved his head. He was becoming enchanted and there was nothing he could do about it. "Sister Taishin, I didn't know you were a secret calligrapher. These *kanji* are neat. Where did you learn?"

Taishin sniffed, wiped her nose on the back of her hand, then wiped the back of her hand on the back of her robe, "A monk came into our village school every week and taught us for an hour. We drew our *kanji* in the sand with sticks."

Yosu looked at Taishin. Something was struggling behind her eyes. "Is something troubling you Taishin?"

She answered a little too quickly, "No. No, I'm fine."

Yosu remembered how Nami looked at her. Lust had poked its head out from behind the curtains, then swiftly hidden itself again.

"Is Abbot Nami bothering you?"

"When I took my vows and set out on the monastic life, my path was clear. I didn't want to carry the world on my shoulders. I wanted to follow the path of the Buddha. Be released from the superficial nonsense of this world and achieve enlightenment. But now I find I'm having to deal with so much idiocy I can no longer see the path. Why should my life be messed up by this insincere fool?"

"Listen, Taishin. Part of the journey is to get battered by waves and pushed onto the rocks. But don't jump off the ship. Hang on there

52

and wait for the waves to calm down, which they surely will. Nami is an idiot. God only knows how he came to be an abbot. His only concern is himself. For him, 'the path' is the path to luxury, wealth and pleasure. He thinks Zen is a kind of soup and *dharma* a type of cake. He's full of crap, but he keeps it well hidden. Crap is mainly what comes out of his mouth when he opens it. How often do you have to attend on him?"

"Every morning. Before breakfast. He likes me to serve him."

"Well, instead of going to serve him tomorrow, go to the meditation hall and serve Lord Buddha. Meditate. If he queries this, tell him that the reason you became a nun was to serve the Bodhisattva, not anyone else. Then stamp your heel, turn around and walk back to the meditation hall. Meditate again and see if he has the nerve to disturb you."

Taishin felt a weight lift from her shoulders. She had someone to help and advise her on how to deal with Nami. She was happy. She had an ally and a strategy for keeping Nami's hands away from her.

Yosu felt like a fraud. He couldn't deny the feeling he felt when he was close to Taishin. Giving her advice on how to deal with Nami felt like he was simply trying to win her affection. His feelings were becoming unruly. He sensed the ulterior motives beneath his altruism.

Abbot Nami was struggling with what to do about Yosu. He'd calmed down a bit since hearing about the cartoon from Polo. He'd just taken delivery of his new cashmere robe from Kyoto, paid for with the money from the cartoon. The robe was his pride and joy. He'd never come across an abbot with such fine attire. He simply couldn't just get rid of Yosu, no matter how much of an irritating, obnoxious prick he was. He needed the money his pictures were bringing in. But at the same time, Yosu was out of control. He had to be brought back into line. Order must be maintained. If behaviour like his was tolerated it would spread like an illness through the other monks. He'd seen it before. All that was required to let the sheep out of the pen was a few moments of carelessness and neglect. But once they were out, it was impossible to get them back again.

Talking to Taishin made Yosu think about his own life in the monastery. He could relate to the nun who had renounced the world to follow the Buddha, but somehow found herself being herded along by the oaf Abbot Nami. Yosu wasn't stupid. He realized the reason Nami tolerated him was because of the money his pictures were bringing in. He loved the way his art took him to the heart of Zen. The painting of the turnip he'd produced all those years ago, when his uncle had taught him about the wave going up and down the beach, was pinned to the wall of his hut. The turnip's shoot was still straining up to the sky, reaching for the knowledge that was hidden within every brushstroke of an enlightened calligrapher.

Meanwhile, Nami was demanding "Something artistic, people and nature stuff". Stuff that would sell and keep him in opulent privilege.

Taishin's rebellion was spreading.

"Stuff Nami," Yosu thought. "It's time for a change."

Just as something unseen had moved his brush when the turnip appeared, something unseen was moving Yosu. This was the real magic of life. It wasn't a God in the clouds. It was something buried deep within him. You could never see the hand of the player placing the stones on the board, but you could see the enemy being surrounded and captured before he realized what was happening.

Yosu knew he had to devise a strategy to get away from Nami and the monastery. The path of the Unsui was a solution. He could live as a wandering monk for a while. He'd carry everything he needed in a small bag: his begging bowl, brush, ink-block and ink-stone. Last time he saw Lord Takamori the Daimyo had invited him to his palace, ostensibly to do a couple of pictures, but in reality because he wanted to spend more time with him, talking. He could go and visit the Daimyo and then go to Mount Kugami, and visit Ryokan, his old master. He'd take a couple of bottles of saki and maybe play a game of Go with him. Once he'd made his decision, a weight lifted. He could feel the turnip shoot stretching upwards. Life felt good again. He'd go and tell Abbot Nami what he'd decided.

He walked through the monastery to Abbot Nami's *hojo*. Nami was having a heated conversation with Polo. Yosu wasn't the only person who was annoying him. He stood by the corner of the balcony, almost out of view, and listened to the conversation.

"What do you mean she's not coming? Go and tell her to get here at once. I'm waiting for my breakfast and I'm hungry."

"She said to tell you she's meditating. That's the reason she became a nun."

"Well go and tell her that she became a nun to learn how to serve. Serving makes you humble. So she'd better serve me. I'm the abbot. I want her here now. Doing her duty. Serving my breakfast." Polo hesitated. Nami screamed, "Go and get her. Even if you have to drag her by her hair."

"She's bald Lord. She shaved her head when she…"

Nami's voice, which was high anyway, rose another octave, "I know she shaved her head. She's a bloody nun you idiot. In case you hadn't noticed, they all shave their bloody heads. Go and get her." He paused and took a deep breath. His voice came back down the scale and began to sound human again'. 'Reason she became a nun.' I'll bloody tell her why she became a bloody nun."

Nami was agitated. He needed to calm himself down. He thought the best thing he could do to feel better was wear his new cashmere robe. It was white, symbolizing purity. Simply touching the soft new wool was soothing and satisfying. It would restore his serenity and command respect from the monks and nuns. It was fitting attire for someone who was probably enlightened and almost a Buddha. He pulled his new robe over his head and smiled contentedly. He was enjoying being an abbot again. Unfortunately the feeling wouldn't last long.

Polo arrived with Taishin, who was agitated.

Nami walked out onto the balcony in his new robe. Polo was quick to react, "Lord Nami. your new robe is magnificent. It truly complements your spiritual level."

"Thank you Polo." He lied: "Abbot Nami insists I wear it as an outward sign of my personal realization." He lowered his voice just enough so everyone could still hear what he was saying, "The Abbot says all the signs say this will be my final incarnation on Earth before I join the Buddhas of the past in eternal paradise.

"Sister Taishin. You've been neglecting your duties. Where were you this morning?

"I was fulfilling my duty to Lord Buddha. He instructs us to meditate, live purely and like the moon, come out from behind the clouds and shine."

"Yes, but you have your duty here. It is to bring the abbot's breakfast. Not to sit around in the meditation hall, avoiding work."

"Buddha said, .' There is no meditation without wisdom, and there is no wisdom without meditation. When a man has both meditation and wisdom, he is indeed close to Nirvana. Much as I respect you, I did not renounce the world to serve you Abbot Nami. I became a nun to serve Bodhisattva, not anyone else. I'm going to complete my spiritual duties. They take priority over worldly pleasure." She stamped her foot, spun on her heel and marched back to the meditation hall. Nami let her go. He was shocked. He'd made the mistake of thinking because she was quiet and modest, she was weak and would be easy to manipulate. He suspected he may have underestimated her. It didn't look good dragging a nun from prayer to serve you breakfast. He'd sort her out later. She needed to come down from her high horse. Nami hadn't realized how very attractive she was when she was angry. What would he give to hold her close? He needed to spend time with her alone, away from the monastery. But before he could do that he needed to repair the damage he'd caused. He'd be nice to her. He'd stroke her spiritual ego, tell her how wise she was and how he'd been ingesting her interpretation of the Buddha's words.

And then there was that sneaky little peasant shit Yosu. He'd been considering what to do with him. He knew Yosu had been thinking about leaving the monastery and going on a pilgrimage, maybe even taking up the life of an *ensui*. If he left the monastery, who knew when he'd be back? And what would happen to the cash he brought in? Nami estimated he needed to sell four or five of his pictures a year to keep everything running along smoothly, including his personal well-being. The solution was simple. He'd set Yosu a target. He needed enough pictures to keep them all comfortable and well fed for about twenty years.

He'd send out for 100 sheets of rice paper. When Yosu had done a picture on each one, he was welcome to *ensui* off to wherever he wanted. But they had to be good quality pictures, plants, animals, monks, lay people and drawings where you could tell what they were. No splodged circles or crooked squares. Nami was sitting on a goldmine, and he didn't intend to let it walk out the monastery with a begging bowl in one hand and an ink-stone in the other. He'd hold Yosu in the monastery until every sheet of rice paper was decorated with a cartoon or piece of calligraphy that could be sold. Even if it meant locking him in a cell.

Every calligrapher had his or her own signature. This was a unique seal, or "chop" which the artists used to sign their work. It is pressed onto an ink pad, usually red, then onto the paper. Once Yosu's ink was stamped on the 100 sheets of his artwork, they would be worth a small fortune. He smiled, pleased with himself for solving the problem.

Polo scurried onto Nami's veranda. followed by his two stooges. "Master, he's on his way. Yosu is coming for an audience. You can reprimand him about his cartoon."

"Listen, Polo. Keep your mouth shut about the cartoon. It's important he doesn't know that I've heard about it. I want him off guard. Understand?"

Polo and the stooges nodded in assent.

"Brother Yosu, it's a pleasure to see you so early in the day. How can I help you?"

Yosu bowed to the Abbot. "Lord, I have something important to discuss with you about my life here."

"What is it brother Yosu? You know I'm always here to advise on spiritual matters."

"Yes Father. I've been meditating long and deep on the path my life is taking. I have come to the understanding that, like my master Ryokan, I should take the path of the Unsui. My Zen is becoming covered in cobwebs. The life I spend within these walls would be helped by some time outside on a pilgrimage. I need to meet the world again and refresh my spirit."

"I understand Yosu. I envy your freedom to take such a path. How I wish I could meet the world with only a begging bowl. My role as Lord of this monastery weighs me down. I often pray for the life of a simple monk again."

Yosu thought, *"Like Hell you do. You want the simple life as much as a chicken want to visit the butchers' shop. And what's going on here? Nami can't let me go as easy as this. I feel like I'm walking into a trap."*

"We just need to sort out a few minor matters before you leave."

"Here it comes."

"Your time with us had always been one of mutual benefit for all of us. We've given you your own room and studio, we've fed and clothed you, and encouraged you to pursue your artistic calling, and supplied you with all the materials you required without interfering with your work."

"Yes, Lord Nami. I appreciate that."

"The only thing remaining is for you to provide us with a few more illustrations before you leave, to tidy everything up and make sure everything is in harmony and balance when you go."

"Of course Lord Nami."

"Polo. Go and get Yosu's rice paper."

Polo disappeared into another room for a moment and returned carrying a large sheaf of rice paper tied up with bamboo string.

The door of Nami's trap slammed shut.

"There's one hundred sheets there. The monastery requires good quality artwork on every one. I don't want any of your wishy-washy circles and triangles, Yosu. I want proper pictures that will sit nicely on the wall of Lord Takamori's palace. Nature stuff. Frogs jumping into ponds, that sort of thing. Bamboo, pine trees, reeds. Plant stuff. And monks and people doing things. Someone walking over a bridge. You know, Zen stuff. No rubbish. And no circles floating around in mid air."

"You mean the moon?"

Nami pretended he hadn't heard. "And as soon as you've finished my hundred pictures, you can pack your begging bowl and wander off down your holy path."

That evening Taishin was summoned to see Abbot Nami again. This time she wasn't in the meditation hall but helping out in the kitchen, washing rice for the evening meal. Polo arrived with the request. She reluctantly went around to Nami's *hojo*.

Abbot Nami was determined to get close to Taishin. He was smitten. The attraction he felt for her was overpowering him. He had become obsessed and was used to getting his own way. He was an Abbot after all. He had decided to begin wooing her, in preparation to taking her out of the monastery on a "pilgrimage", out of sight of critics and gossips. He was sitting at the table on the balcony when she arrived.

On the table was a tea-caddy, made of the bark from a cherry tree, containing powdered green tea. Next to it were two delicate ceramic tea bowls, a bamboo tea-scoop, a bamboo tea-whisk, and a silk cloth. On the floor next to the table was small portable brazier with a small iron kettle over the hot coals. The only sound was the chattering of the crickets and the murmuring of the kettle. It was as if they were having a discreet conversation about why Abbot Nami was about to perform the tea ceremony for Taishin. Both the kettle and the crickets agreed that his intentions were far from honourable.

Nami pointed to the chair opposite, "Please sit down Sister. Let's take some tea together. There's something I want to talk to you about."

Taishin was justifiably suspicious. Recently, she'd become aware that she didn't always have to react to the will and whims of those around her. Her life was her own and wasn't there to be used and abused by anyone else. She belonged to Lord Buddha and to herself. And she didn't like the way Abbot Nami looked at her. She sat down.

Nami picked up the silk cloth and wiped the tea caddy and the bamboo tea scoop. He then removed the lid from the cherry wood tea-caddy. Using the bamboo tea scoop, he placed a spoon of powdered tea into each bowl. He poured hot water onto the tea, then, using the bamboo whisk, gently beat the tea until it was frothy.

"Is the tea to your satisfaction Sister?"

"Yes. It's very nice. What did you want to discuss with me?"

"Well, there are a couple of things. I intend to go on the Shikoku pilgrimage, in the steps of Kobo Daishi. Because of my delicate condition, I will need someone to accompany me. It will only take five or six days. We will be staying in monasteries and guest houses along the way."

59

Taishin thought, *"Oh no. He wants me to go with him. He is so shallow. He thinks I'm stupid."*

"Taishin, I find you incredibly attractive. I'm drawn to you, as if the Lord Buddha was pushing us closer together for some reason."

" I think I know what that reason is. It's not the will of the Lord Buddha, but the will of a dirty old mon, you Nami. Well your fat fingers won't get near me. "

Taishin, I have to share with you what is in my heart. I've never felt this way about anyone before. I'm attracted to you like I'm drawn to the Buddha. I'm in love with you. Every hour of every day you inspire me to dedicate myself more. Will you join me in following the steps of Kobo Daishi? With you at my side, there's no limit to where this love may take us."

Including into your bed. Careful what you say here sister.

"Lord Nami. I'm greatly moved by your words. In fact they are overwhelming me. I need to contemplate what your intentions are, meditate and tell you my answer tomorrow. If that's alright, Master?"

"Of course, Sister Taishin. But I give you my word as a Buddhist, my intentions are only honourable. I seek nothing but to obey the *Dharma* (truth) and following the teachings of our beloved Bodhidharma. Tomorrow is the full moon. It is Dharma day, when we remember Lord Buddha's first sermon at the Deer Park in Benares in India. Come and see me after we have finished our prayers in the main hall.

The monks and nuns assembled early the next morning to remember when Buddha first explained the doctrine of the four noble truths to five disciples by the side of the river Ganges.

Abbot Nami gave the same old sermon every year. Some of the congregation almost knew it by heart. Most of them were thinking about their breakfast as his squeaky voice rambled on about the existence of suffering, the cause of suffering and the end of suffering. The only difference this year was that he was wearing his new white cashmere robe.

By the time he'd reached step four of the noble eightfold path several of the faithful had fallen asleep. They wouldn't be asleep much longer. And neither would Nami's new robe remain white much longer.

The abbot finished his sermon, mumbled a short prayer. and was about to end the proceedings when Taishin rose to her feet. She had been sitting with a brood of words amassing in her abdomen. Once they were assembled they rose slowly to the back of her throat. "Abbot Nami."

At the sight of her the Abbot became uncomfortable. His memory of last night filled his head. He had a bad feeling. He spluttered, "Come and see me after breakfast, Sister Taishin."

"No Lord Nami. I need to say this now. I have a question that must be answered now. Last night you summoned me to your *hojo*. You performed the tea ceremony and expressed your deep love and affection for me. You asked me to accompany you on the Shikoku pilgrimage. Just the two of us."

A rumble ran through the congregation. Everyone was suddenly wide awake. Abbot Nami had turned bright red and was spluttering. His Zen was nowhere to be seen and he could happily add another item to the Buddhas list of the causes of suffering.

"Lord Nami. My question is this: Do you still love me with the passion you expressed when we were alone last night?"

Nami tried to reply, but something like a carrot was blocking up his pharynx. He could only groan, gurgle, splutter and squeak. The carrot disappeared. Nami tried to speak, but all that came out of his mouth were a couple of high-pitched shrieks. His face had turned the colour of a ripe carrot. He closed his address with a childish giggle.

Taishin said, "Abbot Nami, if your love only blossoms in the dark, and hides away when the sun shines, it is not love. I won't be joining you on the Shikoku pilgrimage."

A breeze of grateful satisfaction blew through the room. There was plenty to discuss over their rice porridge that morning. Abbot Nami couldn't get his breakfast down. A fat root vegetable was blocking the path, still waiting for an answer.

61

Zen Face

Yosu was outside his room. On the floor was a pile of charcoal and a bowl of powdered ox-hide, or Waco ox-glue, a bunch of fresh herbs, a bucket and a couple of sticks- a thin stick for stirring and a fatter stick with a rounded end for grinding charcoal. His memories of working with his uncle making ink came flooding back. He'd enjoyed his time mixing ink and making ink-blocks. It was an extremely useful skill for an artist to possess, and his uncle had taught him well. Calligraphers and artists came for miles to obtain his products. He was glad Ryokan had told him to finish his apprenticeship.

The ink he was making was from charcoal. This was ideal for the purpose he had in mind. It had less glue than inks made from soot, and spread more easily on paper. He needed water. It was a lovely day, so he decided to walk down to the river instead of going to the barrels behind the kitchen.

As he was passing the cherry orchard, he saw Brother Jo, the dreamy gardener, examining the leaves on a cherry tree. Yosu was in a much better mood than he'd been the last time he spoke to him, when he had given him the *koan* about the place where the sun doesn't shine.

"Jo, good morning. How are you and how are the cherry trees?"

"Brother Yosu. It's good to see you. The cherry trees are fine. We should get a good crop this year. And I'm fine too. I seem to learn something new every day."

"Have you learned anything yet today?"

"Oh yes I certainly have. Remember the place where the sun doesn't shine?" Yosu nodded. "Well if love only blossoms there in the dark, and not out in the world, it's not real love."

Yosu remembered the morning exchange between Taishin and Abbot Nami. He grinned, "How true Jo. How true."

Jo grinned too. They didn't have to mention the events of the morning service. Yosu repeated, "If your love only blossoms in the dark, it is not true love." They both chuckled and Yosu continued down to the river, filled his bucket and went back up to his room. He ground up the charcoal, added some powdered ox-glue, ground the herbs and added them to the mix. Then he slowly added water, constantly stirring with the thin stick. He went inside and came out with a brush and piece of scrap paper. He dipped the brush into the bucket of ink, and then drew a line on the paper. It flowed perfectly. He hadn't lost his touch. He went back into his room and collected the sheaf of papers Nami had given him. He selected his largest brush, which was as wide as his fist, went out and picked up the small wooden bucket containing the fresh ink. He paused. He'd forgotten something. He put the bucket down and went back into his room, where he picked up his ink, chop and inkpad. He'd forgotten he would have to sign his work when he was done.

As it was a bright sunny day, Yosu thought he'd work outside. He went to the front of the main hall. He put his brush and bucket of ink down on the paving stones.

Abbot Nami's bad day was about to get worse. Three monks who were passing stopped to see what Yosu was doing. They thought he was going to practise his calligraphy by painting the characters with water, onto the stone slabs. It was always interesting to watch someone doing this. If the artist found his or her rhythm it was almost like observing a dance. There was a bamboo broom leaning on the wall nearby. Yosu took the broom and began to brush the floor, making sure each paving stone was clean. When he was satisfied, he picked up the sheaf of rice paper that Nami had handed him with the order to paint a picture on each one. He untied the bamboo string and carefully began to lay the sheets of paper, side by side, in a row on the floor. He stopped them from blowing away by placing stout bamboo poles along the edges.

By now a small crowd had gathered. One of Polo's cronies saw what was happening and thought he'd better fetch Polo. Polo arrived just as Yosu finished laying the row of paper. He'd used half the sheets. He then arranged the remaining fifty sheets next to the original row.

Word had spread and the crowd grew. Sill nobody knew what Yosu was doing. Polo rushed off the tell Abbot Nami that Yosu was up to something.

63

Nami and Polo arrived just as Yosu was laying the final sheet. There were now two neat rows of paper, with all the pages shoulder to shoulder.

The group of monks and nuns gathered on the pavement. They all knew that Nami was refusing to allow Yosu to leave the monastery until he had completed one hundred pieces of art and calligraphy. They suspected that this was something to do with what they were witnessing but didn't know what. They held their breath.

Yosu picked up the bucket of ink in one hand and the large brush in the other. He held the brush up and said, "One hundred pieces of art in one brush stroke. This is the essence of Zen."

He dipped the brush into the ink, placed it on the first sheet of paper and slowly walked down the line, dragging the brush across each sheet. When he reached the end of the first row, he paused, turned around, dipped his brush into the bucket again, and started to walk back down the next column, leaving another broad path of black ink in his wake.

He reached the end, put the brush and bucket down, then took out his chop and red ink pad and began stamping his signature on each piece.

Nami, looked at the two rows of rice paper. He was fuming. "What is this?"

"This is one hundred pictures, my Lord."

"One hundred pieces of toilet paper, covered in shit."

He picked a sheet up, looked at it for a second, then ripped it in half. "This isn't Art, Yosu. It's pure crap. You can't get away with it." There were still a few blank pieces of paper on the floor. He picked a sheet up and held it out to Yosu. "You did a real picture for Lord Takamori, so do one for me." He kicked the torn paper on the floor.

"And now there are only ninety-nine." He lowered his voice, "So listen, you little turd," He picked a piece of blank paper up, "You do me a real picture, right now, or you'll be pushed into a barrel of piss so deep you'll never get out. I'll make sure you choke first, then drown in it. I'll enjoy watching you go under for the last time. So do me a picture. A proper picture. Like you did for Lord Takamori Not a big splodge that looks like you spilt the ink and couldn't be arsed to wipe it up. This is a Buddhist monastery. I want a fucking real, artistic Zen picture. Geddit?" He stroked his white cashmere robe for comfort.

Yosu looked into Nami's eyes. He wanted a real artistic Zen picture did he.? He studied Nami's face. "You have a real Zen face Lord Nami." Lord Nami mistook this for a compliment. "How would you feel if I painted it?"

"A portrait. Yes, that's a good idea. Something that will go on the wall and be there for years. My Zen face. Yes, I like it. I remember seeing a picture of Shakyamuni coming out of his mountain retreat. He had the most serene Zen face. Yes, yes. My Zen face. Paint it. And make sure you get my new robe in the picture too."

Yosu dipped his brush into the paint, and before Nami could move, painted a broad, black line from his forehead to his navel.

"There. From your third eye to your third chakra. That's covered the main bits. A real Zen face."

The hole below the nose on Nami's shining black Zen face, emitted a squeal like a pig stuck with the butchers knife.

He looked down at his beautiful white cashmere robe. A black highway to Hell ran down the front all the way to the third *chakra*.

Nami stumbled back to his room. Yosu was walking along the highway to perdition. Nami wasn't so hot on the Buddhist scriptures, but when he was a boy he'd memorised all levels of Buddhist Hell (*Naraka*). He knew they'd come in useful one day. He imagined Yosu's journey through *Naraka*.

He was welcomed by the duty demon Mahakala, known as the the Great Black One. She looked him up and down with her three eyes, pointed to the entrance with one of her four arms and said, "Brother Yosu, welcome to Hell. I'll be your guide for the duration of your visit. Any questions, don't be afraid to ask. You'll go through a series of routine procedures while you're here. Don't worry; you're in the hands of fully trained professionals who only have your long-term, well-being at heart. Any discomfort you feel will only be temporary. Hell has an undeserved reputation, caused by centuries of misinformation from world religions, but I assure you our treatments and short courses are purely for therapeutic reasons. You'll feel much better when they're complete. If at any time you become worried or upset, there is always one of our trained assistants on hand to help.

Our first stop is the room here on the right. The Tongue Ripping Department. It's mainly for gossips, but what the Hell, who hasn't gossiped once in a while? Sit down over there and put your tongue out. There, that wasn't so bad, was it? Would you like a drink of water?

Don't worry if you have trouble talking, You won't be required to speak for a few days. Let me wipe that blood off your chin.
Next the Scissors Department. This is where we remove the fingers of anyone who destroyed someone's marriage. I think the damage you did to the relationship between Abbot Nami and Sister Taishin qualifies you for this. Put your hand on that wooden block on the table, and I'll tighten the clamps before I remove your fingers. You don't want to bleed to death before they're all removed. There that wasn't so bad was it? Just hold your arms in the air. Your stumps will eventually stop bleeding. Try and keep them clean. You don't want them to get infected. Follow me down the corridor. Next stop Steamer Hell. We couldn't decide if you should be brought in here, or be chained to a red-hot pillar of copper. In the end we thought the best solution was compromise. So we're going to use both. Personally, I think the blasphemous cartoon you did of Abbot Nami tipped the balance. That really upset him, you know.

"Ah, the Mountain of Ice. We all agreed this was a fitting response to your ruining the Abbot's brand-new cashmere robe. Have you any idea how much that cost? Well you can think about it tonight, as you slowly freeze solid on the side of the mountain. You'll need to remove your robe for this one. You can put it on the chair in the corner. Come and collect it when you've thawed out. After your journey on the mountain, you can warm up while you're being submerged in the pool of blood. That's just along the corridor. I know you're a vegetarian. All Buddhists are vegetarians. You don't have to swallow it. Just drown in it. We respect our customers' religious beliefs.

"Next door to the Blood Baths are the Cauldrons of Boiling Oil. Because you haven't actually raped anyone, you'll only spend an afternoon in there. I hear the oil is very good for the complexion. We only use ingredients of the finest quality.

"Next is one of my favourites. The Hell of the Crushing Boulder. This one sorts the men out from the boys. After completing it, when you've been reconstituted, you look on the chart to see where you are on the table. An abbot from Okinawa held it for almost a whole day once. Most people don't last much longer than an hour. You raise the massive boulder over your head. Don't worry, we'll help you lift it up. Then you hold it there until it slowly crushes you, and turns you into *amai* sauce. It's supposed to be a punishment for those who have killed children, but it's really a spectator sport. We like betting on how long before the contestant gets turned to mush. We enjoy it so much we let everybody have a turn.

"After that, it's the Hell of Dismemberment. That's self-explanatory. Bit expensive. Costs an arm and a leg. Ha, sorry about that. Then there's the Hell of the Mountain of Fire, where you are thrown into a live volcano. I don't know if, strictly speaking, a volcano is a mountain. But you get the idea.

"And to finish off the tour, you can get crushed by stone grinders in the Hell of Mills. They use the same sort of mechanism that grinds grain for flour, or you can skip the Hell of Mills and be repeatedly sawn in half in the Hell of Saws. That's up to you. The workers in the Hell of Saws are a bit dozy, and sometimes go on well in advance of the allotted time. If it were my choice, I'd go for the Hell of Mills. A bit of crunching and grinding and it's all over. The idiots in the Hell of Saws sometimes go on all night. By dawn they're up to their necks in blood.

"That ends our little tour. I hope you're a little wiser about what goes on down here. Rest assured we're all experts and every piece of you will be safe in our hands. Any questions? Good. You'll pass the gift shop on the way out. Feel free to buy any souvenirs. We've a wide selection of mini-torturing devices, blood baths, crushing boulders, tools for tongue-ripping and so on. Feel free to spend as much time in there as you like. Well, that's everything. We hope you've enjoyed your visit. Do come again."

Abbot Nami had reached the end of the line with Yosu. He had run out of patience. He genuinely, sincerely, wholeheartedly wanted to kill him. What he'd done to his cashmere robe alone deserved the death penalty. Never mind the cartoon that was hanging in Lord Takamori's castle, making him the laughing stock of the region, or the humiliation of his 'Zen face'. There was no doubt about it. He had to go. Nami prayed that the attendants at every level of Hell would be ready and waiting for him when he arrived. He'd send a prayer to Buddha, asking if he could go and watch. He was, after all, an abbot and master of Zen.

Yosu saw Jo, his friend from the cherry orchard, standing nearby, He waved him over,

"Jo, will you do me a great favour please?" Jo nodded. "Gather up these sheets and look after them for me. It's important that you keep them in the order they're in on the floor. Is that alright? I'll be most grateful. I'm not sure how today is going to end up, and I'd like to make sure that the pictures are alright."

"Brother Yosu, I'll be happy to take care of them. I must say, most of us like the final picture you did, 'Zen Face."

Yosu realized he wasn't alone. Jo had cheered him up ready for the next round.

Prison

Abbot Nami beckoned to Polo, who trotted over with his two acolytes. "Polo, you know that small store room behind the kitchen?" Polo nodded, "Take the bastard and lock him in there. There's a bolt on the outside."

Polo and his deputies walked over to Yosu, still standing holding his brush like a samurai ready for another decapitation.

As we now know, the *fude* (ink-brush) is mightier than the *katana*. (samurai sword)

Polo sneered parodying Yosu's own words back to him, "You must come with me you fucking idiot, from a Buddhist perspective of course. The two lickspittles forced out a couple of sycophantic laughs.

Yosu was riding high. There was no stopping him. "Polo, speaking of the Buddhist perspective, have you ever seen your Zen face?"

Polo looked puzzled. He hated *koans*.

Yosu dipped his brush into the ink bucket.

"Wave comes up the beach." He said quietly.

He gently smacked Polo with the brush. One side of his face became black, like a Tengu who couldn't decide if he was good or bad.

"Wave goes back to the sea."Polo shrieked, "Grab him!"

The acolytes took an arm each. "To the kitchen store-room."

The three Tengus dragged Yosu off to his new home. This wasn't the first time Yosu had encountered a Tengu. The last one was much friendlier and taught him how to make ink. These three were simply spiteful, sycophantic schmuks. Polo pushed Yosu through the doorway, threw a bucket in after him, slammed the door and slid the bolt. "Enjoy yourself brother Yosu. It's a bit dark in there for painting, but you can sit on your lazy arse in the puddles on the cold floor and meditate all day." The acolytes laughed at Polo's wit.

There was a small window, high up the wall. It had been boarded up. A little light forced its way into the room through the cracks between the planks.

Abbot Nami could also play Go. He knew that attacking head on was a fruitless and dangerous tactic. You had to quietly saunter around the outside of the board, then tie up with a few of your stones that had previously ended up behind your opponents defences. Once isolated, they were dead. He had to punish Yosu severely, but he had to get his hundred paintings delivered before Yosu was defeated and his stones were removed from the board.

His first move was clear. He'd use the *katana* and rice pudding method. Beat the subject with the *katana* from the rear, and lead them forwards by waving a sweet rice pudding in their face. It worked for both stroppy mules and stubborn monks.

Yosu's first night in the storeroom was spent sitting in a puddle, leaning against the damp wall, meditating and shivering.

Early in the afternoon, he heard the bolt slide, and the door creaked open. The light dazzled him. All he could make out were two silhouettes standing in the doorway. When he got used to the glare, he recognized Abbot Nami and Brother Polo.

Nami glanced down at the floor, which was covered in half a centimetre of water. "I trust you had a comfortable night. I'm pleased to see you seem to have calmed down somewhat. It's a bit damp in here." Polo sniggered."So, Brother Yosu. Are you ready to get back to work, and do me some decent pictures?"

Yosu knew his pictures were currency, and he was going to have to buy himself out of prison."Abbot Nami, I realize I've been headstrong and impetuous. I apologise and hope we can put the past behind us and start with a clean sheet and a fresh pot of ink, so to speak."

The Abbot smiled. "Yes, I hoped you'd see sense. And you're happy to try again and paint some proper pictures? Something that will raise some funds for the monastery. You are, after all, an artist. Trained by none other than the great Ryokan himself. So when can you start work?"

"Well, Father. I could start today, but first I'll need some equipment and so on."

"What will you need?"

"Obviously, I'll need paper, my brushes, water, water containers, materials to make ink, my chop and inkpad. I'll need a table and a stool, and if you don't want me to drown while I'm asleep, a bed."

"We'll sort everything out. When will you deliver the first painting?"

Yosu realized what Nami was doing. He was trading paintings for materials and whatever Yosu needed. This would probably include food and drink. Yosu had to admire his cunning.

Yosu spent another night sitting and shivering on his wet arse trying to meditate. Next morning Polo opened the door and delivered a small bamboo table and stool. He returned later with a sheaf of rice paper and pot of water.

"Polo, I'll need a brush, ink-stick and an ink-stone. Then I'll do you a list."

"Yosu, stick your brush, your ink-stick and your ink-stone where the sun don't shine." He laughed as if it was his own joke, "And enjoy your breakfast." He laughed again, a little more sadistically. Then he went to report back to Abbot Nami."So I told him to stick them where the sun don't shine. Then I told him to enjoy his breakfast." They both laughed. Nami said, "I'll go and see him again in the morning. He'll have had three nights on the wet floor and three days without food. He should be ready to cooperate by now."

"Well, at least he'll be ready for his breakfast."

Yosu spent another day in the damp and the dark. He drank the water that had been delivered for his painting. It tasted slightly of soot, but he didn't mind.

Next morning the bolt slid open again. Abbot Nami entered, followed by Polo. "Brother Yosu, they still haven't brought you a bed. Polo, get it sorted out today. Yosu can't be expected to sleep on a wet floor. And how can he paint in the dark? Get those planks removed from the window."

Yosu coughed. He was catching a cold. He looked ill. He had dark rings under his eyes, which had lost their sparkle. He found it difficult to concentrate.

"So when shall I see your first picture?"

"Well Father, I've got some paper, although it's getting damp. But I'll need my brushes, ink and ink-stone before I can begin." He coughed again.

Nami considered the situation. He didn't want Yosu dropping dead before he'd finished his hundred pictures. Living in this room with next to nothing to eat would slowly kill him. That wouldn't be a bad outcome, but he needed his pictures first, so he had to keep him alive a bit longer. He considered sending him back to his old room where he was used to working. Then he remembered the nasty cartoon of "The Wise Abbot" he'd heard was hanging on Lord Takamori's wall. And there was the time when he attacked him and the other monks with a large paint brush. No, he could stay here and stew for a while longer. He needed to learn his lesson. Although he was getting ill, he'd survive until the weekend. They'd better let him have a bit of food today. After all, you can't torture a corpse.

Halfway through the day, Polo's sidekicks entered the storeroom and tore down the thin planks of wood covering the window. The light flooded in. A little later, one of them arrived with Yosu's brushes, ink, ink-stone and another pot of water. That afternoon there was a knock on the door. Jo entered carrying a small tray. On it was a bowl of cold miso soup, a small mound of rice and a cup of cold green tea. Because Yosu had been starved for three days, it was feast. Before he left Jo reached inside his robe and pulled out a handful of ripe cherries.

"Don't eat them all at once, Yosu or they'll give you stomach ache and get you moving faster than you want." He pointed towards the bucket with his foot.

No bed arrived, but Yosu was able to fashion a narrow platform on the floor using the planks that had been taken down from the window. He built a base from the low table and wet cushions, then lay the planks across them. If he was careful, when he stretched out on his construction he was held a couple of inches above the water. The table

72

end of the bed was fairly dry. For the first time during his confinement, he had a reasonable night's sleep.

On the eighth day his brushes, ink-stone, ink-block and water pot arrived. But he didn't feel like painting. The world and everything in it seemed farther away. A gap was growing between what he saw, heard and felt, and the person behind his senses. Even the simplest tasks, like putting his table upright in the morning, seemed almost beyond his capabilities. His skin was starting to flake off, and although he was obviously losing weight, his legs were swelling.

Jo arrived with Yosu's food, a small handful of cold rice and a cup of cold green tea. When he arrived, Polo's two lieutenants were on guard duty outside. Nami didn't want anybody entering, seeing or communicating with Yosu. One of the guards poked through the rice with his finger, to make sure who knows what wasn't being smuggled into him. Jo was shocked and concerned by Yosu's condition. He thought, "If Yosu continues like this, he won't be painting any pictures for Abbot Nami, or anyone else.

After his visit, Jo went back to see Abbot Nami. He was sitting on his balcony, stuffing himself with cubes of *goma tofu*.

Jo was soft and gentle, and this was often mistaken for docility and stupidity, but he wasn't stupid.

"Lord Nami, I've just taken Yosu his rice and I'm worried that he won't be able to deliver your one hundred pictures. In fact he may not be able to deliver any of them?"

"Why not?"

"Because he'll be dead. He's starving to death."

"Don't be ridiculous. He's faking it. He's been eating rice every day."

"Yes, Lord. But the amount is so small that it's not preventing him from starving."

"Well, that's his own fault. He should have thought about that when he attacked me and the brothers with his paint brush. Or when he gave that disgusting picture of me to Lord Takamori. You know about the Law of Karma, Brother Jo. Well, you're seeing it in action. As you sow, so shall you reap. I'm not an idiot. I know people will remember Yosu's obscene degrading cartoon, and his attack with the paintbrush for many years. But I'll make sure they remember how he paid for his stupidity. I'll call in later and see how he's getting along. If he's started my pictures yet. Thank you, Brother Jo. You can go now."

All Jo could think of was how he'd love to see the picture of "The Fat Abbot." He'd be looking at it a lot sooner than he realized.

Jo returned to Yosu's cell. He asked Yosu if there was anything he could do for him. Yosu was getting worried. He could only think of one way out. He remembered Lord Takamori's offer of assistance. He didn't imagine things would have become this bad. Takamori's offer was the only way he could think of to escape. He spoke to Jo with a whisper.

"Take four of my Zen face pictures and deliver them to Lord Takamori. You collected them in order?" Jo nodded. "Take the first four pictures from the pile and tell Takamori they are a gift. Carrying the pictures will make it easy to get into the palace and get an audience. Otherwise it could take days getting past the officials. Last time I saw him he told me to get in touch if there was any trouble and I needed help. Tell him what's been happening here, that I'm imprisoned, starving and need to accept his offer of assistance."

"I'll leave this morning."

Joe was relieved. Yosu's slide towards death seemed to be reversing. He hoped Lord Takamori could pull Yosu back from the brink.

Taishin

Taishin was also reaching a crossroads in her life. After she confronted Abbot Nami, her work in the monastery changed. She was no longer required to serve Nami personally every day and was given a string of more menial jobs. She really didn't mind cleaning, washing and preparing food. She was no longer in the presence of the fat abbot's grasping gaze and his leering lips. This was a more desirable way to spend her time. She was happier in her new line of work but she felt that it wouldn't last long. It was a welcome intermission. However, she knew how duplicitous Name could be, and felt that he would definitely want some revenge on the humiliation she had laid on him. Kaki confirmed this view. She told Taishin that when the incident where she'd publically rejected his advances was forgotten, he would be out to get her. He was nasty and vindictive and had a long memory.

She spent more time alone, meditating and in contemplation. Taishin was close to Kaki, a much older nun. Kaki had been a member of the aristocracy, and had become a favourite concubine of a rich Daimyo. She gave birth to his son, who also became Daimyo after his father died. After his death, Kaki became a nun. Tonight she had invited Taishin for tea. Besides writing poetry Kaki was an expert at conducting the tea ceremony. Young nuns like Taishin, loved to take tea with her.

Taishin and Kaki enjoyed each other's company. Kaki had lived a happy rewarding life. She had loved the Daimyo and had seen much of Japan. She was experienced with the politics and wrangling of the court. She had been an advisor to her husband as well as his favourite concubine. She was a good judge of character. The Daimyo always made sure she was present on social occasions, so afterwards she could tell him her opinion of their guests. Like Ryokan, Kaki was oblivious to what others thought of her. She was reaching the end of a long and contented life. Kaki was happy to share her wisdom, experience and opinions with Taishin. She taught Taishin, and many others, the subtleties and nuances of the tea ceremony without their realizing she was teaching them.

Kaki complimented Taishin on confronting Abbot Nami, who she called "an ignorant pig grubbing about in shit, dressed up as a monk". "Kaki, I became a nun to experience freedom from the burdens of the world, but Nami makes the monastery seem like a prison. I'm not happy here. I don't know what to do."

"Well, leave, my dear. Go and see what surprises the world has waiting to show you. You are young. And you don't know what life will do next."

"But Elder Sister, I'm happy being a nun. I know this is the life for me. It's just that I can't live here. It's Nami. I know it's wrong, but I hate him. I know I should be detached, but I sense him everywhere. And when I see him it's even worse. "

"Taishin, you have good reason to hate him. But you know you can leave this place and still be a nun. Be a different type of nun for a while. You could take the path of the *Unsui*, travelling around visiting different Masters. Drifting from place to place like the clouds in the sky or petals floating down a stream. Then you really will have detached yourself from the ignorant little pig. To Hell with him. All seventeen levels of the place. Do you know much poetry Taishin?"

"I've heard very little."

"Good poetry can inspire a person just as much as the sutras. Some of the greatest teachers are also poets. Their simple words can sometimes lead you out of confusion as surely as the Three Baskets of Wisdom. Wait here a minute."

Kaki disappeared inside for a few minutes, and returned with a small handwritten book. She flicked through the pages, stopped and handed the open book to Taishin. "Read this one. It's relevant to what you're going through."

Children,
let's go to the mountain
to view the violets.
If they scatter away tomorrow,
what can we do?

76

The way the words came together made them more than the simple sentences they sat in. They gently pushed at her soul. Her eyes opened a bit wider and the world grew a little larger. The poet had used the words to make something beautiful, the way that an artist uses paints to make more than simple colours. They had also entered her mind and given her a new perspective on life. Taishin decided to write some of her own poetry. If she didn't like it, she could always throw it away. And who knows, maybe it would work magic like the verse about viewing the violets?

A voice was telling her to seize her opportunity to go to the mountain. A door had opened for Taishin and a beam of light shone through. Who knew how long it would be open? She could walk out of the monastery tomorrow. She could leave and drop the weight from her shoulders and walk on . Her heart soared. Her mind was made up. She would walk out tomorrow. She took a deep breath. She knew everything would work out.

"That verse was written by our brother Ryokan. Good advice eh?"said Kaki.

"Thank you Sister. You have pointed to a way out of my suffering. I'll think hard what you've said. If I walk out of here as an *Unsui* maybe I'll find out what the world has to offer. If I go, I'll miss you Kaki."

"I'll miss you too Taishin. And take a stout staff with your blanket and your begging bowl. You are very beautiful, and who knows what beasts and trolls you might have to deal with. A sharp crack on the head with a strong staff should cover most situations. Abbot Nami isn't the only turd in Japan."

Next morning Taishin went to visit Jo in the cherry orchard. He was eager for her to taste the new crop of cherries. They were delicious, sweet and juicy.

"These are delightful, Brother Jo. How do you do it?"

"I'll tell you, but don't tell anyone else. It's my secret. I watch."

"You watch?"

"Yes, that's all I have to do. I simply watch them grow. It's wonderful. I don't have to do anything. Sometimes to look busy I do things like clear the dead branches away. In autumn I burn them, but

77

that's just a disguise. I don't want anybody to find out that the cherries grow themselves. If I wasn't here, they'd grow just the same. That's my secret. They know how to grow on their own. They don't need my help. Occasionally, if there's a drought I give them a drink, or if they get attacked by pests I help them out. But usually I just watch them. So keep it to yourself. Now, have you just come to taste the cherries, or is there anything I can do for you?"

"Well Brother Jo, I too have a secret which I'd like you to keep. I'm going to leave the monastery soon. I'm going to follow the path of *Unsui*, and travel around and meet different Masters. One of the sisters told me I need to take a stick, or a staff, in case I need to defend myself when I'm travelling alone. You spend your time in the orchard and I thought I'd come and ask you if you had one."

"I'm the wrong person to ask, Taishin. You need to see Brother Reigen, our carpenter. I'll take you round to his workshop and introduce you."

Taishin didn't even know there was a carpenter's workshop in the monastery. The place seemed full of secret paths, corridors, rooms and annexes.

Jo took Taishin down a winding alley and into a large room containing half a dozen monks and nuns. The room was filled with the aroma of freshly cut wood. It was delicious. Taishin took a deep breath. Jo introduced Taishin to Reigen, the chief carpenter. He remembered her from her confrontation with Abbot Nami. She had impressed him by standing up to the abbot, and he was happy to help her in whatever way he could. She explained that Kaki had advised her to take a staff on her travels.

"What you need is a *bokken*." Taishin was puzzled. "That's a piece of hardwood, shaped like a sword. But don't be fooled. It's not a toy. A whack to the shin and it can break your leg. One to the side of the head will knock you out. One of our brothers here is well acquainted with the *bokken*. He knows how to make them and is an expert at using one." He took Jo and Teishen through the workshop to meet Kanzan.

Kanzen said, "You went to ask Jo for wood for a bokken. Cherry wood is good for furniture, chairs and tables, but it's not really good for a bokken. For that you need a nice length of red oak. We've

78

got a couple of pieces somewhere. I'll sort something out for you. Come back in a couple of days and I'll have one ready. Do you know how to use one?"

Taishin said, "Close my eyes and swing as hard as I can? "She shrugged.

"You'd better come round after breakfast tomorrow and I'll teach you the basics. If you try on your own you'll probably send the *bokken* flying in the air, maybe into the river, or bouncing off some innocent monk's head. You can use one of mine until yours is ready ."

Next morning she had her first lesson, which was mainly how to hold the *bokken* so you didn't hurt yourself or throw it up into the air. Kanzan explained, "The *bokken* represents a sword, so you never touch the edge of the blade." He taught her to hold the blade very lightly, and see it as an extension of her body. "You and the bokken are one," he said.

He taught Taishin to point the blade at her adversary's eyes, so all they could see was the tip of the blade. He explained the importance of balance. She understood she had to stay relaxed and not force the blade.

On the third day, she had her own *bokken* and was ready to face the enemy. After a week Kanzan had taught her the three basic strikes: straight down, straight forward and across from the side. "That should be enough to fight off an idiot or two." Only time would tell.

She felt confident with her "stick" in her belt, and was ready to begin her pilgrimage. She walked around the monastery and said goodbye to Kaki, Jo, and Kanzan. Jo told her where Yosu was imprisoned. She went round and knocked on the door, but it was silent inside. She thought she heard a moan, but she wasn't sure what it was or where it came from. She continued to the dining room for her last meal at the monastery. She sat at the bench in the dining hall eating her rice porridge, looking around at everyone she knew, wondering if she'd ever see them again.

Then she set off towards the north, heading for Echigo Province. Kaki had told her about the poet who wrote the poem about going to the mountains, about looking at the violets before they disappeared. It was written by Ryoken, a Master who lived in Echigo, on Mount Kugami.

He was a Zen Master, poet, artist and calligrapher. He sounded like someone she'd like to meet. And there were lots of other monasteries and Masters she could visit on the way.

Many monasteries had an entrance protocol. Visitors were asked a *koan* at the gate. If your answer was satisfactory, you were welcomed in, given a bed and fed. If your answer wasn't acceptable, or simply rubbish, or you clammed up and couldn't reply, you were refused entry and had to sleep in a field outside or walk on to the next abbey.

Some monasteries allowed travelling supplicants entrance without evaluation. Taishin was looking forward to her encounters at the monastery gates. Her mind was like her new *bokken*. She was a child with a new toy. She was eager to test both her mind and the *bokken*.

Her enthusiasm for her new life didn't last very long. It began to rain. At first she marched on, telling herself how beautiful and refreshing the rain was. She was a Buddhist. The outside world was manufactured from illusion. The unspeakable mystery of Enlightenment drew her onwards. But after an hour, she wanted the mystery to draw her onwards out of the wet. She wished she was back in the monastery, sitting in the dining room with the other renunciates, drinking green tea. Eventually, she came across a small hut, where a farmer kept his tools. It was cold and draughty, but at least it was out of the rain. She had a small ball of cold rice in her bowl. She was saving it for an emergency, and this surely was an emergency. She ate it as slowly as she could. She would have to beg tomorrow. She still hadn't got used to begging, but there wasn't a lot to it. You usually sat there with your bowl and occasionally said something like, 'Alms please," followed by "Thank you Sister," or "Thank you Brother."

There were a couple of bales of dry grass at one end of the hut, which the farmer had obviously stored to feed the animals in winter. Placed end to end, they made a comfortable dry bed, provided you didn't mind sharing it with a few mice.

Taishin was woken up by a third bale of dry grass next morning. The door opened, and a hay bale wearing a large conical bamboo *kasa* (hat), stood staring at her in shock. Taishin was just as shocked to be woken by a man-sized hay bale. Between the bale and the hat was an amazed human face, stunned by the surprise in his tool-shed. It was the farmer. He was wearing a *mino*, a traditional straw rain coat that went from his shoulders down to his ankles. *Minos* were good for keeping out the rain. Anyone who wore one resembled a walking haystack.

"Good morning sir, I am sister Taishin, a Zen nun. I took shelter from the storm last night and sheltered in your hut. Thank you for your kindness. I hope I haven't caused you any problems."

"Not at all Sister." The farmer knew his manners and his duty to the monastic orders. Besides, he had been in dire need of a monk or a nun for over two weeks. Sister Taishin appearing in his shed was an answer to his prayers. It was truly serendipitous.

"Sister, you must be hungry. Please join me in my house for some breakfast. I'll wait outside for you."

Things were looking up. She had been soaked and found a dry hut, she was tired and found a bed, and now she was hungry and she'd found a breakfast, or rather the breakfast had found her.

The straw man led her down to his house, sat her down at the kitchen tableand served them both a cup of green tea. When they'd finished the tea, he placed a bowl of rice on the table, followed by a black lacquer tray. The tray stood on legs and was covered with a variety of food. There were boiled and pickled vegetables, a small bowl of miso soup, tofu covered in sesame seeds, toasted wheat cakes and more tea.

After they'd finished eating and were sipping the second cup of tea, the farmer asked Taishin, "Sister, I've been praying for someone like yourself to pass by. My wife died recently and there has been nobody to recite some *sutras* for her. She was a devout Buddhist and I don't think her soul would be able to continue its journey without some ceremony to send it on its way. Would you be so kind as to repeat some of the words of Lord Buddha, to guide her on to the next world?"

"Of course dear Brother. Show me your shrine and fetch some incense."

The farmer showed her into the next room. In the corner was a small altar with a carved wooden statue of the Buddha, sitting meditating in the lotus position. Behind the statue was a black and white woodblock print of the Buddha seated on a lotus, with a rose

81

growing behind his back, peeking over his shoulder. A nervous hare sat at his feet gazing up at his face. Buddha seemed to be looking down at the hare. The print was slightly blurred. It had been cut from a page of four, which in turn had been torn from a book.

Taishin sat before the shrine. The farmer lit a stick of incense and stood it in a small incense-holder next to a pot of wilting wild flowers. They bowed to the nervous hare.

Taishin recited the words of the Buddha, from the *sutra* "Mindfulness of Death": *"Monks, mindfulness of death -- when developed and pursued -- is of great fruit and great benefit. It plunges into the Deathless, has the Deathless as its final end. And how is mindfulness of death developed and pursued so that it is of great fruit and great benefit, plunges into the Deathless, and has the Deathless as its final end?"* Taishin continued quoting the *sutra* for another ten minutes, advising reflection on death should inspire extra effort: *"…should put forth extra desire, effort, diligence, endeavour, undivided mindfulness, and alertness for the abandoning of those very same evil, unskillful qualities."* She finished by saying *"If your turban caught fire you would put forth extra endeavour to extinguish it. In the same way you should apply extra effort to abandon those negative qualities which condemn you to death."*

Taishin especially liked the section of the *sutra* where the turbans caught fire. The farmer had quite enjoyed that part too. He asked Taishin, "Do think my wife will gain merit from this ceremony?"

"Not only your wife; everyone who is alive will benefit from reciting the *sutras*. The smallest action affects the greatest events. Think of an archer in battle, who is bitten by a mosquito. It causes him to miss his target, which was the Daimyo of the opposing army. If the mosquito hadn't bit him, he would have hit the Daimyo and killed him, winning the battle. Because of the tiny insect the Daimyo lived and the battle was lost. When a stone is thrown into a river, nobody knows where the ripples will end. Yes, every living being benefits from the recitation of the *sutras*."

The farmer thought for a minute, something was clearly bothering him. "You say all living beings will benefit. But my wife may be very weak. Others may be much stronger than her. They may take advantage of her, and get the benefit she should have."

"Brother, the next world isn't like a queue at the baker's when he is running out of fresh bread. It is like a huge lake of clear, cool water, where everyone may come and fill their bucket and the level never goes down. Because somebody fills their bucket, doesn't mean there's not enough for everyone. Don't worry. She'll get all the benefit she can carry."

The farmer's face relaxed for a moment, then became worried again. "That is a good lesson. You say the *sutra* benefits everyone. But please could you make just one exception? My neighbour is nasty and mean. He swears and spits at me and lets his goats eat my vegetables. Would you mind excluding him from all those living beings?"

"I'm afraid that's not possible. If people could be excluded, there would be chaos in Heaven. All the prayers would be arguing all the time. Only positive blessings are allowed entrance. Thank you for your kindness." Taishin picked up her bowl and blanket, stuffed her *bokken* into her belt and left, leaving the straw man to his own devices.

The weather had improved and she was enjoying life again. She chuckled when she remembered the straw man's request to exclude his neighbour from humanity. Late that afternoon, she reached a small monastery, where she thought she'd request shelter for the night. This was a traditional place, where you had a win a debate on Buddhism to gain entry. Two brothers were always on duty at the gate. One of them was well educated. His younger brother was stupid and only had one eye. There was knock on the door. The older brother opened it.

"Hello Sister. How can I help you?"

"I was hoping you might be able to give me shelter for the night."

"Well, we have a long tradition here of sheltering travelling monks and nuns. But to qualify, you must make and win an argument about Buddhism."

"I will enjoy that Brother."

"And you will make the argument with my younger brother." He omitted to tell Taishin that his brother was crazy. "Do come in." Taishin entered the gatehouse. "I'll just fetch my brother." He went into the next room, where his brother was waiting. "I'm exhausted, I've been working since sunrise, so I'd like you to debate with the nun. Listen, before you begin, request that the dialogue takes place in silence."

The one-eyed younger brother made the request and Taishin agreed. They both sat down before the shrine. The older brother waited next door. Because the debate was in silence, he couldn't hear what was happening, so he became extremely curious. Then he heard his brother roar in anger. The next moment Taishin appeared in the room. She said, "Your brother is very wise, he defeated me."

The older brother was even more intrigued. "Tell me the details of the dialogue."

"We agreed the debate was to take place in silence, so I wasn't sure how to begin. I held up one finger, to represent Lord Buddha, the enlightened one. He held up two fingers to represent Buddha and his teaching. So I held up three fingers, representing Buddha, his teaching and his followers, living the life of Dharma. Then your brother shook his clenched fist in my face, showing that all three come from one realization. Thus he won the debate, proving that I have no right to stay here."

His brother entered the room, angry and flustered. "I hear you won the debate. Well done."

"Won nothing. I should have given her a good beating. But because she's a woman I held myself back. But at least I should have given her a good slap before she left."

"Tell me what happened in the debate."

"Well, as soon as she saw me she held up one finger. She is insulting me by saying I only had one eye. Because she was a visitor, I was polite. I was kind to her. I held up two fingers, saying it is good that she has two eyes. Then she becomes very rude by holding up three fingers, telling me between us we have only three eyes. That made me really angry. So I raised my fist to give her a punch, but she ran out the room. And that was the end of it. Nobody said anything."

"Well done brother. You were right not to hit her. You gave her a good enough beating in the debate."

Taishin set off down the road to the next monastery, still trying to work out what had happened with the one-eyed monk.

Jo the Gardener

Jo left Giso to deliver Yosu's message to Lord Takamori. He had four of Yosu's pictures, his blanket and his bowl. As Yosu had requested, he rolled up the pictures in the order in which they were painted. Lord Takamori's palace was usually three days' walk, but Jo was worried was worried that Yosu wouldn't last much longer. So he was determined to make the journey in two days.

This was the first time Jo had been outside the monastery for three years. He'd forgotten what it was like out in the big wide world. What made the greatest impression was the huge amount of people everywhere. He couldn't believe how many there were, travelling along the roads, sitting by the roads, buzzing around the villages, working in the fields, playing in the streets. The planet was infested with them. From morning to night they were chattering, rushing about their business, and wandering around. But when he thought about it, he realized they were doing nothing more than keeping themselves alive. He couldn't imagine where they all came from.

By the end of the second day, he was exhausted. His legs were tired, his feet were sore and he was suffering from an overdose of humanity. He longed to be back in the cherry orchard in the monastery.

He needed another night's sleep before reaching the palace. He left his comfortable field at dawn and walked into the town. He felt like an animal whose cage door had been accidently left open. He had wandered out and got lost. People were wandering about everywhere. He didn't even know there was this amount of men and women on the whole planet.

"What do they do all day?" he asked himself. He couldn't imagine. The only attention he received was odd glances. Occasionally, someone would put their hands together and bow their head in greeting. In response, he dipped his head like a bird.

It wasn't difficult to find the palace. It towered over the town like a giant monarch surveying his realm. People were scurrying around the palace like mice. They got on with their business as if the great building wasn't there. It was beautiful, covered with splendid symmetrical curved roofs, all different sized versions of the same shape. The curves resembled drifting snow, gently sloped against a wall. The roofs were sometimes stacked three or four high, each smaller than the one below. The entrance was a massive arch, with stacked roofs the same design as the rest of the palace. The palace soon became part of the scenery, and after a while you didn't notice it.

An armed guard stood either side of the gateway. Jo thought he could simply walk in, but before he could enter, a tall spear swung down in front of him blocking his entrance.

"What is your business with Lord Takamori monk?"

"I wish to have an audience with him. I have a message from Brother Yosu, at the abbey at Gisu. I also bring him some papers from Brother Yosu." He pulled the roll of pictures partly out of the bag on his shoulder.

"Wait here." The guard walked into the palace, leaving Yosu beneath the arch. He turned around to see that the samurai who was taking his message had been immediately replaced by another guard. After a couple of minutes, the guard reappeared accompanied by a man who was obviously one of Takamori's officials. He was wearing a splendid silk jacket and carrying a small stick and an air of authority. He walked up to Jo and asked, "Are you Brother Yosu?"

"No, sir. I bring a personal message and some papers from Brother Yosu."

"Where is Brother Yosu?"

"He is imprisoned in the abbey at Gisu."

"Come with me."

Jo had never been more aware of his poverty than when he walked through the palace to see Lord Takamori. He had slept in fields for the previous four nights. He had been in such a hurry he hadn't taken time to take care of himself. His robe was dirty owing to sleeping on the ground. He hadn't stopped to bathe. He felt like he was being escorted out rather than welcomed in.

Jo felt as if every step his muddy feet took on the beautiful silk carpets was somehow causing irreversible damage. The official spoke to him as they walked through the corridors towards the reception chamber, "When you get into the chamber, bow and kneel on one of the cushions on the floor before Lord Takamori's throne. Don't stand unless he tells you to. Don't speak to him unless answering one of his questions. And don't get nearer to him than ten paces. The samurai guards have strict instructions to behead anyone who gets any nearer to him unless Lord Takamori requests it. Understand?"

Jo involuntarily rubbed his neck. He liked his head where it was. He was hungry and he wouldn't be able to eat his breakfast if his head was rolling on the floor or decorating the garden stuck on a stick. A shudder ran up his spine. "Yes I understand."

"You haven't had breakfast yet?" Jo shook his head "We can sort that out after you've had your audience with Lord Takamori."

They walked into the hall. Lord Takamori was seated at the far end, on a raised dias. Two of his concubines sat on the floor behind him gently fanning themselves. Josu had expected to see the daimyo seated on a magnificent chair, but his seat was covered by his generous black silk cloak. Six or seven court officials were seated on cushions in rows on the floor on either side of the hall. They reminded him of two rows of plants in his garden at the monastery. Some of them looked like they needed watering.

The official, who had accompanied Jo, bowed his head. Jo followed suit.

"Brother Jo. Welcome to my court. I believe you have something for me from Brother Yosu."

Jo reached into his bag. His arm was immediately grabbed by one of the Daimyo's samurai guards, who had mysteriously appeared at his side. He looked and felt around in the bag, checked the roll of Yosu's paper pictures, then nodded to the Daimyo and stepped back.

"Forgive my guard, Brother Jo, but lots of people would like to kill me, so I have to take precautions. You wouldn't believe how many of my ancestors have been poisoned, stabbed, shot, drowned and met messy ends to their lives. I don't want to be another daimyo suffering from an early death. Nice as it may be in Heaven, I'm in no hurry to get there. Now, what's the gossip from the monastery? I hear brother Yosu may be in prison."

Jo explained that Yosu was unhappy in the monastery. Abbot Nami was trying to force him to produce artwork the way the Abbot wanted, not the way Yosu painted them. He kept saying he wanted "proper paintings, nature scenes, people, landscapes, bamboo, that sort of thing." " Well, even the most ignorant person knows that an artist must be allowed the freedom to work in their own way. So Yosu decided to leave the monastery and follow the path of the Unsui. He told me he'd like to travel north and drink a few glasses of saki with Ryokan, his old master."

The Daimyo smiled and nodded. He'd met Ryoken. He admired and respected him. He had a couple of pieces of his calligraphy on the wall. He too would like to travel north and have a few glasses of saki with him.

Jo told the Daimyo how Nami had demanded one hundred works of art which Yosu had to produce before he left. And they had to be 'proper paintings.'

"What did he do then?"

"Yosu took a hundred sheets of paper and carefully lay them on the floor in a straight line. He'd already mixed up a bucket of black ink. He dipped his biggest brush into the ink and walked along the row, dragging the brush over the paper as he went. He finished Nami's hundred paintings in five minutes."

"How did the Abbot react?"

"He hated it. He said the pictures were toilet paper covered in shit. He ripped one of the pictures in half and said now he only had ninety-nine pictures. He demanded Yosu make the hundred up with a 'proper painting'. He said he wanted a real, artistic Zen picture. Like those he did for you.

"Yosu told the abbot he had a real Zen face, and asked him if he'd like it painting. Nami fancied his portrait on the wall, so he said, 'Yes'. Yosu dipped his brush into the ink and, starting at his forehead, painted a broad black line down Abbot Nami's face and body. Unfortunately for Nami, he was wearing his brand new cashmere white robe. In a few seconds he looked like a striped weasel. Yosu said, "There is your Zen face. And there is your one hundredth painting."

Takamori roared with laughter.

"The Abbot was apoplectic. He ranted and raved like a monkey with a bad-tempered scorpion up its arse. He wanted to kill Yosu there and then. He'd heard about his picture 'The Greedy Abbot.' so he already had a motive. I think it was really there and then that he decided to kill Yosu. The trouble was Yosu's pictures were the main source of income for the monastery. Without the money from his art, how was Nami going to afford new cashmere robes from Kyoto? He needed one hundred pictures. The paintings were better than money. He couldn't get rid of Yosu if there was no money in the chest."

"What happened next?"

"Well, Nami had Yosu locked up in a storeroom behind the kitchen. It's a real dump, no furniture, not even a bed, water on the floor and all sorts of creatures trotting around the place. He is trying to force him to paint some 'proper pictures' by starving him."

"How is he?"

"Not very well. Last time I saw him he looked quite ill. That's when he asked me to come and see you, give you four of his 'Zen face' pictures and ask for help."

Takamori thought for a moment, then said, "Don't worry, Brother Jo. I'll take care of everything. You must be tired and hungry after your long journey." The Daimyo looked at his assistant. "First get Shimazu and Tomoe in here. Get their horses prepared for a long journey. Take Brother Jo to the kitchen and feed him. Then show him the bathhouse, get him a clean roble and have this one washed. And give him a bed." He looked at Jo. "And when you're fed and rested, come and see me again. Don't worry about Yosu. I'll take care of that." He then sent for his doctor.

Menko

Shimazu and Tomoe were two of the Daimyos' senior samurai. Takamori told them what was happening to Yosu. "That Nami is a real shit, as you'll no doubt discover. According to Brother Jo, Nami is starving Yosu to death. It sounds like he is quite ill, so I'm sending my doctor with you to take care of him. Brother Yosu is an artist of rare talent and a monk of wisdom and integrity. I don't want his life snuffing out by an oversized idiot who thinks he's Lord Buddha. Sort him out. Whatever is necessary."

The two samurai and the doctor left the palace on horse, and set out on the road to Gisu. The journey took three days walking, and about ten hours on horseback. Shimazu and Tomoe's horses were fitter than that of the doctor. So not to delay, the samurai agreed to meet the doctor at the monastery in Gisu when he arrived.

They trotted into the monastery just before sunset. They tied their horses up and asked to see Abbot Nami. They asked where Yosu was. At first nobody knew, then a nun said she would take them. They told a monk to look after their horses and then walked through the monastery with the nun. She led them to the store room where Yosu was locked up. The door, which had previously been bolted, now had a lock on it as well. Polo was on duty in front of the door. He'd been sweeping up.

"Open the door." Demanded Shimnazu.

Polo saw their hands on the hilts of their swords and stammered, "I d' d' don't have the k' k' key. Abbot Nami has it."

"Get it."

Polo leaned the broom against the wall and stood the bucket by its side. He then hurried off to find the Abbot.

Tomoe rattled the door but it remained locked.

Abbot Nami reappeared with Polo, standing diligently behind him. He was wearing his recently laundered cashmere robe. If you looked carefully you could still see the ghost of the black skunk stripe down the centre.

"Who are you and what do you think you're doing?" he asked.

"Open this door."

"I am the Abbot of this monastery. I'm responsible for everything and everyone around here. I'm in charge. You can't just walk in here and give me orders. I don't' even know who you are." Nami's voice became louder as he became more confident.

"We are representatives of Lord Takamori. We are here on his orders. Now open the door."

Polo opened the door and the two samurai entered.

Abbot Nami puffed himself up and said, "While within the walls of this monastery, you do what I say."

Shimazo barked, "Take us to Brother Yosu."

Nami picked up the broom and jabbed the handle towards Tomoe. He had no idea what a big mistake this was. "Nobody gives me orders. I am the Abbot."

Shimazo said, more quietly, but with greater threat in his voice, "Take us to Brother Yosu. Now!"

Nami was incensed. And he didn't want anyone to find out how he'd been treating Yosu. He jabbed the broom at Tomoe, hitting him on his chest. How could Nami be so stupid? Did he know nothing about Samurai? He'd spent too long living in a monastery, giving orders and having people bow and scrape to him. He had lost touch with the world outside. He had no idea how to conduct Samurai diplomacy. It was safer to poke a poisonous snake than a Samurai.

He shouted at Tomai, "I am head of this monastery!" and jabbed him again. This was the last mistake he made.

There was sound like a brief gust of wind blowing through the leaves of a cherry tree. Tomai's sword swept through the air and the head of the monastery flew up in the air too, propelled by a brief fountain of blood. It landed on floor, eyes and mouth wide open, staring at Polo, still maintaining a look of disbelief. The look of disbelief changed to one of terror. He pissed himself. Tomae pushed the end of his *katana* into Nami's mouth, and deftly flicked his head into the bucket by the wall.

Shimazo cried, "*Menko.*"

Menko was a game played on the floor with wooden discs. If you flipped an opponent's wooden disc over by hitting it with your own disc you shouted "*Menko.*" and won the disc.

On the other side of the wall where Nami lost his head, Yosu lay on his improvised bed. He'd been starving for over two weeks. He'd run out of energy and found it difficult to concentrate. His temperature was jumping up and down like a frog in a hot wok. He felt faint, dizzy and had stomach ache. The top of his body was getting thinner, but his legs and stomach were getting fatter. For the first week he'd thought about nothing but food. He'd mixed up his fish glue with water and rather than waste it as ink, he'd drunk it as soup. By the end of the first week, he'd finished eating all his glue. He slept more and spent more time inhabiting his dreams than the room.

Everything in the world was made of snow. Silently, the sun appeared and the snow began to melt. Whatever had seemed so important to him was slowly disappearing. He didn't even mind. His faith had always told him that nothing was real. Reality was beyond the pieces of the world that surrounded us. They came and went. Only the truth, our true self remained. His meditation kept him centred while the world he was sitting in was holding his cushion up but crumbling around him.

Yosu spent more time practising meditation, known as zazen. The world was fleeing, but his breath remained. Once he'd thought that meditating pushed the world away, but sitting in the damp prison, he had a different perspective. The world seemed to be leaving of its own accord. His experience of meditation however, remained. It was always there, beneath whatever else was going on.

Breath came and went. But one day it would leave and not return.

Wave comes up the beach.
Wave goes back to the sea.

He remembered his first painting lesson from Uncle Toshio. Laying on his bed, he had nothing else to do but breathe.

Out breath
and in breath-
know that they are
proof that the world
is inexhaustible

Ryokan

Yosu felt like a magician had shown him where he hid the coin which had magically disappeared. Things were much simpler and more straightforward than he imagined. In his mind, he'd made Zen and Buddhism into an endless spiritual path that he had to walk for the rest of his life. But really it was a bench where you could sit down and rest. What was there to worry about? The wind would soon blow it all away.

Our bodies will rot and fade away
But the fruits of the Buddhist Law
Cannot be discarded.

Ryokan

He remembered his childhood. Playing with friends in the village. Where did those precious days go? Life was so simple then, so safe.

As I watch the children happily playing
Without realizing it
My eyes fill with tears

Ryokan

Breathing. It really wasn't any more complicated than that.

Wave comes up the beach.
Wave goes back to the sea.

On the other side of the wall, in the evening sunlight, Shimazo turned to Polo, who was sweating and shaking, "Get the key." He pointed with his bloody sword to Nami's hand, which was still clutching the key, "And open the door. Fast."

Polo jerked into action. He closed his eyes and removed the key from the abbots' lifeless hand. He went to open the door, but his hand was shaking so much he had difficulty getting it into the lock. Tomoe leaned over and cleaned his blade on Nami's cashmere robe. He held it up and examined it for any remaining abbot blood, and replaced it in its scabbard.

Polo managed to unlock the door. There's nothing like the fear of losing your head to concentrate your mind. The door opened and the smell of shit stumbled out. Yosu lay on his homemade bed. His skin was flaking, his hair had turned grey and his legs and stomach were swollen. His cheeks were sunken and his wide eyes were staring at something nobody else could see. He was breathing. The wave was going back to the sea.

Polo's acolytes had heard that something exciting was happening, and hurried to discover what drama was unfolding how it involved their role model. When they arrived at the store room they found Polo, two samurai and the head of the Abbey in a bucket. They wished they'd stayed gossiping in the library.

Shimazo looked at them for a moment then pointed to the pool of blood on the floor and splashed on the wall. "Get rid of that mess." He gave Nami a casual kick. "And do something with this piece of meat."

Yosu couldn't walk or even stand up under his own power. Tomoe helped him out of the store room. Shimazo barked at Polo, "Get him a chair and some tea."

Polo scurried off to the kitchen and returned a couple of minutes later with a bamboo chair. He was followed by a nun carrying a tray with a jug of tea, another jug of hot water and a cup. This wasn't the time for the tea ceremony.

Yosu sat on the chair, accepted the cup of tea from Polo, and took a deep breath. He felt like a young boy peeking over the monastery wall. He wasn't a character in the play, merely an observer. He sipped the tea. He felt the day forming around him, as if he'd been lowered into a big bath of water. He could feel the day everywhere. The day wobbled from side to side and he passed out.

When he came round, he was in a clean robe, on his old bed in his old room, with his old turnip on the wall, still reaching up to heaven. The Daimyo's doctor sat beside him, along with Brother Tosui, the monk who dispensed herbs and cared for the sick. "Brother Yosu, Lord Takamori sent me to take care of you. Because you've been starved you'll need some careful looking after for a while. Eat miso soup and drink plenty of green tea. I've talked to Brother Tosui about what herbs will help you recover. No solid foods for a couple of weeks, then only small amounts. An elephant has stepped on your stomach and you need time to recover."

Yosu was watching a play. Centre-stage was a bed with a monk in it. Two doctors were discussing the patient. "Give him plenty of ink to drink."

"That will bring the colour back to his cheeks. What colour do you suggest?"

"Well, obviously black. He's a calligrapher and artist."

"Which black?"

"I've always liked ivory black. "

"What about peach black? In his condition the fruit will help his recovery."

"Yes, good idea What do you think about Mars Black. Yes. That contains Waco Deer Glue, very nutritious."

"We could always mix in some rabbit glue. Help build his muscles up."

"What if it makes him run away?"

"Good point. If we use rabbit glue, we should tie him to the bed."

"So we agree: a mug of Peach Black and a mug of Mars Black, with deer and rabbit glue?"

"With deer and rabbit glue in his ink, he'll be out of here in no time. We'll never catch him."

96

"But we won't lose him. We can follow the trail of ink on the floor."

Then the world containing his vision of the two medical men began to distort. The walls bent and moved together. A gap opened in the ceiling and a turnip shoot rose up to escape the world with the bendy walls. Except it wasn't a turnip, it was Yosu.

The turnip had slid down from the paper on the wall and sat on the pillow by his head.

Turnips and Zen monks,
Are both best when they sit well.

Sengai

The turnip spoke to Yosu, "So where's all your Zen realization gone now? Enlightened yet? Why don't you knock out a little haiku about it?"

"There's nothing there, is there Madam Turnip?"

"Oh, by the way, I'm not actually a turnip. I'm a rutabaga. Lots of folk confuse us. We're sweeter than turnips. They're more radishy. But you're quite correct Yosu. There's nothing there. The Zen cupboard is empty. It always has been. Not even a mouldy old turnip."

Yes. When he looked there the cupboard was bare. The rutabaga climbed back onto the paper and slid up the wall, where it had sat since Yosu first put it there.

Yosu listened to Takamori's doctor giving advice to Tosui about his diet. "If you give him solid food now it will probably make him ill. He'll probably want to eat anything and everything in a couple of days, but don't let him. It's an irony that lots of starving people are killed by food. Not lack of food. Give him plenty of miso soup. You can mash vegetables and add them to the soup. Small meals, but frequent. Beans and lentils are good if they are cooked well. Rice of course. Turnip is good."

97

Yosu murmured, "Not turnip. Rutabaga. They're sweeter." Then he went back to sleep.

For the next few days the Daimyo's doctor and Tosui concentrated on Yosu's diet and supplementing it with herbs. He slowly began the journey back to health. The doctor massaged his skin with sesame oil and it stopped flaking. The swelling on his stomach and legs receded. He stopped getting the sweats. His concentration improved. He slept for long periods.

After a week, the doctor was satisfied with his improvement and was happy to return to the Daimyo.

"How are you feeling, Brother Yosu? You seem to have made a rapid recovery."

"Yes doctor. I think this is mainly because of your care."

"Yes, me and Brother Tosui. Do you think you're up to taking a walk outside? It's a lovely day out there."

Back at the palace Jo was preparing to return to the monastery. The Daimyo Takamori asked him if there was anything he needed before he left. He requested to see the cartoon of 'The Wise Abbot' that had caused all the fuss, and asked if he could look around the palace gardens before he left. The chief gardener gave him a tour. They discussed plants and gardening, with no mention of Buddhism. The gardener gave him several cuttings of plants he had admired but never seen before. Before Yosu left, the official who had met him at the gate when he arrived appeared to escort him out.

On the way out, he took him down a wide corridor where most of the Daimyo's art collection was on display. Saigo Takamori had one of the most comprehensive collections in Japan. The paintings lined the corridor in chronological order. Some of the early works were over a thousand years old. Bright, intricate mandalas on silk, decorated with Bodhisattvas and Buddhas gazed down at the people walking along the corridor. The thousand-year-old Vairacona Buddha hung next to Fugen Enemei, the Bodhisattva of Universal Virtue who prolongs life. He sat there on a piece of seven-hundred-year-old silk in his gold and silver ink. Fugen and the Buddha hadn't spoken to each other for five hundred years. By the 14th century they'd run out of things to talk about.

Further along the wall, Shaka (Guatama Buddha) was rising from his coffin. When he died, his mother was pissed off that she hadn't been contacted before he went off into Nirvana. She rushed back from her holidays to see him. When she arrived, he was already dead, and having a massage in the next world. His mother began hammering on his coffin and woke him up. Afraid of his mum's wrath, he opened the lid and rose up with a thousand rays shining out of his head. She immediately started telling him off. "What the bloody hell did you think you were doing, trotting off to Nirvana without telling me, or even saying 'Goodbye'? You might be Siddhartha Gautama, Sage of the Shakyas, Lord of the Three Worlds, Buddha of the past, present and future who has transcended the cycle of birth and death, but I'm your mother and you'll still do what you're told or you'll get my fist round your ear."

He told his mother he was sorry. He'd been really busy and it had slipped his mind to inform her he was off to the promised land. Then he muttered something or other about laws being imperishable, jumped back into his coffin and closed the lid. A sign appeared on the top saying,

"DO NOT OPEN UNTIL FIRST FULL MOON IN MAY 5059."

Near the end of the corridor was a hand scroll depicting the life of the priest Muromachi. It contained beautiful drawings of the priest and his exploits. Some pictures were set in breath-taking landscapes, some in gardens and some in the forest. The pictures were separated with pages of fine calligraphy, telling the story of the love affair between a Buddhist monk and an attractive young male acoloyte. The monks lived in separate monasteries but loved each other so much they couldn't stay apart long. The got together again and began a journey up the mountain towards the monastery. On the way, they became exhausted. They were offered help by an old man in a palanquin. As soon as they climbed into the palanquin, they were abducted. The old man was a Tengu in disguise. Things went from bad to worse. The monks from the two monasteries blamed each other for the disappearance and went to war with each other. One group assumed that the older monks father was involved and burned his mansion to the ground. The other monks took revenge by burning their opponents' monastery down.

When the fires had gone out, and tempers were cooled, the monks repented their carnal pleasures. Everybody shook hands, made up, attained salvation and lived happily ever after on a diet of rice porridge, sutras and miso soup, peppered with the odd *koan*.

Jo finished his tour of the Daimyos art gallery and set out on the journey home. The cuttings for the garden at Gisu were wrapped in wet cloth, and he was given a bag of food for the journey. The weather was good, and he didn't hurry. The crowds became less dense as he moved away from the city, but he was still amazed by the amount of people everywhere. He spent five days on the road and when he got back to the monastery everything had changed.

Yosu was on the road to recovery. He'd exercised every day with the doctor. Abbot Nami was beneath the ground pushing up flowers. The cherry blossom had come and gone.

The first thing Jo did was rush to the garden and plant his new cuttings. After he had finished in the garden he received a message that Abbot Shinran wanted to see him. Shinran was a well-respected abbot who had come to the monastery to sort out the mess left by Abbot Nami. Shinran had discussed the situation with two other senior abbots of their order before he set out. When he arrived he talked to the older monks at Gisu, and got a clear picture of what had been going on behind the walls. It was plain that shouting at a samurai and jabbing him in the chest with a broom handle was enough to cost Nami his head. Samurai lived by a strict code of honour and were beyond the law. They were entitled to behead someone for simply omitting to bow. Jabbing one with a broom handle was unforgiveable. Nami was yesterday's gossip. Abbot Shinran had been sent to the monastery to find a new abbot to replace Nami. The order needed someone who wasn't a bully, a glutton, a lecher, a thief or wallowing in earthly desires.

The most difficult quality to ascertain was the sincerity of the aspirant. Nami had been very deceptive. If asked a question he would

100

answer with what he thought the enquirer wanted to hear. He subtly tried to give the best impression of himself, regardless of the truth. Abbot Shinran knew he had to trust his instinct rather than what the candidate said. By the time he'd whittled down the list of possible replacements, he was left with a list of one - Brother Jo, the gardener.

Jo wasn't the brightest lotus floating on the pond, but he was sincere, honest, warm-hearted, committed, dedicated and devoted. There was no competition. Least of all Brother Polo, who was sure he would have made a better abbot, but had learned enough to keep his mouth shut. Seeing the previous head of the monastery flying into the air had a sobering effect. He had begun to appreciate the quiet life.

At first Brother Jo tried to refuse the position. But he soon realized it didn't involve doing much. His main job was to act as a figurehead. He could get on with his gardening. There was nobody to order him around and he could pretty much carry on as before, which he did. He continued sleeping in the small house in the cherry orchard, continued eating in the dining room with the other monks and nuns. Occasionally he'd don his orange robe and officiate at some ceremony or festival, but by and large life went on as usual. He was well liked, and the senior monks advised him without being domineering or controlling. Both Abbot Jo and the monastery garden flourished and flowered.

Yosu, however, wasn't doing so well. Starving almost to death had taken lots out of him. He looked older, his hair was grey and lines had been etched into his face that weren't there before his confrontation with Nami. His health had returned, but his spirit was still away on pilgrimage. He'd stopped painting and practising calligraphy, and showed little enthusiasm for anything other than sleep. His big questions about life were still there. The turnip on his wall, which had always symbolized his rising spirit now looked like it had been punctured and was slowly floating down back to the mud from whence it came.

His walks down to the river became less frequent, and he found it difficult to talk to Abbot Jo. He simply couldn't see the point any more. His "get up and go" had got up and gone. He spent hours laying on his bed staring at the ceiling. When he looked at his paint brushes, it seemed they belonged to somebody else, someone he knew many years ago who'd left the monastery. His problem wasn't physical. Brother Tosui had followed the advice of the Daimyo's doctor and made sure he stuck to his diet, and his body seemed to have recovered quickly. It was his spirit that had postponed its return to health.

Abbot Nami had almost destroyed Yosu's faith in everything. His path towards enlightenment was no longer visible. It was as if a snowstorm had covered every recognizable feature that had been guiding him through the forest. He didn't know which direction to take or even what his destination was. When someone tries to kill, you sense and reason have already left. And when that person is the representative of Lord Buddha, your desire and understanding crash and shatter like an ice statue. Then the pieces melt. Before long they can no longer be put back together. The water starts to evaporate. Soon there will be no trace of what once was his life.

About three weeks after Brother Jo had been installed as the new Abbot, a skinny, scruffy old monk appeared at the gate of the monastery requesting admission. Polo, who was on duty, was reluctant to let him in. He was old and needed a bath. His robe was torn and muddy. He carried an unopened bottle of saki in one hand, and a Go board under his other arm. He told Polo he was here for, "a drink and a game of Go."

"I'm sorry Brother. We don't drink alcohol and we don't gamble."

"As that so? Well ye'd better fetch the abbot then. Before I kick you up the arse you poor excuse for a monk."

Polo thought fetching the Abbot was a good idea. He didn't think he could cope with the visitor on his own. He offered the old monk a seat and went to fetch Abbot Jo. "He's dirty, scruffy and smells. What's worse is he's carrying a bottle of sake and wants to bring it into the monastery. We had a little stand-off, and he suggested I went and fetched you before he kicked me up the arse."

Polo and Jo entered the small room in the gatehouse. Abbot Jo froze for a moment, then his face broke into a smile. "Master Ryokan. It's been a long time." The old monk stood up and embraced the Abbot.

102

Jo said, "It's good to see you Master. I thought you'd disappeared forever in the mountains.

"No such luck." He held the bottle of sake up. "I ran out of sake and had to come down from the mountain to the world of illusion, delusion and confusion to get some more."

Polo was confused. Jo laughed. "Ryokan, you're a breath of fresh air. Come on in. Have something to eat. You look like you've been travelling for a while. You can have a bath. We'll give you a clean robe while we wash that one."

Half an hour later, still in his tatty robe, with his Go board under his arm and the bottle of sake in his hand, he was knocking on Yosu's door.

"Go away. I'm busy."

"Busy my arse. Git your hands off your prayer stick and open this door."

"Ryokan."

Half a minute later the door slowly opened and Yosu peeped out. "Master Ryokan. What are you doing here? What do you want?"

"Can I come in?"

"Of course, Master." Yosu stepped back and welcomed Ryokan into his room. Ryokan placed the Go board and the bottle of sake on the small table. He reached into his shoulder bag and removed `a jug, two small sake cups and two cloth bags, each containing a pot of Go stones. He placed them on the table with the board and bottle.

"I was getting a wee bit bored. So I thought you might like a game of Go and a wee drop of sake."

Before Yosu could answer, Ryokan removed the two bowls of stones and placed one each side of the board. Then he pulled the stopper from the sake bottle and threw it into the corner of the room. "Can we warm this up?"

Yosu placed a pan of water on the stove and lit it. Ryokan placed a cushion each side of the table and motioned for Yosu to sit down. He sat facing him. He looked into his bowl and saw that the stones were black. He placed them on Yosu's side and took the bowl of white stones onto his own side. "Now, how many stones would you like. I remember last time we played, you had eight. You died a slow and painful death. You'd better take nine this time."

He removed a handful of Yosu's black stones and placed one on each of the nine highlighted intersections on the board. Unlike chess, Go has a handicap system to allow players of different ability to have an even game. The highlighted intersections on the board indicate the nine positions for the extra handicap stones.

Ryokan filled the two small cups with sake, placed one in front of Yosu and raised his own cup, "Let battle commence. Banzai."

They both sipped. Yosu looked at the board and placed his first stone. Ryokan banged his white stone down in the opposite corner.

The stones seemed to know where to go. It was like building with bricks. No philosophy or insight was required. You didn't need to think about anything. The patterns began to appear as the stones clicked on the hard wood. After a couple of dozen stones, black's position began to look hopeless The pieces were made of black slate and white clamshells. They had no feelings. The only thing that could happen was they would be removed from the board and returned to their bowls.

"I called in and saw your Uncle Toshio last summer. He still makes the best ink in Japan. He told me about the time when you and your friend thought he was a Tengu and ran for your lives."

Ryokan refilled the saki cups. They both laughed.

"Yes, we were worried he was going to eat us."

Yosu placed a stone and captured four of Ryokan's pieces.

Ryokan place his stone outside the dead group, creating an escape route for half a dozen adjacent threatened stones. He repeated a well known Go proverb, "Four die and six live."

Yosu replied with another Go proverb, "Four is five and five is eight and six is twelve." He paused. "I never really understood what that one meant."

"Me neither."

They laughed.

There was a knock at the door. It was Abbot Jo.

"Everything alright? I must make sure my guests are happy."

Ryokan picked up the sake bottle and gently shook it. "Well the bottle's been leaking."

Abbot Jo smiled. "I'll send Polo down to the village to get another one."

"Splendid."

"I'll come and let you know when the bath is ready. It takes a while to heat the water up." Abbot Jo went to find Polo and send him down to the grog shop.

They finished the Go game. All territory was occupied and it was time to total the scores. Ryokan won. "Well that wasn't too bad, Yosu. You've done a lot worse. I just wish I'd been playing you for money." Ryokan stood up and stretched his back. He noticed the picture of Turnip on the wall. "That's a wicked turnip, Yosu. And the first thing you did? I remember you telling me about it. You never actually did it, right?"

The memory of painting the turnip blossomed in Yosu's mind. He recalled watching the brush take over and do the painting for him. It had been a magical moment.

"No, Master. The brush did it all by itself. All I did was hold it and watch."

"That's the only way to do it, laddie. Anything else is just interfering."

Ryokan poured two more cups of sake. "Do you fancy another game of Go?"

"No thanks, Master. That sake's made me a bit pissed. I'd probably miss the board and fall off my cushion."

"Ha. Don't worry, laddie. I'll pick you up and put you back. "

There was a knock at the door. Yosu wobbled up to the door and opened it. It was Polo, with a bottle of sake in his hand. "Polo. How nice to see you. Come in. Have a cup of sake."

Polo looked confused. He glanced behind Yosu and saw Ryokan sitting at the table, squeezing the last few drops from the old bottle. "Abbot Jo said to give you this." He held out the bottle.

"Will you no come in and have a cup with us?" Ryoken asked.

"Er..no thank you Brother. I don't touch alcohol."

"Well you're touching it now. Better give me the bottle before it bites you."

Polo stuttered, handed over the sake, then spun on his heel and disappeared into the night. Ryokan opened the second bottle, threw the top into the corner, and put the bottle in hot water. When the sake had warmed up he filled their cups. "Do ye not find that the second bottle always tastes better than the first?"

"Maybe the third bottle will taste better than the second."

"We'll never know, because we'd be totally pissed before then. In fact, I'm a wee bit pissed right now. Do you know what I like to do when I'm pissed?"

"Have a piss?" They both roared with laughter.

"No. If I'm a bit woozy, I like to knock out a few lines of calligraphy. Do you have some paper and ink and all that stuff?"

Yosu moved the Go set from the table and replaced it with a few sheets of rice paper, an ink-stone, ink-stick, a pot containing brushes, standing side by side and hairy side up, like guardsmen in bearskins waiting for orders, ink-well and pot of water.

Yosu watched Ryokan prepare the ink. He hadn't touched his calligraphy set since he'd been freed from his storeroom cell. He felt like a small boy again, watching his teacher paint for the first time.

Ryokan was completely relaxed. He didn't appear to be making any effort at all. Yosu felt calm and fulfilled. He recognized the feeling from when he'd first met Ryokan. It cut through his worries, his loneliness, his confusion and the effects of the sake. Ryokan mixed the ink, selected a brush and began writing one of his poems. The words appeared magically on the paper.

> ***Out breath***
> ***and in breath-***
> ***know that they are***
> ***proof that the world***
> ***is inexhaustible***

He poured a couple more cups of sake, took a sip and placed the paper on Yosu's bed to allow the ink to dry. He paused for a moment. "Somebody's coming round to tell me something. But for the life of me

I canna remember who it is." He sat down again, picked up the brush and wrote:

Waiting for a visitor, I drank four or five
cups of this splendid sake
Already completely drunk, I've forgotten who is coming.
Next time be more careful.

There was another knock on the door. A female voice said, "Your bath is ready brother Ryokan."

"All right. I'm on my way. That's who was coming. A good bath and something to eat will do the trick. I'll see ye later, Yosu. Thanks for the game and the company. You'd better take ten stones next time." He chuckled and wobbled out the door.

Yosu looked at Ryokan's poem. The tranquillity that constantly leaked from the old monk still filled the room. *Out breath and in breath. Proof that the world is inexhaustible.* "Wave goes back to the sea."

He breathed deep. Ryokan had lifted a weight from his heart. He sat down and placed a sheet of rice paper in front of himself. He picked up the brush laying on the ink-stone and dipped it into the well. It began to draw.

Catch Bull at Four

Taishin had a hard time growing up, but she was tougher than she looked. She was very attractive, but this wasn't such an advantage in life as it first appeared. In fact she began to see it as a burden. It attracted lots of unwanted attention, shallow praise and affection. It also brought on jealousy and unwarranted dislike. It appeared that boys liked her, but she slowly realized that what they liked and what they wanted was to get hold of her and roll around on the grass in the cherry orchard. By the time she became a teenager the unwarranted advances she received became more threatening. Fortunately she had a elder brother who taught her what to do when a bullying boy laid his hands on her. He gave her a large egg-shaped stone. "Hold it like this. Then swing your arm like this. And hit them on the side of the head just here." He touched his temple. "One good wallop should knock them out. Believe me, they won't come back for more. Don't hit them with anything bigger, and don't hit them anywhere else on the head. You don't want to kill them. Keep the rock wrapped up in a cloth. You don't want them to know your secret. Let them think it was your fist that hit them."

By the time she was fifteen, grown men started paying attention to her. More difficulties arose when she discovered she could use her looks to manipulate men and get her own way. Whenever she did this they wanted something in return. Life wasn't fair. She felt like she'd been given something that looked good but didn't work properly. It was a like a jar of honey without a lid. She became more ill-tempered and snappy. She began to look forward to the next idiot teenage boy or drunken farmer who tried to force his hand inside her *kimono*, so she could smack him with her rock. Things weren't going too well.

She'd had enough and wanted out. She didn't like growing older. She hated her body which did nothing but cause her trouble.

Nobody understood her problems and no-one appeared to have the answer.

Two lifelines were thrown to her. One afternoon, she was pulling a few weeds from the family garden when she heard a hauntingly beautiful melody coming from the other side of the fence. She stopped and listened. The tune tugged her heartstrings. It bypassed the trivia and nonsense that littered her existence and touched her deep, inside, beyond her thoughts and concerns.. It was like listening to a beautiful sunrise, or a flower opening. She rushed out the garden to see where the music was coming from. She saw an old man sitting by the path, playing a small bamboo flute. She sat down and listened to him for a couple of minutes. He stopped, held his flute out, pointed to his bag and said, "Would you like to buy one? Only one *mon*. Make beautiful music yourself."

Taishin disappeared back into her house and returned clutching a small round coin with a square hole in the centre. She handed it to the peddler, who selected a bamboo flute from his bag and handed it to Taishin. He then spent a few minutes showing her where to put her fingers to play a simple scale. She took to playing it like a flautist takes to a flute, and was soon playing simple enchanting melodies, without thinking about it too much. She felt more satisfied playing unscripted airs than she did sitting trying to still her mind by meditating. The flute became a permanent fixture of her bag and was an essential accessory on her journey to view the violets in the mountains.

After Taishin had lost the debate with the one-eyed monk she continued her trek through the countryside. She was much happier living the life on a Unsui now she'd escaped to soul-destroying influence of Abbot Nami. She loved the country and was fond of the people who lived there. They were less sophisticated than the folk who lived in the city. They spoke plainly and were usually lacking ulterior motives. What you saw was what you got.

The morning sunlight warmed Taishin both inside and out, as she wandered down the lane between the tall grass of the fields on either side. Her mind, however, was far from tranquil. It was jumping all over the place like a frog that had eaten a hot chilli. She was rummaging through ideas and asking questions "What is enlightenment? Does it really exist or is it another fairy story? All I hear at night are the locusts chittering away. And I've been hearing them all my life. Maybe I've been fooling myself."

She heard someone in the long grass, moaning and swearing. The moaning turned into wailing and a distraught farmer appeared on the road ahead of her.

"What's the matter Brother? Why all the noise?"

"I've lost my best bull. He wandered off into the long grass an hour ago and he's gone. How will I plough my field and pull my cart now he's disappeared? I'm ruined. My children will starve. What's to become of us."

Taishin said, "Don't give up, Brother. He must be somewhere. Be patient and keep looking until you find him. I'll help you. Don't give up."

Taishin and the farmer set off through the fields, searching for the errant bovine. The fields ended at the bank of a small river. Taishin walked east, the farmer walked west. She removed the bamboo flute from her bag and played a few notes. Her mind stilled and she looked down at the muddy floor and noticed cloven footprints in the loam. She called the farmer and they set off following the trail beneath the willows that lined the bank. Taishin played another short melody on her flute. She heard a *hototogisu* call in response. She felt the sun on her face and the mild wind across the top of her head. She told the farmer, "I think we're on the right track. He won't be lost for much longer."

Suddenly, the grass parted and Taishin saw the ox. She held her hand out to the farmer, who placed a coiled rope in it. She moved through the tall grass and placed the rope around the animal's neck. He had been enjoying his freedom wandering around by the river. The grass was sweet and the water was cool. Taishin tugged the rope, but the ox didn't want to return to its dark shed. Taishin pulled harder but the ox resisted. The ox could see the mountains in the distance, and wanted to visit them before he went home. He lurched towards them, jerking Taishin with him. He was undisciplined and stubborn. Taishin decided he needed a wallop on the arse to bring him into line. She pulled out the *bokken*, and holding the rope firmly with one hand, whacked the oxen's behind with the swordstick. The animal got the idea and immediately began to behave himself.

Taishin took advantage of her new authority over the ox. She slowly hauled herself up onto its back and began to enjoy the ride home. The farmer walked happily beside her. She reached into her bag, took out her flute and played a soundtrack to the setting sun. The farmer gently clapped his hands in time. The woodmen in the forest heard her beguiling melody and put down their axes. The children rushed from their games to see where the music was coming from. They were enchanted by the nun riding the ox and playing the flute. They followed her to the cowshed. She looked up at the clouds tinted pink by the setting sun. She was satisfied and serene. She untied the rope from the ox and replaced the bokken in her belt.

She was up at dawn the next day. Taming the bull had tamed her mind at the same time. She no longer felt the desire to achieve enlightenment. If hundreds of birds had strewn her path with flowers, it would have been meaningless. She felt invisible. There was nothing to desire. Like a baby coming into the world, she was satisfied with the warmth of her mother and the sweet taste of her milk. There was nothing more to do and nowhere else to go. He mother would keep her close and carry her everywhere. She walked on towards the emerald mountains. The water in the river was clear. Some grass was turning yellow and bending down towards the earth which was pushing up fresh green shoots. The flowers were blooming bright red. The soft warm clay squeezed itself between her toes as she walked. The trees stood proudly upright as she passed before them, alive in the morning sun like servants waiting to be inspected by the mistress..

She walked into the village and entered the marketplace. She went into the wine shop and came out with a small bottle of sake and continued on her way. Every face she looked at appeared to be Lord Buddha in a flimsy disguise. Taishin was happy to be back in the world and the bull was happy to be back in its shed.

Catch Bull at One

Yosu, however, wasn't happy to be back in his shed. Ryokan's visit had snapped him out of his deep depression and pulled him gently back into life, but it wasn't enough. Once Ryokan left the monastery, Yosu felt like a little boy whose father had deserted him and left him in the middle of a busy market. Yosu didn't, know where to go next. All he wanted to do was find his father again. He was still confused. Nami's ill-treatment had thrown him into turmoil. Everything he had taken for granted had been thrown up in the air and not all of it had returned to earth. Most of what he'd believed had been dismantled. The path he'd set out on didn't seem to be going anywhere. What was solid and dependable was liable to disappear without warning. And to throw oil on the fire, he had become haunted. Taishin's face kept drifting into his consciousness. No matter how hard he tried to banish her from his mind, she kept reappearing. He was going insane. He remembered how he felt when he was with Ryokan. This was the only connection he had back to sanity. And one day even Ryokan wouldn't be around.

Priest Ryokan must fade
like this morning's flowers.
But his heart will remain behind.

Ryokan.

There was only one solution. The peace and contentment he'd felt when he was with Ryokan had left its footprint in his memory. If Ryokan couldn't help him, he couldn't think who would. He'd long since abandoned talking to pictures and statues. It was time to turn the page. He decided to leave the monastery. He'd take his begging bowl down from the shelf and follow the familiar path of the Unsui. He'd head north and find Ryokan's hut. This was the final throw of his *menko* card. If it failed, all he could foresee was darkness.

Since Ryokan left, he'd tried to make some marks with his brush and ink, but he was as empty as a dry ink well. His brush was too heavy and the ink had set solid. He never knew if he'd ever be able to paint again. If all else failed, he could always go back to his uncle and make ink sticks. In truth, he didn't have a clue.

He went to see Abbot Jo, who had been concerned about him. He didn't know what Yosu was going through and thought it best to leave him alone, give him space and help if he asked for it. He had been pleased to see the effect Ryokan's visit had had, but after he left, Yosu seemed to slide back into his isolation. Jo had faith that something would come along and lead Yosu back out of the shadows. Maybe this was it.

"Brother Jo. My experience with Nami has thrown me into a pit that is very difficult to get out of. I've been cooped up here, thinking about things, and I've decided the best course of action is for me to take the path of the Unsui once more. I'll go north and look for Master Ryokan's hut in the mountains. Maybe he can help me clamber out of my hole."

"That sounds like a good idea, Yosu. What have you to lose? I'm sure the journey will benefit you greatly and if Master Ryokan can't help you, who can? Why don't you take your brush and ink with you? You may find you'll decide to use them again. They take up so little space in your bag. Come back here when you're ready. I'll make sure your room stays free. This is a big place, we've plenty of space. And I'll look forward to seeing some of your paintings again one day."

Yosu went back to his room and collected together the few items he'd need on the road: his begging bowl, a blanket, a small cloth, a razor to shave his head and a small bamboo water strainer. He glanced up to the shelf, saw his paintbrush, ink-stone and ink-block, and remembering what the abbot, said, placed them in his bag, along with a couple of sheets of paper. He set off on the road to the north. He felt better already.

Yosu avoided built-up areas and happily wandered through the countryside. People in small villages dropped enough food into his

begging bowl to prevent him going hungry. The day to day necessities
of survival kept him busy enough to prevent him from tumbling back
into depression. The weather was good, and he'd forgotten how
beautiful the sky could be at sunrise and sunset.

One morning, as he walked through the long grass by a river, the
air was filled with the frantic buzzing of insects. Swallows swooped
down devouring them for breakfast, as he disturbed the long grass and
sent them up into the air. The peace of the morning was punctured by a
dismal wail. Yosu looked along the path and saw a farmer sitting on a
rock with his head in his hands, occasionally making a noise like a
stuck pig.

He drew nearer and asked the farmer what the matter was.

"I've lost my best ox. He wandered off this morning before I
was up. And now he's gone. I need him to pull my cart and plough my
field. I'm ruined. We'll all starve. You're a monk. It's your duty to help
people. Help me find my bull Brother, or we'll all starve. Lord Buddha
said you should help even the smallest, weakest creature."

"You're a farmer and it's your duty to look after your animals
properly. Buddha said, 'If you don't lock the stable door at night, your
ox will wander off and become lost.' So get up off your lazy fat arse
and go and find him."

Yosu smiled at the farmer, dipped his head and continued on his
way. The farmer got up off his fat lazy arse and went to look for the
bull.

Yosu heard the song of the *hototogisu*, (Japanese cuckoo). The
sun was warm, the wind was mild, willows were green along the shore,
but still Yosu was troubled. The foundation of his life had seemed so
solid. He'd believed he'd discovered the true path to enlightenment, the
true meaning of a worldly existence. But it had crumbled beneath his
feet. The monks and saints and masters and scriptures were full of
advice on how to reinforce *dharma*. It was the basic principle of
existence, the Divine Law. It was the only way to discover your true
nature. But the wonderful image he'd carried was peeling away, like a
neglected painting of a mandala on an ancient temple wall. The saints,
gods, goddesses and rows of meditating Buddhas were flaking from the
wall. The delicate thin paint was drifting to the floor. *Dharma* was

blowing out through the temple door. Dharma means to uphold: uphold the teachings of the Buddha, which is the foundation of dharma, uphold the family, uphold the natural order of the universe. Yosu felt alone and abandoned.

The people he passed on the road were different creatures from himself. They were under a hypnotic spell that was hiding them from reality. "Where is your Zen now?" he asked himself. After three years as a monk, all he could think about was another bottle of sake and a game of Go with Ryoken. When he stopped to take stock of himself, the house started collapsing around him.

A Cup of Tea

Taishin felt that the world had woken up and was humming a happy tune. The sun was pushing its fingers through the branches and illuminating the path before her. The birds had formed a choir, and their gentle song was serenading her through the forest, to a small hut at the side of the path.

The hut was larger than a shed but smaller than a cabin, The frame was made from bamboo poles and was covered with strips of sliced bamboo, The roof was thatched with rice straw, tied to the bamboo rafters. A wisp of smoke beckoned Taishin inside. As she approached, the sign swinging gently from the edge of the roof demanded she come in.

A cup of tea.

The inside was divided into two rooms by a paper screen. There were a couple of low bamboo tables inside, and two more outside. The tables had cushions around them. A small iron kettle muttered happily on a charcoal stove inside the door. The floor was covered with *tatami* (straw mats).

There was a small alcove built onto the wall near the entrance. It was like a small art gallery. Three shelves and a piece of calligraphy hung in a simple frame on the wall opposite the entrance. Each shelf displayed a delicate piece of beautifully decorated pottery: a blue plate where two lobsters drifted between strands of waving seaweed, a heron standing in a lake patiently waiting for its lunch to swim by, a jovial sailor standing on a boat sailing through a rough sea.

116

Taishin studied the calligraphy. The poem hypnotized her.

What is the heart of this old monk like?
A gentle wind
Beneath the vast sky.

Ryokan

"Beautiful. My friend wrote it."

Taishin turned around with a start. An old woman stood behind her, smiling at the poem. The story of her long rich life was engraved on her face, a work of art that had improved over decades. Taishin only saw a kind, loving grandmother who wouldn't hurt a fly. She had shaved her head and wore a simple red robe. It was threadbare in places, but clean.

"Would you like some tea, dear?"

Taishin nodded, "That would be wonderful, grandmother. Thank you."

"Sit down dear. My name is Aiko."

"I'm Taishin." She bowed her head.

Aiko placed a tea bowl, bamboo tea-scoop, and whisk neatly on the table. She took a small white linen cloth and wiped the bowl to clean it. She then took a small lidded tea caddy down from a shelf, opened it and carefully filled it with powdered green tea which she tipped it into the tea bowl.

Taishin was captivated by the old woman's actions. She was performing a sacred ceremony, not merely making a bowl of tea.

She took the kettle from the stove and poured the boiling water into the cup. She replaced the kettle, picked up the bamboo whisk and hastily stirred the tea, until it was well mixed and slightly frothy. She then placed the cup on the table in front of Taishin and gave a gentle bow, which Taishin returned. The old lady then took the kettle outside and refilled it with fresh water. She returned and placed more charcoal on the fire.

Taishin had heard about an old lady who was a teacher of Zen, and ran a tea-shop. She was known as the tea lady. Taishin didn't have to ask. She realized that Aiko was the person she'd heard about. She was well known. Sometimes a monk would send one of his students to Aiko's tea house to sample her Zen.

Most people respect monks, whatever path they follow. They have devoted their lives to a higher purpose and that alone demands acknowledgment. However, some people adopt the life of renunciation for purely selfish, materialistic reasons. Idle, freeloading parasites often appear, along for the free rice. A monk doesn't have to work every day in the fields in the baking sun. He doesn't have to cook all his meals or look after children. He lives rent free, and usually has someone to cook for him. As a lifestyle, renunciation has plenty of temporal benefits. Any spiritual rewards are perks of the job. The main disadvantage of asceticism is celibacy; and that isn't always adhered to. In some cases the maxim "What the abbot doesn't see won't hurt him," applies. Life contains a non-negotiable clause that compels it to reproduce itself. Otherwise there'd be no life. Every insect, bird, animal, fish, flower and tree must obey the command from its genes and try to release more editions of itself. It's been going on for millions of years. What chance does a poor little Zen monk stand of halting the unstoppable tide of life? No sex means no more monks and nuns. (Religions that enforce strict rules of celibacy inevitably die out.) Fortunately, renunciates make up a small fraction of most religions so the human race marches on relentlessly.

Taishin was halfway through her cup of tea when a monk entered the tea-shop. He clomped through the door and looked around. Aiko was in the back room. The monk caught Taishin's eye and she felt lust leaking from his face. He tried to impress her, "Where's the old biddy who's supposed to know Zen? I've come to give her a lesson and find out what she really knows."

"Would you like some tea?"

The monk, Oshin, turned around surprised. Aiko had emerged from the room at the back. He sat at the table on the other side of the room to Taishin and turned his answer into an order.

"Yes. Get me some tea,"

Aiko took down a cup, tea-whisk, scoop and tea-caddy. She wiped the scoop and strainer with a linen cloth and placed them on the table. She picked up the cup and carefully wiped it with a slow, circular motion.

"I hear you're an expert on Zen, old lady. I hope your Zen is faster than your tea-making. I could be dying of thirst here."

"Wanting Zen to hurry up is a sigh of ignorance. It is like telling a tree to grow faster. It has its own pace and grows in its own way. If you tell it to hurry up it will simply laugh at you, as will the birds sitting in its branches and the wind blowing through the leaves."

Aiko removed the lid from the caddy and scooped some tea. She tipped it into the empty cup and fetched the bubbling kettle from the stove.

"Oh, very clever. Your fancy words might fool a dumb stupid novice but they don't fool me." He raised his voice, " I see right through your act, you old sham. If you're so wise, where do the flowers come from? What is the sound of one hand clapping?"

Aiko poured the boiling water into his cup. It reached the rim and she continued pouring. It flowed over the table and onto Oshin's knees. He shrieked and jumped up in the air.

"It's full, you idiot. There's no more room."

"Just like you are full of your own opinions and ideas. You will never understand Zen until you empty your cup."

The monk growled and grabbed Aiko by the neck of her kimono. He raised his free hand, "I'll show you what's the sound of one hand clapping you stupid old bat."

But before the monk could strike, he saw the light. It was the brief flash of luminescence when Taishin's bokken walloped him on the side of his head. He slowly sank back onto his cushion.

"The sound of one hand clapping, you ignorant monk. Can you hear it now?" said Taishin.

He got to his feet and staggered towards the door. Before he left he turned around and said, "I'll be back. I haven't finished with you two bitches yet." He wandered off the way he came.

Taishin said, "He's not a happy rabbit."

119

Aiko replied, "I think he's in the wrong job. Maybe he should look for something less stressful." She paused, "Would you like another cup of tea?"

"That would be lovely, grandmother."

"I think I'll join you. I've got some rice cakes in the back."

They had tea and rice cakes and got on very well. Taishin told Aiko about her days in the monastery. She told Aiko how Yosu had done a hundred pictures with one brush stroke and how he had painted the abbot's Zen face and how Abbot Nami, already angry because of Yosu's cartoon, became upset, imprisoned him for his cheek and then began to starve him. She told Aiko how Polo had gone to see the Daimyo for help and he had sent two of his samurai to sort the mess out and Nami eventually lost his head.

If you shake rice flour through a sieve, any lumps in the flour rise to the top. Taishin had finally allowed herself to take a look at her life and where it was heading. She was having doubts about living by begging. She was quite capable of work and felt guilty about taking from the poor. In theory monks and nuns give spiritual sustenance and inspiration in return for being fed. Following this guidance, inspired by the teachings of Buddha, a person isn't reborn on a lower level of existence. A person without *Dharma* has no direction and is a prime candidate for the Tongue-Ripping Department in the Second Level of Hell, and may well end up eating from a bowl on the floor on their hands and knees in the next life.

Questions had risen to the surface in the sieve. Taishin wondered how necessary it was to live as a nun. At the core of Buddha's teaching was the dictum that you should do no harm to others. But you didn't have to be a renunciate to understand that. Taishin had lots to think about. She knew she wanted to be fulfilled in life. She wanted to experience Peace. She wanted to learn where to place her feet so she wouldn't destroy anything precious. But what had seemed so simple once was now shrouded in fog. The questions were lining up to interview her and Taishin didn't have any answers.

"Are you alright my dear?" Aiko placed two cups of tea on the table and sat down beside her.

"I don't know, grandmother. Not long ago, life was a walk in the sun. I'd committed myself to the eightfold path and the journey to the end of suffering. But now I'm dragging my feet through mud in a rainstorm. I believed that the world inside the monastery was a shelter from ignorance, conflict and strife..." Taishin paused.

Aiko said, "But it turned out to be just as corrupt as the world outside..."

"Everything I trusted and believed in seems to be falling apart. "

"My dear, everything crumbles. All that is good, all that is bad will one day be blown away. If you try to keep hold of anything, or stop the wind, you will suffer. You can't stop the sun rising, or a tree growing, or the tide turning or the wind blowing. We are all part of the same parade, and we'll all finish in the same place, no matter which route we take."

"So what do we do?"

"We sit back and enjoy the ride. Stretch out on the hay. Feel the sun on your face. Enjoy the gentle rhythm of the cart as it carries you along the track. Your journey will be over one day soon. All our worries and problems will have dropped from the cart and blown away long before that day comes."

"But what about *Dharma* and realization and walking the path to the truth?"

Aiko paused and gazed into her empty cup. "Well, can you think of anything better to do? I can't. Would you like some more tea?"

Aiko and Taishin got on well. She told Taishin she was welcome to stay as long as she wanted. Taishin, for her part, was happy to share Aiko's hut. She found plenty to do, collecting firewood, cleaning, washing, and it wasn't long before Aiko began teaching her how make and serve tea. Taishin understood that the purpose wasn't to make a nice cup of tea, but to achieve harmony, purity and encourage a meditative state of mind. A cup of tea was the magnet to draw you into the present moment and still your mind. Taishin noticed that when she experienced this, the feeling was transmitted to whomever was sharing the tea.

Taishin didn't realize that Aiko was teaching her without saying a word. Taishin was simply living her life, day to day and was happy again. The peace she achieved working as an assistant in the tea-shop was far greater than she had experienced in the monastery. Contentment was like a shy wild animal or bird. If you approached it, it fled. But if you remained still and quiet, it came nearer.

However, not all animals were so shy. One afternoon Taishin heard some unruly noise outside the tea-shop. Someone was knocking the tables over and shouting. It was Oshin of the scalded knees and two companions. They had been to the village sake shop and drunk a couple of bottles on the way to the tea-shop. Oshin was kicking the cushions around, shouting, "It's an illusion. All an illusion, See this table?" he kicked it over. "It's not real. Watch and learn. Look and learn."

Aiko stood in the doorway and stared at the three buffoons.

"Ah, here she is, Brothers. The wise old char woman. Why don't you try her out with a *koan*? Hey, old lady, where do the cups of tea come from? What is the colour of a cup of tea? What is the sound of a cup of tea clapping?"

The three monks shrieked with sake-fuelled laughter.

Aiko asked, "How can I help you three young men? Would you like some tea?"

Oshin looked at his companions as if Aiko had insulted them. "Yes Granny Coot. I hope it will be better than that piss you served me last time." The two goons laughed.

Aiko nodded towards the upturned tables and chairs. "Sit down and I'll bring you some tea out." She headed back into the hut, then paused and turned around. "In answer to your questions, the tea comes from the back of my hut, from out the teapot. The colour depends how strong you make it. It's a shade of green."

Aiko went back into the hut and gathered the utensils. Oshin looked around and said, "Get a table ready. I fancy a cup of tea, unless she's got a bottle of sake stashed in there."

Oshin's companions arranged a table and three cushions. Oshin picked up another cushion and placed it beside the table. "Maybe that tasty young tart will join us." A leer crept across his mouth and tugged his eyes.

One of the lickspittles asked, "Is she the one who whacked you with her wooden sword?"

"Yes, but she won't do it again. I'll be ready next time. The bitch will get a surprise. I'll steal her stick and smack her arse with it. After I've had a bite of her mango." The three monks laughed the sake snicker, and one of them hooted.

Taishin appeared in the doorway carrying a tray with the tea utensils. She placed the tray on the table.

Oshin asked, "Are there any other customers today miss?"

"No. You're the first."

Oshin pointed to the extra cushion, "Then why don't you sit down and join us?"

"That's very kind of you to offer, but I'm afraid I've got other things to do right now. Although you're the first customers, you won't be the last today. So we need to prepare for the extra guests. But thank you for asking."

While she was talking, Oshin was undressing her with his eyes. Taishin felt uncomfortable, bowed quickly and went back into the hut.

Aiko came to the table, carefully wiped the cups and placed them back on the table. Then she went in to get the kettle from the stove. Oshin followed her inside. Taishin stood at the back of the room. "Can the girl serve us?"

"No. Taishin is busy. Please go and sit down so I can serve you. The tea is almost ready."

Oshin turned to leave. On his way out, he quickly grabbed Taishin's *bokken* and concealed it under his robe. He was ready for the little bitch this time. On his way back to the table he leaned the bokken by the door where it was partially hidden by the door frame.

Aiko came out, served the tea then returned inside. The monks sipped their green tea.

One of Oshin's hangers-on asked, "What are we going to do next."

There was silence for a few moments. The two goons looked at Oshin. He cheerfully replied, "Well, we could go in and fuck the slut. There's plenty of mango for everyone. You two will have to wait your turn though."

123

One of them was keen, the other looked worried. "Err, I don't know about that. I mean, I'm not..."

Oshin said, "Hey, don't worry. If you don't want to dip your joss stick in the honey, you can watch us. You might learn something. Maybe you'll change your mind when you see what fun we're having. She's an ignorant peasant who's spent her life looking at the arse of an ox, whacking it with a stick. She knows nothing about nothing. I can tell she'll be begging for it once she gets a taste."

Oshin stood up. "Ready for some exercise?" He nodded towards the doorway. The hesitant monk said, "No. This is disgusting. I'm going back to the monastery."

"Oooer. Worried that a *Jikininki* will creep into your cell while you're asleep and frighten you to death?"

"I'm not scared of a *Jikininki* Oshin, but I am scared of you. You're fucked up."

Oshin bared his teeth, growled and stepped forward with his arms raised. His companion spun on his heel and set off back towards the monastery. "Pussy. His loss is our gain. Come on."

Oshin checked that the *bokken* was still leaning by the door outside and entered the tea-shop. Taishin turned, saw the two monks, and looked for her *bokken*.

"Lost your stick, sweetie?"

Taishin started to walk past him, but he grabbed her arm.

"No need to rush, darling. We've got something for you."

Taishin tried to jerk her arm away from him, but he held tight.

"Grab her arms."

The rapist's assistant went behind Taishin and took hold of her arms.

"Hold her tight. I want to see what she's hiding under that robe."

Taishin struggled and shouted to no avail.

"It's payback time. Where's your big stick now, pretty young miss?"

There was a sudden crack. Oshin's lights went out and he slid to the floor.

"Her big stick's here, you little shit." It was Aiko, taking care of her staff's welfare.

124

Oshin's accomplice froze with his mouth open. Aiko looked at him for a moment, then swung the *bokken* with all her might. Another crack and another monk bit the dust. *Devi* and the *Shaktas* in heaven gave a mighty cheer.

Going Home

Yosu was going home. Like a dog who has snapped its lead in a strange town, or the snipe, who winters on the warm coast of Australia every year and flies thousands of miles back to Japan for summer. Neither has to look at a map or follow instructions. The snipe's wings, the dog's legs and Yosu's *waraji* (straw rope sandals) knew where to go automatically.

The *waraji* led him towards Osaka, on the west coast, then east to the smaller town of Nara, and finally down the lane to the village where he grew up.

It had been almost twenty years since he'd left to learn the art of making ink with his uncle. His mind was full of memories since leaving the village where the storyteller had put down his mat and frightened them all with his tale of the Tengu. The lessons his uncle had taught, the visit of Ryokan, learning to paint, and most significant of all, his awareness of Zen, abandoning thoughts of 'good' or 'bad' had worked their way into his soul. "Enlightenment" or "illusion" was no longer a burning question. He had learned how to paint a simple shape without interference from his thoughts and desires. Sometimes the clouds cleared and he could see that he had already arrived at his destination. On other days, his mind was unruly, kicking up enough dust to make him question why he was sitting by the road begging, wondering if he shouldn't get a conventional job, or become a simple farmer. He had imagined that enlightenment would be instantaneous, like walking into a room and taking up residence. But it seemed more like walking through rain showers between the occasional sunny periods.

As he entered the village, memories of his childhood returned. He recognized the houses and remembered their inhabitants. He had been inside many of them, playing with the children who lived there, or occasionally visiting with his mother. He glanced from side to side, registering, "Been in that one. Been in there. Had lunch in that one. Played in there." He wondered what had happened to that world of long ago. It had been too big and too vivid to exist only in his mind. But that was its dwelling place now. The traces and echoes of his childhood were everywhere and nowhere were they more vivid than in the place where he grew up.

He stood in the entrance at the end of the path to the hut. The gate was gone and the garden had been neglected. He looked at the grass by the path and remembered hiding with his friend from the black-faced Tengu walking towards them. He smiled and walked up to the doorway. He heard his mother's voice. She was talking to someone inside. Yosu hoped it was his father. Her words danced like cool spring water on a dry tongue. It had been too long.

"Hello. Anybody home? Can you spare a cup of tea for a poor monk?"

There was silence. Then a skinny old lady appeared in the doorway. "Yosu. You're home." She grabbed him with both arms and held him tight. A tear escaped from his detached Buddhist reserve and ran for freedom down his cheek.

"Mother, it's so good to see you."

"Yosu, I thought I'd never see you again. I prayed to *Daruma* and the seven lucky gods that one day you'd walk through the door again, And look, my prayers were answered, "

She called to the back of the hut, "Jimmu, come and see who is here."

A skinny, bent old man hobbled into the room. He squinted to make out who the visitor was.

"Father, it's me, Yosu."

"The seven lucky Gods have answered our prayers. Our son has come home."

Yosu hugged his father. He was so skinny and frail Yosu was gentle with him. He was afraid he'd crush him like a rice cracker. His mother made some tea and asked how long he could stay. She was pleased to discover he wasn't in a hurry.

Yosu realized quite quickly that his parents were poorer than when he had lived at home. There was very little rice, a few straggly vegetables, some miso paste in the bottom of a cup, and a little watered-down soy sauce in the bottom of a bottle.

Yosu woke up early next morning and knew straight away what he had to do. He'd had no desire or inclination to paint for months, but now there was a good reason. His parents needed fattening up.

When he lived in the monastery, his artwork and calligraphy had become valuable and made Abbot Nami fat and prosperous. What the Daimyo gave him for one drawing would feed Yosu's parents for months. It was time to get back on the Tamari Train. He was glad he hadn't thrown his painting gear away. He still had three sheets of rice paper. He laid out his equipment on the small kitchen table, woke his ink block up with a thimble of water and watched the waves come in and out on his ink stone.

He untied the string and unrolled the rice paper. He flattened a sheet out on the table and placed his ink-stone at the top and his mother's wooden spatula along the bottom, to prevent the paper from rolling up again.

He closed his eyes and breathed slowly. He understood enough to know that the picture wasn't going to come from his mind, rather from the end of his brush.

He watched the ink form into an old man and an old woman, both bent and small, but with large smiles on their faces. In the space above them he wrote:

Where we came from
Where we're going to.

The couple were his parents, the place he came from. They were old and nearing the end of their lives, the place we are all going to. He took a small block of red ink, wet a piece of cotton and wiped it on the ink.

He then rubbed the cloth on his chop and pressed it beneath the old man and woman, leaving his signature.

He lay the next sheet of paper on the table and closed his eyes. He opened them and immediately knew what to do. He needed an *enso*. The *enso* the ultimate Zen character. A single stroke of the brush

128

created a symbol of the moment of Enlightenment, when the world becomes nirvana. To Yosu it was simply a circle, but if he was going to Osaka, he would need an *enso* to prove his credentials to the gallery owners who didn't know who he was. He pressed his chop beneath the circle. This painting didn't need any words.

When the ink was dry Yosu carefully rolled the sheets up in the remaining blank sheet of rice paper. He told his parents he had to make a journey to Osaka. His mother was worried that she wouldn't see him again, but he promised he would come straight back as soon as he finished his business.

It took him two days to reach Osaka. The weather was good, and he enjoyed walking at a leisurely pace. He was surprised by the crowds and the hustle and bustle of the city, but he managed to find his way to the street of galleries.

He walked the length of the street, looking in each gallery. They displayed a variety of types of Art, some colourful and detailed, some simple pieces of calligraphy, black ink on white rice paper. At first he tried some of the larger, more prosperous galleries. Because he had been travelling and sleeping in the open they assumed he was begging and threw him out. Some gave him a few coins and sent him on his way. Eventually, he entered a small gallery called Gazan Graphics, displaying simple black ink drawings and pieces of calligraphy. He waited patiently at the counter at the back of the shop. Gazan the gallery owner, a middle aged man in a plain silk kimono was talking to a young couple who were interested in some calligraphy to put in the entrance hall of their new home.

When he had finished, he showed them to the door and returned to Yosu.

"I'm sorry to keep you waiting Brother. Can I get you some tea?"

"That would be generous. Thank you."

Gazan went into the back of the gallery and returned a few minutes later with a small lacquered try holding two cups of green tea. He motioned to a couple of cushions on the floor. They both sat and sipped.

"That's lovely tea. Thank you."

"My pleasure. Now, how can I help you?"

"I've just moved into the district and I'm looking for a gallery for my work. I wondered if you'd be interested in taking some of my pictures?"

"Do you have any with you?"

"Yes, I've a couple."

Yosu removed the roll from his bag and handed it to Gazan, who walked to the back of the gallery and returned with a small table which he placed between them. He slid the string from the roll and unrolled the rice paper. He let it curl up again, went behind the counter and returned with two pieces of bamboo. He carefully flattened the picture and placed the bamboo at either end. It was the *enso*. He studied it for a moment and said, "That's very good."

Yosu couldn't help himself, "It came from the brush of its own accord, like all good ensos."

Gazan smiled for a second then unrolled the second sheet. He studied that for longer, then turned to Yosu, "Parents?

Yosu nodded. "Where we came from?"

The owner asked, "But where are we going?"

Yosu pointed to the couple, "Old age."

"Of course. Yes. That's very clear now. Yes. Very good. Very good."

Gazan stared at the pictures for a few seconds then said, "We have to talk about numbers and price. But first I'd like to talk one of my friends. May I take the pictures for the evening?"

"Of course. When would you like me to come back?"

"Tomorrow. Any time after lunch. Where are you staying tonight?"

"I was going to find a monastery and have a koan fight with the gate-keeper."

"There's no need for that, Yosu. You're welcome to stay here. I'll put a mattress in the back for you. There's a bathroom out there. I'll heat some water up."

"You're too kind, Gazan. That would be wonderful. I'm exhausted."

Next morning, over a breakfast of rice porridge, Gazan told Yosu, "You're a dark horse Yosu. You didn't tell me the Daimyo is one of your patrons and you had a falling out with the fat, lecherous Abbot Nami. The story has spread the length and breadth of the country. Of course I'll be happy to sell your work."

"How many pieces will you want?"

"I'll handle just as many as you give me. Your work is well known, but you stopped painting for a while so your pictures are rarely seen. They will sell like hot sake. How much do you want for them?"

"I'll leave that up to you, Gazan. You're the expert and I trust you. I'd appreciate it if you could give me something for the two pictures I brought with me. I need to get a few things for my parents."

Yosu arrived home pulling a small wooden trolley with a sack of rice, a large bag of beans, a pot of miso paste, a large jug of soy sauce, tofu, four bundles of noodles, a box of dried fish, a large pot of tsukemono pickles, a generous bag of green tea and a large bottle of sake.

His mother thought he'd been moonlighting as a bandit until he explained that calligraphy was more lucrative and much safer.

He stayed with his parents for two more weeks. He tidied the garden, planted some vegetables, did a few minor repairs on the house and a couple of dozen more pictures. These would generate enough money for his parents to live well for the rest of their lives.

Word spread around the village that a monk was staying in his old house with his parents. Several visitors appeared during his sojourn, many surprised that he remembered them. He enjoyed sitting in the garden in the sunshine talking to them about old times and what had happened since. He and his old friend shrieked with laughter remembering the black-faced Tengu who scared them to death.

Eventually, Yosu felt it was time to become an *Unsui* again, and continue his journey. He would deliver his pictures to Gazan in Osaka, arrange for the money to go to his parents and then visit his uncle the black-faced Tengu before returning north. He said 'Goodbye.' to his parents and gathered his few possessions together. His mother gave him a small woven bamboo basket, containing *dorri* (rice crackers), pieces of tofu rolled in sesame seeds and deep fried, a parcel of sunflower seeds roasted in soy sauce and a packet of crispy seaweed. It kept him going until he reached Gazan Graphics in Osaka. Gazan was pleased to see him again. His appearance in Osaka had caused considerable interest, and Yosu of the "Zen Face" paintings and the "Wise Abbot" notoriety had become a minor celebrity of the Art world. Gazan could sell his work faster than hot rice cakes fried in sweet chilli oil and tamari and coated in sesame seeds. Yosu handed over the bundle of his latest work and arranged for the proceeds to be delivered in regular amount to his parents. Gazan fed and watered Yosu and sent him on his way the next morning with a sheaf of blank rice paper in his bag.

"Do what you want with it, Yosu. You can use it as a plate and eat your dinner from it if you want."

"Will it fetch a decent price?" They both roared with laughter and Yosu set out to meet the black-faced demon again.

He was glad of the food his mother had put in his bag, and glad of the coins Gazan had given him. He was happy to walk through the streets without begging. He'd always felt a bit uncomfortable about taking food and money from those who could least afford it, and he'd noticed that it was often those who had least who were most generous and the wealthiest who were the meanest. He was sure there was a lesson hidden somewhere in there, but he couldn't work out what it was.

A couple of days after leaving Osaka Yosu arrived at his Uncle Toshio's ink workshop with a bottle of sake in his bag. Six years had passed since Yosu left the ink factory. Toshio had grey streaks in his hair and the lines on his face were more pronounced, but you couldn't tell because his face was still black.

Toshio was pleased to see Yosu and eager for news of what he'd been up to for the past few years. Reports of his success as an artist had dribbled through to Toshio from the visiting artists who had arrived to buy ink. The story of the picture of the fat Abbot and Abbot Nami's violent demise had spread far and wide. Toshio was keen to hear it all directly from one of the leading characters.

Toshio decanted some of the sake into a smaller stone bottle and stood it in pan of boiled water. They sat by the stove in the kitchen and he asked Yosu to tell him the whole story of the fat Abbot, leaving

132

nothing out. Toshio wanted to hear all about it. Yosu didn't disappoint him.

His nephew had become famous. By the time Nami's head flew into the air the small bottle was empty so Toshio replaced the pan of water on the stove and waited for it to boil. He took the pan from the stove, refilled the stone bottle with sake and stood it upright in the hot water.

"Have you noticed Uncle, how the second bottle of sake always tastes better than the first?"

"Yes Yosu. A bottle of warm sake makes me feel like a new man. Then he wants one."

Yosu immersed himself in the world of ink again. It was like taking a warm bath. He loved the smells, the textures, colours, and the whole process of ink-making. Toshio had a new apprentice ink-maker and Yosu slightly envied him. He missed the dark world of mixing ink but he suspected it may have been his youth that he regretted passing.

They sat by the stove and relaxed. The sake loosened their tongues and the hours past as they talked.

Neither of them had seen Ryokan for a couple of years. Toshio told Yosu that he'd heard the old master had a young girlfriend and they went for walks together and wrote poems to each other.

Yosu laughed, "That sounds like the Ryokan I remember. He must be older than the hills nowadays. I wonder if he still lives in the little cabin on the mountainside."

"Yes, and his paintings and calligraphy are as much in demand as they ever were. What about your work? I heard that was selling well. Didn't the Daimyo start buying it? And isn't there one of Abbot Nami that everyone wants to see?"

"Oh, don't talk about it. Nami, that little fat bastard got greedy and tried to turn me into a painting factory. I did a sketch of him and really pissed him off. You know the story had a bad ending. It ended up with his head rolling around on the floor. I thought everybody knew what happened if you tried to shove samurai around. They use idiots like Nami to test the sharpness of their blades."

Yosu thought for a moment, "He was a nasty little bastard. Even so I wouldn't have wished that on anyone." The image of his head laying on the floor in a pool of blood, with his mouth open, looking stupid, flashed through Yosu's memory. He shuddered.

Yosu said, "Fancy another sake? We can toast Ryokan."

Toshio filled their cups and raised his and held it still for a moment. "Here's to the old fool, Ryokan, wherever he may be."

"And his new girlfriend."

"And his girlfriend."

They emptied their cups and Toshio refilled them, adding, "Before it gets cold."

They sipped the sake. "Do you know where your next stop is, Yosu?"

"Yes. I'm heading north to the Snow Country, to Echigo province. I want to reach the mountains before the snow starts falling. I want to pay Ryokan a visit and have a game of Go and a glass of rice wine. Meet his new girlfriend."

"Give him my felicitations. I'll sort out some ink-blocks for him. That will save him a journey next time he runs out. Last time he was here he left me a brilliant poem. I'm going to get it frames next time I go into Nara. Would you like to see it?"

"I certainly would. I love his poetry."

Toshio went into the back of the hut and returned with a sheet of rice paper, covered with Ryokan's beautiful spidery calligraphy. Yosu read it carefully.

Too lazy to be ambitious,
I let the world take care of itself.
Ten days' worth of rice in my bag;
a bundle of twigs by the fireplace.
Why chatter about delusion and enlightenment?
Listening to the night rain on my roof,
I sit comfortably, with both legs stretched out.

Ryokan

Daruma Doll

Back in the Tea shop, Taishin had become comfortable serving Aiko and her customers. She was happier and more fulfilled making tea than she'd ever been when she was in the monastery. Aiko loved her company and was grateful to her for lightening the workload. Some customers simply came for tea, but many of them had heard of Aiko's reputation as a Zen teacher and were keen to see her in action. She could see quite clearly who had come to learn, and who had come to show off their own understanding.

Aiko enjoyed herself. She didn't see herself as a teacher. She was simply a follower of Zen. Everything happened by itself, without her will being involved. She never intended to give anyone a lesson. She simply enjoyed watching events unfold on the stage of her tea shop. When a visitor simply wanted tea, her preparation was almost ritualistic. The approach was the same as that of an artist dipping a brush into the ink and letting it run across the paper. For Aiko, making tea was a form of meditation. Not that she made the tea in an atmosphere of austere concentration. She was usually happy to chat to her guests in a relaxed atmosphere.

When Taishin watched Aiko catering for the customers she received a lesson in how to live. It was a joy to see her deal with the arrogant young monks, disarming them with her down-to-earth simplicity and sending them home with their egos in a bag. It was a pleasure to witness her attitude and disdain for "spiritual wisdom". As Ryokan said, "Why chatter about delusion and enlightenment?"

A couple of years rolled by and gradually Taishin took on more of the duties of Aiko. Aiko sat in the back of the tea shop and was happy to watch Taishin make the tea and chat to the customers. As she became older, she grew more frail. She looked like a leaf in autumn. Any pressure and she would crumble to dust. But behind her eyes and delicately engraved skin shone a defiant beacon that wouldn't be quenched.

One warm summer evening, when business was finished for the day, Aiko asked Taishin to make some tea and bring it outside. "It's such a lovely evening, I hate to leave it and go to bed."

Taishin brought the tea outside and they sat at a table, watching the sun sink behind the trees.

Aiko sipped her tea and looked at Taishin. "The taste of tea and the taste of Zen are the same."

When Aiko said something like this, Taishin understood exactly what she meant. She felt the meaning in her being. But when she was alone, she ran the words through her memory and their exquisite flavour wasn't quite so strong.

Aiko pointed to one of the cushions, "Look. A Daruma doll. Somebody must have left it here."

Sitting on the cushion was a small round wooden doll. It was red and had one blank white eye and one coloured. There were no arms and no legs. Taishin picked it up and put it on the table.

Aiko asked, "Do you know what happened to the Daruma Buddha's arms and legs?"

Taishin shook her head. Aiko said, "He sat and meditated for nine years. Blood stopped flowing into his limbs and they fell off. You would think that with no legs he couldn't stand up. But try and knock him over."

Taishin flicked and pushed the doll. But whatever she did, because of the round, weighted base, it bounced upright again. Aiko laughed as if the Daruma was whispering her a secret about life.

Taishin said, "Why does the Daruma have only one eye? The other one is plain white."

"Bring me a pen and ink and I'll show you." Taishin fetched a short stick, the point carved into a nib and a small block of ink-stone. Aiko wet the stone with a drop of saliva and worked the stick back and forth in the spit until it became ink. She picked up the Daruma and carefully painted a small dot in the middle of the blank eye. "Now he can see properly. If you have a goal in life, or a wish to fulfil, on the day you achieve your aim, you give Daruma his missing eye. Now we can all rest in peace. Can you bring another cup of tea please, Taishin?"

She went into the back of the hut and made a fresh pot, When she walked back outside with the teapot Aiko was sat frozen, holding the wooden pen. It took Taishin a minute to realise what had happened. She said, "Aiko, are you alright?"

Aiko didn't move. She was dead. She'd restored the Darumas' missing eye and quietly passed away in the fading sunlight. The birds were singing and the Daruma was staring up at the bright blue sky. Taishin took him back into the tea-shop, placed him on the charcoal stove and watched while he disappeared in the small flickering flames. Tears trickled down her cheeks.

Taishin laid Aiko out at the back of the tea-shop. She placed candles at her head and feet. She placed a small statue of Buddha on a block at her side and surrounded the body with burning incense. She collected wild flowers and arranged them around Aiko. She placed a bowl of fruit at the side of the body.

The next day, three monks arrived to carry Aiko to the monastery, where, like the Daruma Buddha on the stove, she was cremated.

The day after the funeral, Taishin was tidying up the hut and found a poem on a piece of paper.

Empty-handed I entered the world
Barefoot I leave it.
My coming, my going —
Two simple happenings
That got entangled.

Kozan Ichikyo

Taishin sat and meditated. What was gone and what remained? Aiko had painted the empty eye on the Buddha. She had achieved all her ambitions and had left. There were plenty of things Taishin could tell herself, "Aiko had moved on to the next life. She was here in spirit. Like ripples in a pond, her essence was moving out through the world, still creating more Karma. It was one of the tenets of Zen that nothing was permanent. But there was a difference between believing it and experiencing it. Taishin wasn't aware that she'd had a great realization. She just felt sad. Something beautiful had gone from her life. Aikos' beautiful weather-worn smile was gone forever.

Since time began
the dead alone know peace.
Life is but melting snow.

Nandai

Taishin understood that her Buddhist wisdom wasn't worth a grain of rice. Life was drifting along, day by day, but as Shinsui said, it was like dewdrops on the leaf of a flower. One day it would vanish. Whatever Taishin said, saw or felt would evaporate like the dew, leaving no trace. Everyone was a prisoner in their own skin, guarded by their thoughts and ideas and tortmented by their desires. The *koans*, the words of wisdom, the sermons, the haikus, would all be blown away down the road with the autumn leaves. Nobody would be around to speak them and no-one would be there to listen. Wherever the world came from before people walked on it, that's where it was going back to.

The spiritual and philosophical aspects of death, and the passing life of the deceased filled people's minds, but first there was a very practical, down-to-earth problem that needed to be dealt with. In times of mourning, natural instinct pushed people away from worldly concerns and they took refuge in their grief and mourned, but there was a very practical matter that urgently needed to be dealt with: what to do with the corpse. We treat it with love and respect, but we need to get rid of it before it becomes a health hazard.

Taishin was in a haze for a few days afterwards. The world was there as before, but she was removed from it. It was a play performed on the stage and she was the audience. In her heart she knew everyone was acting. Guests still appeared at the tea shop, but Taishin was marooned between two worlds. When Aiko was there, everything had happened naturally, as it should. But alone, she no longer felt like she belonged there. She was a bird living in a stranger's nest. It was time she moved on. She was out of harmony. Her life needed to regain its balance.

She returned to the monastery and met the abbot again. He gave her space in a store to house the materials from the tea room. She didn't want to burn her bridges and thought that one day she would return. So she packed the charcoal stove, tea pots, ladles, strainers and the framed calligraphy. She carefully wrapped the cups in clean cloths, put everything in a bamboo basket and placed it in the store room. Back at the tea-shop she swept the place clean, moved the furniture inside, and placed a sign on the door saying, "Closed", tied the door shut and set off with her *bokken*, bag, blanket and begging bowl. The sun tickled her eyes and she walked to the north. She was glad to walk the path of the Unsui again. Her life as an assistant in the tea-shop slipped from her shoulders into the grass by the path and she wondered what the coming days would do to surprise her. She was learning to be silent again.

A little later in the day, she saw a Zen monk walking towards her. When he reached her, he stopped, dipped his head and said, "Salutations Sister. The Buddhas of the past, the Buddhas of the present and the Buddhas of the future all take the road to Nirvana. Where does that road begin?"

Taishin smiled and said, "I haven't a clue," and continued on her way.

139

Hamamatsu

Yosu had changed. He looked like a monk, but he felt like a fraud. Outside was a humble Buddhist mendicant, inside was a confused little boy, rattling with illogical desires. If the kind, simple souls feeding him every day could have looked inside his head, they'd have retrieved their offerings and chased him out of town.

He saw that the world was rolling relentlessly forwards, like a boulder on its way down a mountainside. It would sail over the edge of a cliff and splash into the river in the valley below, where it would sit for millennia, silently being washed away by the water.

He approached the next village. The sky was filled with strange creatures and birds flying above the people below. There were dragons, flying fish, a variety of sea creatures, every type of animal, demons, ghosts and samurai warriors. There were even a few Tengu flipping about in the air, switching between red and black. As he got nearer, he realized that the flying creatures were made out of bamboo and paper. It was the annual Hamamatsu kite festival.

There were competitions and prizes for categories like the biggest kite, the smallest kite, the best decorated kite and the champion fighting kite. Fighting kites battled two at a time. The winning kite either dragged its opponent to earth, or cut its string and set it sailing away into the sunset. Many fighting kites had their strings coated in powdered glass, to make it easier to cut the opponent's string when the cords dragged against each other.

Yosu sat in the shade beneath a cherry tree and enjoyed the spectacle. He remembered Hamamatsu from his childhood, making kites days before the festival, and when he was old enough, entering his own fighting kite into combat. As he watched the aerial battles, he remembered the techniques of using one kite string to cut through another, pulling it fast and firm, like a saw.

The alternative method way of bringing down your opponent was to surround the kite, tangle the strings and haul your adversary down to earth. Yosu was fascinated. Some kites crashed down to the ground, others flew off into the blue sky. And the kites themselves had nothing to do with their fate.

The kite festival is held to show the awakening of the Gods from their deep sleep. It wasn't working on Yosu. The only time he could follow his dreams was when he was sleeping like a log. When he was awake, he travelled in the opposite direction. Something in his life didn't fit properly. He felt like a jar with a lid that was too big.

The wind was blowing to the north. Yosu had given up trying to sort everything out. He could let life tug him along with the wind or he could come crashing down to the floor and see what happened next.

He closed his eyes, enjoying the warm sun.

"Excuse me, Mr Monk."

He opened his eyes. A small girl was standing before him, holding a small, hexagonal kite. On one side was the face of a black Tengu, on the other side a bright red face stared menacingly. The kite was made from rice paper, stretched over a thin bamboo frame. Yosu had learned from Ryokan, to treat children with the same respect as he treated adults.

"Yes, young lady. How may I help you?"

"Can you please write something on my kite?"

"And what would you like me to write?"

"Well, the Tengu won't fly. So could you write something to call the wind and lift it up into the sky?"

Yosu went into his shoulder bag and removed his ink-stone, ink-stick, and bamboo brush. "Could you go and fetch me a little bit of water please? I don't need much. Half a sake cup will do. It's to make the ink."

The girl ran down the path. While she was away Yosu examined the kite. The string was connected too far down the central spa. He slid the knot along the piece of bamboo and tightened it. The girl appeared with a sake cup full of water. She stood silent as Yosu mixed the ink. The girl was mesmerized by the act of turning water into ink. Yosu lay the kite flat on the grass and watched the brush draw four characters on the kite. The ink dried quickly. He pointed to the first character and looked at the girl. "Sky."

The girl repeated, "Sky."

Yosu pointed to the second characterand said, "Above." He looked up.

The girl repeated, "Above."

He pointed the third character, lowered and raised his voice, "Great."

The girl imitated his voice and said, "Great."

The fourth character caused Yosu to jerk the kite around as though he was having difficulty holding on to it, "Wind".

The girl repeated, "Wind."

Yosu said, "Can you read them all?" He pointed to them one at a time. She remembered to growl when she got to "Great".

The girl read,

"Sky Above Great Wind."

"That's wonderful. Did you know you could read?" The girl shrugged. "Now, what's your name?"

"Yua."

"What a lovely name." He turned the kite over, dipped the brush into the ink again, read aloud as he wrote, "This kite belongs to Yua." A smile as bright as the sun lit up her face. Yua clasped her hands together and bowed her head. "Thank you, Mr Monk."

Yosu waved the kite and examined the ink, "That's dry now." He handed it to Yua. She turned to go. Yosu said, "Don't forget the sake cup," He handed her the little beaker. "Don't drink it. I'll get into trouble if you get drunk."

Yua laughed and ran back down the path.

While Yosu sat beneath the branches of the cherry tree, painting poetry on Yua's kite, things were changing in Japan. He would soon be caught up in the drama that was unfolding throughout the country. The conflict between the shoguns and the emperor was evolving into a war. Soon he'd be too busy trying to stay alive. He'd have no time to worry about his dreams.

142

He closed his eyes and enjoyed the warmth of the sun on his face. He could hear the children shouting and the birds singing. Then he heard the jingle of horse harnesses and the clip-clop of hooves. The sound of horses ceased. Yosu was dozing in the sun, drifting towards sleep. Four heavily armed Samurai were riding slowly through the village, casting their eyes from side to side. Yosu heard voices in the distance. "Do you think that's him?"

"Someone said he was dressed like a monk?"

"Well, he looks like a monk. He's even got a begging bowl."

"Does anyone know what Saigo looks like? Has anyone seen his face?"

"Yes, I have. I saw him at a festival last year."

"Is that him?"

"I can't tell from here. He's asleep."

"Well wake the bastard up and let's find out."

"If he was running for his life, I don't think he'd be fast asleep under a tree, in the middle of the day in a busy village."

"Wake him up."

Yosu was roughly shaken awake. He opened his eyes and found himself staring into the face of a fierce Samurai. Unlike Abbot Nami, Yosu knew how to behave with Samurai warriors, who, if the mood took them, were liable to test the sharpness of their sword on your neck. Yosu stood up quickly and bowed respectfully.

"That's not him. He's much too young."

"Who are you?"

"Brother Yosu from the Gisu Monastery."

"Gisu Monastery. Isn't that the place where that little fat fuck of an abbot had his head chopped off?"

"Yes sir. That's the place. It was Abbot Nami."

"Abbot Nami. What was he like then?"

"He was a little fat fuck sir."

The Samurai laughed.

"Well, Brother Yosu, I don't suppose you know the daimyo Saigo Takamori, do you?"

Yosu sensed he had to be careful. A little lie wouldn't hurt.

143

"I saw him once, lord. He visited our monastery at Gisu about a year ago. But I don't know him other than by sight."

"That yokel who said he saw Takamori dressed as a monk must have been talking about Brother Yosu here."

"Most of them can't tell their arse from their elbow."

"Shall we get on our way? You can go back to sleep, Brother Yosu. Sorry to disturb you."

Yosu bowed. The Samurai gave a nod in return.

The insects were still buzzing in the midday sunshine. The children were still jumping up and down, shouting at the kites, which were still flitting around the sky ignoring them.

Yosu sat back down beneath the branches and closed his eyes, but his heart was beating fast and his mind was racing faster.

Why were the Samurai looking for Lord Saigo Takamori? Why wasn't he safe in his palace guarded by his own Samurai?

Many kings, emperors, czars, popes, gurus, kaisers and rulers throughout history and all over the world, suffer from the delusion that they are the personification of the Creator of the Universe on Earth. When they speak, God speaks. This saves lots of time when they want to get things done in a hurry. You'd probably be surprised if you found out how many people are walking around believing with all their hearts that they are God Almighty. It's also surprising how many people follow them and behave like they are the chosen ones, serving the Lord Incarnate.

It was widely believed that the Emperor of Japan was an incarnation of the Creator. He was the ultimate authority on Earth. This made Japan the home of God. Everything seemed to go fairly well for about 700 years, but around the time our story takes place, conflict was brewing between the emperor and the shogun supported by a handful of the shogun's samurai. Both sides were organizing their armies and holding military exercises. Both sides denied they were preparing for war while they moved their warriors into the most strategic positions.

Saigo Takamori supported the emperor. The samurai who were searching for him served the shoguns. Saigo had been instrumental in supporting reforms in the Satsuma region. Power was slowly shifting from the shoguns to a more centralised system, headed by the emperor.

Their land was being seized and distributed to lower ranking warriors and officials were being promoted according to their talent, rather than their samurai rank. The conflict between the emperor and the shogun grew into a war and Lord Saigo Takamori, who had always advocated a peaceful resolution for conflict, had been drawn in. To bring the private, regional armies of the Shoguns under control, Saigo had counselled creating a national force, and the emperor wanted Saigo to return to Tokyo and organize it. This had placed him at the top of the Shogun's wanted list.

Yosu knew little of the politics unfolding throughout the country. His only contact with Saigo Sakamori had been when the daimyo had visited Gisu to buy Yosu's paintings, and later, when he had sent two samurai to rescue him from the clutches of Abbot Nami. Saigo had been instrumental in saving his life and for that Yosu was grateful.

He closed his eyes and meditated, concentrating on his breath entering and leaving his body. The sound of the horses faded into warm sunshine as the swordsmen clip-clopped from the village and continued their search. Yosu relaxed to the accompaniment of buzzing insects and the sound of his breath. He fell asleep.

He was awakened by a child's voice screaming.

He opened his eyes. The black face of an evil Tengu was floating in the air above him, gazing down with malice. Yosu was on his guard. He was still half asleep, rolling between two worlds. He remembered the stories of Tengu tormenting monks and priests. He didn't want to find himself stuck high in the branches of a tall tree, or eating animal dung disguised as a sesame biscuit.

The Tengu swooped down above Yosu and seemed to be laughing at him. Yosu remembered that a large Tengu flying through the sky at night was a prophecy of a military uprising. But it was daytime. The Tengu whipped around in a circle and disappeared behind the trees. Yosu closed his eyes and relaxed. It was a kite, made of paper and bamboo. Tengu only existed in stories. Yosu drifted off back to sleep.

"Mr Monk. Mr Monk."

It was Yua. She had a ball of string wrapped on a stick. It was easier to demonstrate her problem rather than try to explain it. She jerked the string, but it was tangled in one of the bushes on the other side of the path. The more she pulled the string, the more tangled it became.

"Alright, Yua. I get the idea."

Eventually, she stopped trying and started crying for the lost kite with her name on it. Her chin quivered and her cries began to get louder.

Yosu was now fully awake. "What's the matter Yua?"

She snuffled, "My kite. A Tengu flew away with it."

"Don't you worry. I saw where it went. It's hiding over there in the bushes. If you wait here and hold tight onto the string, I'll go and get it for you." He paused, "You know I'm a monk?" Yua nodded. "Well, Tengu trick monks. He won't carry me to the top of a high tree and leave me there will he?" Yua shook her head. "Or trick me into eating animal poo by making it look like a honey cake?" Yua laughed again and shook her head.

"It's only a kite."

Yosu raised an eyebrow, "Are you sure?"

Yua nodded enthusiastically.

Yosu took hold of the string and followed it hand over hand until he reached the bush where it was snarled. He carefully removed it and turned to Yua. "Now you wind it up until it gets tight, and wait there. I'll be back in a minute." He followed the string into the thicket and saw the kite sitting on top of a wild cherry bush.

The kite spoke, "*Sky Above Wind Below.*"

Yosu shrieked and froze. He heard the rustle of a large animal behind the bush.

"It's me. Saigo."

He peered between the branches. The leaves parted. Peering through them was the face of Saigo Takamuri, the man who had saved him from "death by abbot".

A voice from the pathway called, "Mr Monk. Mr Monk."

Yosu replied, "I'm coming. Wind the string gently. I'm on my way."

146

He nodded to Saigo. "I'll be back as soon as I've got rid of this Tengu." He made his way back through the bushes and returned the kite to Yua. Then he returned to the thicket. Saigo had emerged from his hiding place.

Saigo said, "Would you like a piece of honey rice cake, Mr Monk, with a dash of cow-dung?"

They both laughed. Saigo was relieved that Yosu wasn't a samurai with orders to behead him, and Yosu was relieved that Saigo wasn't going to fly him to the top of a tree and leave him there nesting with the crows eating a lump of horseshit disguised as a sweet rice cake.

Yosu noticed that Saigo was wearing a monk's habit. "Have you renounced the world and joined us mendicants? You never seemed the type to wander around with a begging bowl sleeping in fields."

"No, Yosu. The Shogun sent his samurai after me. I grabbed a monks' habit and ran for my life. Otherwise I'd end up in bits on the floor, like Abbot Nami. A lot has changed in our country since he lost his head."

"Yes Lord. I never had the chance to thank you for sending Tomoe and Shimazo and your doctor to Gisu. They saved my life. I wouldn't have lasted long without them. Thank you, Lord." Yosu bowed his head.

"Well, we can't go slaughtering our artists,can we Yosu? And who knows? Maybe you'll save my life before long."

Saigo and Yosu went back and sat in the shade under the cherry tree.

"So what's been happening to you, Saigo?"

"Quite a lot of shit, actually Yosu. It's a long story. Are you sitting comfortably?" Yosu smiled and nodded.

"Then I'll begin. Life is full of surprises. When I was child, our family was poor. Although my father was a samurai, he worked in the tax office and barely brought home enough to feed us. In fact, if we hadn't grown out own food we would have starved. I slept with my six brothers and sisters under a single blanket. I worked hard at school and my fortunes changed. A few years later I was Daimyo Shimazu Nariakira's closest advisor, living a life of luxury in his palace. Shinmazu Nariakira, like myself, believed that the shoguns had taken too much power from the emperor and the balance had to be restored. The country was falling apart. Each shogun had his own army and they were out of control, always at war with each other, always scheming, plotting and changing sides. They were destroying the country, squabbling for power and keeping us in the Dark Ages. The only way to bring the world back to order was to restore power to the emperor. I helped Nariakira work for this. Then Nariakira was poisoned by his enemies. I thought about committing *seppuku* to accompany him into death, but was persuaded it was better honour his memory by continuing his work rather than committing ritual suicide. After all Yosu, what's the hurry?"

"No rush, Lord. All roads, rivers and muddy footpaths eventually drop us back where we came from, into the void."

"Goodbye, cruel world. Well, the shoguns knew I'd been Shinmazu's closest advisor, and they believed my knowledge and experience could be very damaging. The shoguns were out of control. There was nothing to restrain them. I realized we needed a national army under the authority of the emperor. That would stop the bickering, weaken the power and dominance of the shoguns and return power to where it belonged. So the shoguns sent their samurai out to grab me and shut me up. Luckily, I'd been tipped off that they were on the way so I disguised myself as a monk and slipped out of the palace. My guards wanted to come with me, but they would be no match for the small army the shogun had sent out. I thought my chances would be better if I was inconspicuous. Besides, I'd always been secretly attracted to the life of renunciation. No bills. No undisciplined employees to keep in order. Nobody trying to steal your money because you didn't have any. Not surrounded by lickspittles and sycophants. "

"No warm bed. No regular meals. Constantly scrounging and begging from those who can least afford it. Plenty of fleas. Plenty of aches and colds in winter. Lots of mosquitos in summer. No sex. Very little sake. Yes, Lord, it's a great life."

"I decided to go north to Kagoshima, in Satsuma, where the daimyo is a supporter of the emperor and can protect me from the shogun's men. I have friends and allies up there, and think this would be my best chance of avoiding having my neck stroked with tamahagane steel. What about you, Yosu? Are you just wandering about randomly, or have you a destination in mind?"

Yosu said, "Well, I'm heading north myself. When I left the monastery at Gisu, the Go board was kicked over and all the stones flew up in the air. The board was clear again. It was time to begin a new game.

"There was no pressure on me, and I decided to take time and visit my uncle, who taught me how to make ink, my parents, who fed me and kept me alive, and the monk Ryokan who teaches me Zen. I've already visited my parents and my uncle, and now I'm on my way north to see Ryokan."

"Ryokan? I met him once. He's a bit wacky, but a wonderful artist and poet. Do you think we could travel together for a while? Two monks don't look too suspicious. And I'd appreciate the company."

"Yes, I could do with somebody to talk to myself. One slight problem would be we'd have to beg for twice as much food from the same amount of people."

"Don't worry about that, Yosu. I didn't leave the palace empty handed. I've got plenty of money stashed at the bottom of my bag and sewn into the hem.of my robe. I'm only pretending to be a monk after all. I may be an out-of-work daimyo, but I'm not a stupid out-of-work daimyo and I'm not broke."

"You may not be a stupid daimyo, but you could well turn out to be a stupid monk."

Saigo gave Yosu a piercing stare. Yosu smiled and said, "It's time we took the narrow road to the deep north. Let's go up there and smell the rain."

Saigo looked puzzled. "Some of this Zen Buddhist stuff goes right over the top of my head."

"You're lucky it doesn't smack you hard between the eyes and knock you into the void. Then what would you do with all your money and your fancy paintings? Not to mention the headache you'd have when you woke up."

"I'd probably buy a cartoon from a drunken monk and stick it on my bedroom wall next to all the others."

Yosu laughed. "Well, there are much worse things you could spend your money on. And anyway, you don't have a bedroom wall nowadays. Be careful, you could be turning into a real monk. You might start to like sleeping in fields and eating yesterday's cold rice."

"I thought Lord Buddha was supposed to be compassionate."

"He is. And wise. But haven't you heard of the Law of Karma? In the end we get what we deserve."

The monk and the imitation monk slowly walked north. Yosu continued begging, but also ate some of the food that Saigo bought with his secret stash. He looked on it as a different sort of begging.

They had many conversations, which were really just one continuous dialogue, with pauses for eating and sleeping. Yosu was fascinated by the world of politics from which Saigo had escaped. He was amazed by the deception, double-dealing, trickery, lies and cheating upon which it was built. He was surprised that the humans hadn't wiped themselves out long ago.

"You may have walked on silk carpets and eaten the most expensive fish from delicate china plates, but it sounds like you were living in a swamp surrounded by deadly lizards and giant rats. Put me with the hungry beggars in their dirty robes any day."

"Yes brother. At least rats and lizards don't lie and cheat. The richer the Lord, the more he scrabbles for more wealth, more land and more power. The more they have the less satisfied they are. They've more to lose. The Shoguns are their own worst enemy. They are the biggest threat, constantly scheming, deceiving and telling lies. They all have their private little armies so they cause lots of death and suffering, constantly making alliances then changing sides. You're right Yosu. It's a swamp. My old lord Shinmazu was dedicated to cleaning it up and making the world a better place and I was committed to helping him."

"Don't you think all the other shoguns believed they were doing the same thing, trying to clean up a corrupt world? Everybody thinks they know best. That they're the only ones who can see clearly, and know how to sort the mess out. Shinmazu believed that if only the emperor regained his power that order would be restored."

"But the emperor is a divine being."

"Saigo, we're all divine beings. Even the fleas and mosquitos. Japan was ruled by an Emperor for seven hundred years and the country is still full of squabbling lords, daimyos and shoguns. They are like a rat king. Have you ever heard of a rat king?"

Saigo shook his head.

"A rat king is a group of rats that have their tails bound together, usually by sap or gum. The more they struggle to escape, the tighter they are bound. Then they panic and start biting each other. It's a disaster. Any rat that tries to join in and sort the mess out, inevitably becomes trapped itself. It's a nightmare.The only solution is to sit quietly and do nothing. That's hard enough for a monk to do, let alone a prisoner of a rat king that's being eaten alive."

"You have such a lovely way with words, Yosu."

"It's the way I tell them."

"So you don't think anyone should do anything to sort out the mess that we're in, and stop all these little wars that are always breaking out?"

"Sorting out the mess is the same as going to untangle the rat tails. If you try that, you'll just get tangled up with all the others and end up wrangling at the bottom of a rubbish bin in a rat king."

"So you don't recommend a career in politics?"

"You'll be much happier sitting quietly and doing nothing. Hidden somewhere between the armpits is an area of great peace. You won't find it by fighting for the emperor. And you've got far too much hair for a monk. Let me shave your head for you."

"First, you take away my noble political principles, and now you want what's left of my hair as well."

"Shut up and give me some of that miso soup before it goes cold. Have you got any more of those rice balls?"

"I thought you were supposed to be beyond desire."

"I am. But I'm not beyond lunch. Can you afford a bottle of sake?"

"I can. But the wine merchants aren't usually happy selling sake to a monk."

"That's alright. You're not a monk. You just look like a monk. Tell them it's for your dad."

151

All at Sea

Their journey to Satsuma was not the pleasant outing they'd
hoped for. The shogun's men were searching for Saigo, and wherever
they went they had to avoid the samurai. When they finally reached
Kagoshima, they discovered that the daimyo they hoped would help
them was dead. His successor was made nervous by the presence of the
shogun's samurai in the region and refused to help Yosu and Saigo.

During their second night in the palace, they were woken by one
of the old daimyo's retainers. He remembered Saigo from previous
visits. "Sir. so sorry to wake you, but you must leave immediately. The
daimyo has sent a messenger to the shogun's samurai telling them that
you are here in his palace. They will be here before morning to arrest
you. Get your things together and I'll show you a way out that will
avoid the guards. By the way, it's good to see you again, sir. I'm sure
my old master would have looked after you properly. He really liked
you. My new Lord is young and inexperienced. He trusts people too
quickly and often gets sold a pile of junk. He's frightened to do
anything wrong, so he relies on unreliable advisors. They are either
lackeys and crawlers, or ambitious devious rats. He wants to keep
everybody happy. He wants everyone to like him and is scared of
changes. He'll take the side of whoever is the most powerful."

A servant arrived and gave a hessian bag to the retainer. He
handed the bag to Saigo. "There's some food in here. That should keep
you going for a while. There are samurai looking for you all over town,
so be careful and keep out of sight. Your best chance is to go down to
the dock and get on a boat. There have been too many heads rolling
around on the floor lately. I'll send a boy with you to show you to the
quay."

They were soon creeping down the narrow streets towards the
sea, a small boy leading the way. They could smell the seaweed and salt
and hear the occasional squawk from an insomniac gull. Out in the bay

they could see Sakurajma island, topped by a volcano spitting the odd lump of glowing lava into the dark sky. They wandered along the wharf, looking for a seaman to ask about a passage. They weren't fussy about where they went. They just wanted to get somewhere where they weren't being hunted. They came upon a sailor with a small junk. He was loading it with baskets of fruit and vegetables. They asked him where he was going.

He replied, "Sakurajma. Volcano island."

Saiko asked, "Would you take two passengers? We can pay."

"How much?"

"How much do you want? Please don't try to cheat us. We are just humble monks."

"One *mon*." He paused. "Each."

Saigo heard shouting coming from further down the wharf. He looked and saw three samurai, pointing and gesticulating. He nudged Yosu and nodded towards the samurai. Saiko asked the boatman, "Shall we get aboard?"

"Yes, I'm ready to leave."

There was a curved canvas canopy on the centre of the craft, where the boatman had stacked his baskets of fruit and vegetables alongside a couple of small barrels.. Saiko and Yosu worked their way between the baskets, trying to keep out of sight. One of the samurai had noticed them going aboard. He said something to his companions and pointed along the wharf. They paused for a moment, then one of them shouted, "Oi, you there in the little junk. Hey, stop. We want to talk to you. What have you got in your boat? Stop, I said."

The boatman heaved on the single oar that protruded from the back of the boat, and pulled away from the wharf. The samurai ran along the wharf until they were level, and continued shouting. They were already separated from the little craft by other vessels moored along the wharf, and their voices were lost behind the cabins and sails and piles of cargo waiting to be shifted.

The samurai understood how important it was to grab Saigo. He was a long term threat to the authority of their Shogun lord. Now that Saigo was back in his old territory of Satsuma, where he still had friends and allies, he would only become more of nuisance. It didn't look like his head would remain attached to his shoulders for much longer. "We need a boat to catch the bastards. If the Shogun finds out we let them slip through our fingers it will be our heads rolling around on the floor instead of theirs."

One of them pointed along the wharf where another larger boat was being loaded. "That's the one."

They ran along the dock, and were joined by three more samurai. When they reached the vessel, the half dozen crew and coolies who were loading the hold stopped in fear and bowed. "Stop loading and get aboard. This craft is required in the service of the Shogun. Prepare to sail immediately."

The samurai and crew scrambled aboard. One of the coolies unhooked the rope from the capstan and the sail was raised. Four crew and two samurai took their seats next to the oars and began to row.

The samurai in the front of the boat, stood up and scanned the water between the docks and the island. He squinted, pointed and shouted. He'd seen the little junk and urged the rowers to pull harder. He then barked at the warrior carrying a bow and arrows. "Can you hit them from here?"

"I can try, sir. The movement of both craft makes it more difficult. And it's dark. But I'll give it my best shot." He selected an arrow from his quiver, made from woven wood and covered in fur. His bow was a hardwood core surrounded by layers of laminated bamboo. Only trained archers knew how to use them properly. Normal foot soldiers used smaller bows that were easier to handle.

The archer inserted the groove at the end of the arrow into the bowstring. He decided where he was going to aim for on the little junk.

The archer called, "Stop rowing."

The rise and fall of the boat became more regular. Fortunately there was a lamp attached to the short mast.

The archer pulled back the bowstring, remembering his lessons when he was taught to shoot from a moving horse. The secret was not to aim at the target, but where the target was going to be when the arrow arrived. The arrow was released when your breath and was at the top of your lungs, just before you breathed out. Then you remained calm for a couple of seconds until the rise and fall of the horse or the boat was at its peak.

The archer breathed in. His lungs were full and the boat was at the top of a wave. He saw the lamp on the junk rising. He released the arrow.

On the junk, Yosu and Saigo had come out of hiding and were squatting on the deck, talking to the boatman.

There were two small wooden barrels on board for delivery to the island, one containing sake and the other soy sauce. There was a hiss followed by a gently thump as the arrow flew through the air and struck the barrel of soy sauce. The three men looked round in shock as the arrow stopped quivering. There was another hiss, followed by a scream as the second arrow stabbed into the boatman's arm. Saigo and Yosu dived down onto the deck to avoid what was coming next. What was coming next hit the boatman on his shoulder. He fell to the deck moaning. Saigo looked behind and saw the boat with the samurai getting nearer The archer was fitting another arrow to his bowstring.

Saigo snapped, "We've got to get off this junk."

"Where?"

He looked over the edge of the junk into the sea. "There's only one place we can go."

"Saigo, I can't swim."

"Oh shit."

Another arrow thudded into the barrel of sake.

"I hope you're a fast learner." The arrow was pointing at a solution to their problem. Saigo pulled the barrel of sake towards him and twisted out the cork at the end.

The samurai boat drew nearer. Saigo tipped the barrel, and the sake poured out onto the deck.

"Get the other barrel, take out the cork and empty the soy sauce. And hang on to the cork. We're going to need it."

Saigo pouring with one hand, reached into his bag with the other and took out his begging bowl. He put it beneath the barrel and filled it with sake. "Waste not want not." Another arrow hit the deck where the boatman was moaning, terrified as his blood rolled over the planks mixing a macabre cocktail with the sake and soy sauce.

The barrels were soon empty. "Push the cork back in. Make sure it's tight."

Saiko took a gulp of sake from his bowl, then passed it to Yosu, who did likewise. Another arrow jabbed into the deck, next to Yosu's foot, pinning his robe to the bamboo deck.

"Time to go Yosu."

"But I still can't swim." He jerked the arrow pinning his robe, from the deck.

"Don't worry. Just hold tight to the barrel and it will keep you afloat."

Saigo had another gulp of sake, and clutched the empty barrel to his chest. Another arrow thudded into it. He jumped overboard clutching the empty barrel. Yosu saw him disappear beneath the waves for a moment, then bob up to the surface. "Come on."

Another arrow hit the deck. Yosu grabbed the bowl of sake and took a large gulp. He threw his arms around the soy sauce barrel as if his life depended on it. It did. He jumped overboard and joined Saigo bobbing up and down in Kagoshima Bay.

They looked up at the island and saw the volcano throw up a large cloud of ash and steam.

Yosu remarked, "The island's saying goodbye."

"It looks like it's glad to be rid of us."

"As it says in the Sambhogakakya, 'Guests are like fish. After three days they begin to smell.'"

They could hear the samurai boat approaching. The tide was carrying them in the opposite direction out to sea.

Saiko whispered, "Keep still and quiet. Sound carries over water."

As they drifted away the waves became choppier and the wind pushed them further across the bay.

Back on the junk the samurai questioned the boatman, whose life was dribbling out onto the deck. "Your two passengers. What happened to them?"

"They went overboard, lord. They were drowned. They both had arrows sticking in them. One of them cried, 'I can't swim.' The other tried to help him, but he grabbed onto him and dragged them both under."

The samurai in charge looked over the side and saw Yosu's bag floating. He grabbed an oar, fished the bag out, lay it on the deck, where it soaked up the blood, soy sauce and sake cocktail. He looked out across the dark bay. The volcano spluttered. The wind whipped the waves. The night smothered everything. "Take us back to the wharf."

The boatman hauled the craft around and started rowing. The effort caused his blood to pump out into the boat even faster. The nearer land they were, the more exhausted he became. By the time they reached the wharf he was dead.

The samurai captain spoke to his men. "Just so we're all clear about it. The two subversives are dead. Wounded by the Haruto's brilliant archery, then drowned in the bay. There was a witness, also dead, and we have evidence." He held up the blood-stained bag. "There's no way they could have survived. They were far out in the bay. Even if they hadn't been shot they'd never have made it."

The samurai understood what the dire consequences would be for letting the fugitives escape and eagerly agreed with their commander's description of events. "Yes sir. Definitely dead."

"Blood everywhere and no sign of the arrows that hit them."

"Miles from shore. Freezing water."

"That bastard Saigo won't be bothering the shogun anymore."

"Yes. Screw him. He can finally do something compassionate in his life and feed the fish."

"Saiko the *sashimi*."

They laughed, relieved. Their fear of losing the fugitives had passed.

Yosu and Saigo were silently hanging on to their barrels, hoping nobody had noticed them The current was taking them out between two headlands, Ibusuki and MinamYosuki. It was raining and the further away from land they were, the bigger the waves became, and the harder they slapped their faces.

Yosu began to think that maybe life in Gisu monastery wouldn't be so bad after all. Nami the pig was gone. Jo his replacement was an amiable individual. Nobody would be trying to drown him or use him for target practice.

Saigo shouted, "Yosu, look. A boat. Perhaps they'll rescue us." Coming towards them was a medium-sized boat with a large sail. The deck had a beautifully carved balustrade, and there were several cabins and a large hold below.

They shouted and waved. The crew saw them and steered toward them. Two of the crew leaned over the bow and called down to them. "What are you doing out here?"

Saigo shouted back, "Cold."

Both of them had started to turn numb. Yosu had swallowed good helping of seawater and was vomiting. The lack of feeling in their hands was causing them to lose their grip on the barrels.

The crew threw a couple of ropes over the side and hauled the drowning fugitives aboard. The empty barrels wobbled off over the East China Sea towards Shanghai. Yosu leaned over the rail of the ship and looked out over the Pacific Ocean. A brush had been dipped in red ink and was drawing a vivid line across the horizon.

The captain told them he was heading south to Okinawa and said he could drop them off at the next port, which would be the small island of Amami Oshima.

Takamori said, "That sounds ideal. Thank you."

Amami Oshima

A few hours later the boat pulled up to the dock in Amami Harbour. Amami was the largest town on the island. It was not very big. The port was quiet and most days no ships passed through. It was hot, quiet and peaceful. Yosu and Saigo thanked the crew and went ashore. They received a few unobtrusive stares. Monks weren't a common sight on the island. Several people put their hands together and bowed their heads respectfully.

They wandered through the town and found a market. Saigo bought a couple of canvas shoulder bags, two wooden begging bowls, a small metal pan, a couple of firestones, some chopsticks, tofu, miso, tea, soy sauce, water bottles, sake, rice and vegetables. They were still nervous about being discovered and decided to take the road out of town.

"I've been thinking, Yosu. Now we're living in a different place, it might be a good time to change my name. The Shogun and his men are looking for Saigo Takamori. It would be better not to advertise that's who I am. Now we're in Amami I think I'll change my name. How about Saigo Sasuke. "

"Sounds fine to me. Nobody's ever heard of me, so I'll stay being Yosu Gessho."

They asked a few people if there was a monastery on the island. They received a variety of answers,

"No, friend. No monasteries in this place."

"There used to be one on the road to Tatsugo. But the place has been empty for years. There's nobody there anymore. I think they got ill and died, or left or something."

"A monastery. Yes. There's one out on the way to Tatsugo. I've never been there, but I've heard about it."

Yosu looked at Saigo and said, "Tatsugo?"

He replied, "Tatsugo it is then."

It was a beautiful day and a beautiful island. They walked out of Amami along the path to Tatsugo. The forest stretched over the island like a green blanket covering a sleeping giant. The shade kept them out the sweltering sun. They were happy to be walking without looking over their shoulders for murderous samurai. They came to a clearing that was littered with large stones, that had once been part of a building that had long since gone to ruin.

Saigo said, "Why don't we stop here and make some miso soup?"

"Good idea. But we haven't got any *dashi*."

"That's alright. We've plenty of miso and tofu. Even a few spring onions. Anyway I didn't think monks were allowed to eat *dashi*. It's got a bit of fish in it."

"You've got an answer for everything."

"That's because I'm a politician. It comes with the job."

"Yes. I know. If you don't know the answer you just make something up."

"The art of politics."

"Anyway, I'm sure the Buddha said, 'Never look for hidden fish flakes.'"

"He probably ate lots of miso soup."

They gathered a few dry sticks and grass, made a fire and put on a pan of water. Yosu added a large piece of miso, a couple of shredded spring onions and some tofu cubes.

Saigo lifted a tofu cube from his bowl with chopsticks and popped it into his mouth. "Delicious. Could have done with a few hidden fish flakes though."

Yosu half closed one eye and looked threatening.

They both sat on large stones that had obviously been part of a larger structure. Yosu wandered over to some bushes to relieve himself. He was going with the flow when he noticed a familiar stone shape half covered with vines. When he'd finished, he untangled the plants around the stone then stepped back. There was no doubt, it was an ancient, well-worn statue of a seated Buddha.

"Hey, Saigo. Come and see who I've found."

160

"Don't tell me. A samurai looking for a fugitive daimyo to behead."

"No. Try again."

"A Tengu in a bad mood."

"No. Wrong again. It's Lord Buddha."

"Don't you start going all Zen on me again."

"No. Come and look."

Saigo sauntered over to the bushes and Yosu pointed to the Buddha.

Saigo was surprised. He hadn't expected to meet the Buddha in the bushes. He said, "You're right. It's the Bodhidharma. He's been hiding in the bushes."

After their lunch and a snooze in the heat, the monk and a half continued down the road and found themselves in Taiyour village. There was a well in the centre, so they filled their water bottles and sat in the shade of a nearby tree for a drink.

Although they hadn't seen anybody since they arrived in the village, plenty of people were looking at them, peeping out from the their windows and doors. Visitors were rare and always a curiosity. They rarely saw travellers, and those they did passed straight through the village, perhaps stopping for a drink, like these two strangers. Most of the villagers had never seen a monk before, so there was an added reason to be curious.

Many of the villagers had shrines in their homes, decorated with wild flowers and guarded by small statues of the Buddha.

An old lady appeared from one of the huts, carrying a small parcel, wrapped in a large leaf. She knew what a monk was and knew that it was her duty as a Buddhist to donate something for them to eat. She was nervous. The nearer she got to Saigo and Yosu the more she shook. By the time she reached them she was having second thoughts. She wanted to place the small parcel of rice in Yosu's bowl, but her hand was shaking too much. Yosu lifted his bowl with one hand and gently placed his other hand on the trembling fingers clutching the parcel of rice. "Mother, is that some rice you've brought us?" She smiled and nodded, unable to cough out any words. "Well you are too kind. Thank you so much."

Yosu knew what would make the old lady happy. "May I say a prayer with you?"

She was so nervous she could only croak. Yosu took it for a "Yes". He looked into the old woman's face. It was covered with lines drawn by a long, hard, full, selfless life that said, "I am a human being and so are you." She was surrounded by stars. He said his prayer: *In the space before me is the living Buddha Shakyamuni surrounded by all the Buddhas and Bodhisattvas, like the full moon surrounded by stars.*

Once the old lady had broken the ice, other villagers began to appear. Before long, the monk and a half were sitting before a beggar's banquet: rice, dried fish, pickled vegetables, raw vegetables and even a couple of pieces of goma tofu, which Yosu hadn't seen since Abbot Nami was stuffing himself in Gisu monastery.

By the time they'd finished the tofu cakes, the village children had appeared. They were even more curious than the adults. Who were these aliens with bald heads and strange robes? At first, about four or five of them stood at a distance debating who and what the monks were. Gradually, they were joined by other children from the village. The debate became heated. Finally, the biggest boy stepped forward. He carried a ball the size of a coconut, made from rags, bound tight with thin strands of bamboo. He rolled the ball towards the monk and a half. It stopped at their feet. The children and the adults held their breath, waiting to see what would happen next.

Yosu stood up and picked the ball up. He tossed it up a couple of times in his right hand to ascertain its weight then pointed up to the clouds with his left hand and rapidly threw the ball into the air with his right hand. He continued pointing and cried, "There it goes. Up to the moon. See. To the moon."

Then he lowered his arm and relaxed. There was no sign of the ball anywhere. The boy who had rolled the ball took a few steps forward and said, "Where's my ball?"

"I think it went to the moon."

"Can you get it back please?"

"What's your name?"

"Ren."

Yosu looked up into the sky, cupped his hands round his mouth and shouted, "Mr Moon, can Ren please have his ball back? Ah here it comes." He pointed up with his left hand.

Nobody noticed him slip the ball from under his robe with his right hand and flip it up behind Ren. The ball bounced on the floor. Yosu picked it up and handed it to Ren with a smile. The children were impressed. They liked the visitors. The villagers too were warming to them. Nothing this exciting had happened in the village since Fat Yuma got drunk and fell down the well. It took four men and a donkey to haul him out. And the first thing that happened when he got back to his feet was his wife broke a sake bottle on his head then chased him home, beating him with a bamboo cane. Now they had a magic monk who threw a ball up to the moon.

Saigo and Yosu spent the night in the ruined monastery outside the village. They returned to the village the next day and were soon surrounded by Ren and his friends, who were eager to see more magic tricks. Saigo was curious. He asked the children, "What do you do all day long?"

"Oh, we play games. Help our mothers in the home. Sometimes we go to the beach. Sometimes we play in the forest or in the stream, making dams, sailing boats and stuff."

"Don't you ever go to school?"

"What's that? What's school?"

"It's a place you go to learn."

"Learn what?"

"Learn to read. Learn to write. Learn arithmetic. Calligraphy."

"We don't know about those things. Do you know them?"

"Yes, I know them."

Ren asked him, "Why don't you show us?"

Saigo was gently knocked sideways by Ren's question. It was one of those moments when a butterfly flaps its wings and the world changes. Saigo was silent. His thoughts were were shuffling about rearranging themselves like a flock of geese standing by a lake, disturbed by a cat. His plans for the future were shuffling like a pack of Menko cards. Most cards had a picture of a classroom, full of children. Saigo saw Ren was waiting for a reply. Saigo said, "I'll think about it."

163

Ren then asked, "What's calligraphy?"

"It's beautiful writing that you do with ink and a brush."

A small voice piped up, "Can I do some?"

Another child said, "We don't have any ink, or a brush."

Yosu said, "You can do it without a brush and ink you know."

"How?"

"There are lots of ways. You can use water on stone. You can scratch on a slate. You can draw letters in sand with a stick. Because the village is near the sea, the soil here is sandy. So this would be a good place to use a stick. Would you like to try it?"

An enthusiastic chorus of "Yeees," filled the air. This promised to be another good day.

Time for School

Yosu selected a patch of ground near the well and asked Ren if he and his friend could borrow a rake from someone, so he could level the ground and make it flat enough to write on with a stick.

He then told the rest of the children to go and find a stick that they could write with. They disappeared into the bushes. Ren and his friend reappeared with a bamboo rake, carried by its owner, who wanted to check on Ren's tale. Satisfied that Yosu was serious, he handed him the rake. He marked out a square and then asked Ren and his friend to rake the inside. "Nice and smooth and even, so we can write on it."

As they prepared the surface, the other children began to appear from the bushes with their sticks. Some were too small, some were too large. Minato, the smallest of the group, was keen to show his strength and enthusiasm. He appeared dragging a branch that was taller than himself. Saigo explained what size would be more useful and sent the children back to revise their selections.

Yosu went and chose a stick for himself and then scratched lines in the raked area, dividing it into a dozen squares. He called the children and told them they were going to write three numbers: one, two, three.

"Who can show me one finger?"

The older children held up a single finger. The younger children copied them, until everyone had a finger in the air.

"I'll just come around and count them to make sure you haven't hidden any. One. One. One. Yes. Very good." He stopped next to the smallest boy, Minato and checked his finger. "How many fingers have you got up there, Minato?"

"One."

"Are you sure you haven't got another one hidden behind your ear? Let me look. No nothing there. One finger. Very good. Well done Minato. Good boy. Now for the next number. What number comes after 'one'? 'Two' that's right. Who can show me two fingers? Good. I'll come round and check you're not hiding any. One two, one two, one two. Very good. How many have you got there Minato?"

"Two."

"One two. That's right. And none behind your ear. Well done, you're getting good at this."

Minato smiled, happy to be noticed. Yosu was about to start the next part of the lesson when he noticed a group of about half a dozen girls, standing by the well, discussing the proceedings and pointing at the class. He walked over to them, "Ladies, why aren't you in class? Go and find a stick about this long." He held his hands about a metre apart, "And then come and join the rest of us. We'll wait for you." The girls were surprised and confused. They hesitated. "Of course, if you don't want to learn how to write, you can stay here and watch the boys learn and miss all the fun. You'll find some sticks among the trees. You only need one each." Sara, the oldest girl, determined not to miss out, walked into the trees followed by the other girls. They reappeared a couple of minutes later with their sticks.

"We're going to learn to write. The first thing we're going to write are numbers. Who knows the name of the first number? Sara, how many noses have you got?"

"One, sir."

"One. That's the first number. Very good. Thank you Sara. Minato. How many noses have you got." Minato touched his nose, just to make sure, "One sir."

"Are you sure you haven't got any more hidden anywhere?"

The children laughed. They liked Yosu. He was funny.

He organized the children so each of them stood in front of one of the squares on the floor.

An old woman had been standing by the well, fascinated by the goings-on in the centre of the village, She walked with a cane to help keep her balance. She approached Yosu. "I'm sorry to disturb you, Brother, but I have something to ask you."

"You're not disturbing me mother. How can I help you?"

"My name is Akari. I am eighty years old. I see you are teaching the children to write."

166

"Yes, mother. Today is their first lesson."

"Well, sir."

She was nervous and her voice trembled.

"You can call me Brother Yosu."

"Well, Brother Yosu, I wondered if it would be possible for me to join the class and I could learn too?"

Yosu thought for a moment, then said, "Mother Akari, it would be my greatest pleasure if you joined us. You are most welcome."

Akari raised her walking stick and smiled. "I already have my stick."

Yosu called Ren over.

"Ren, Mother Akiri-san is going to join us. Do you think you could find her a cushion to sit on?"

Ren arrived a few minutes later with a bamboo chair. Akiri sat down with the children and the lesson began.

Yosu raised his right index finger, said, "One," and drew his finger in a horizontal line, from left to right, level with his shoulders.

"Now you do it."

Once they'd mastered drawing the line in the air, they moved on to drawing it in the sand. And so they began.

Their home-made school was popular with both the children and their parents. The parents were illiterate and very pleased that their children were learning to read and write. Saigo enjoyed his new role in school. He enjoyed the company of the children. They were open, sincere and good hearted, unlike most of the adults he'd had to deal with when he was involved in politics. The children liked Saigo, which made teaching much easier. He had surprised himself when he discovered he had a natural talent for teaching. Soon he was spending more time with the children than Yosu. There were lots of distractions in the centre of the village, and there was always an audience of curious adults eager to watch the proceedings, often eager to give advice and join in. Saigo and Yosu decided to move their class outside the village to the monastery, where they had taken up residence. They cleared a space for the classroom, and villagers helped build a canopy to protect them from the sun and rain.

More children joined the enterprise, and Akari-san began helping with the younger children. Saigo invested some of the money he had stashed on books from the local market. He told people they needed books for the school, and a small library started to grow. Yosu resumed his old trade as ink-maker for a while, using pine wood and vegetable oil and getting the villagers to collect soot from their lamps. Yosu made some brushes by gently crushing one end of a piece of bamboo to release the fibres. Some of the seamen who travelled back and forth to Okinawa collected wrapping paper and bags which were cut up for the children to paint on. The school in the monastery prospered, and Saigo was happier than he'd ever been when he was fighting for his life in the swamp of politics. The pro-emperor faction seemed to get along quite well without him.

Gogo-An

Ryoken, the poet, calligrapher and monk, had been a disciple of another famous monk, Kokusen. He trained at Kokusen's monastery until Kokusen's death. Ryoken then received authority to take his teacher's place, and become head of his own temple. He wasn't interested in becoming the head of anything however and he turned down this, and several other offers, to run his own monastery. Instead, he set out on a pilgrimage, and lived as an *unsui* for the next decade, supporting himself by begging. He shared any surplus food with children, animals and anyone who was hungry. Children loved him and he would often neglect his begging by playing with them for too long. He usually carried two or three balls made of rags and string in his bag, so the children always had something to play with. He continued writing poetry and practising calligraphy. When he ran out of ink, he made his way to Yosu's uncle Toshio's house, where he could replenish his supplies, play a game of Go and drink a bottle of sake or two. He was well-loved wherever he went. His poetry and calligraphy were highly valued, although if you had see him begging in the street, in his grubby robe, you would hardly believe that years after his death he would be renowned as one of Japan's greatest ever poets and artists.

After a decade of wandering all over Japan, begging and playing with children, writing poetry creating calligraphy, and sitting peacefully practising *zazen* meditation, Ryoken returned to Echigo province, the place where he'd grown up. The places he knew from his childhood were all slightly different from how he remembered them. He felt like a stranger. He was feeling old and no longer wanted to sleep out in the rain, or struggle making a fire when the wood was wet.

He lived in various huts and lean-tos, some in the grounds of local Buddhist temples, and he noticed he'd begun to look at where he slept from a different perspective. Previously he had simply considered if he'd get a decent night's sleep. But now a part of him automatically wondered if the place would be suitable for a longer stay. He found himself at the bottom of Mount Kugami and decided to visit the Kokujoji Temple, a little way up the mountain. One of the resident monks offered him some tea, which he accepted. They got chatting, The monk asked Rykonan if he wanted to join their monastery.

"Well, I've been wandering around Japan for over ten years and I must confess that the solitary life suits me very well. I feel part of the community of brothers without having to live with them. I know I'm supposed to be detached from the ups and downs of this world, but I'm getting old now. Too old to sleep in a field through the rain and wake up soaking wet and shivering with a frozen arse and a cough. So I suppose what I want is a small place big enough to lie down in with a roof over my head. A place where I can practice *zazen*, write poetry and do a little calligraphy."

The monk thought for a moment, finished his tea and waited for Ryoken to finish. Then he said, "Come with me."

Ryoken followed him out the monastery and onto a narrow path into the woods. The path slowly rose upwards. A small hut with a thatched roof came into view. There was a small hole in the thatch. Inside the hut there stood a small bamboo table and a slightly raised bed. The floor was littered with dead leaves and a few dry animal and bird droppings. There was a small balcony outside.

"This hut is named Gogo-an, the name of the previous tenant, who lived on five measures of rice a day (Gogo). Gogo-an was the last tenant, and the place has been left to the birds and the squirrels. I'm sure people would be happy if you moved in and restored it."

Ryokan loved the place. He loved the solitude, he loved the view and he loved its wild nature. His neighbours were monkeys and wild deer, with whom he foresaw no problems. He loved animals and plants, and literally wouldn't hurt a flea. In fact he sometimes gave them free meal on his forearm. Mount Kugami became his new home. He settled down, wrote more poetry and inscribed more calligraphy. When the weather permitted, he made journeys into the local countryside, visiting friends, staying in local Buddhist temples, having a glass of sake with a local farmer or playing hide and seek with the children, who swamped him wherever he appeared. Sometimes he spent the whole day playing with them. When asked why he spent so much time with children, he replied, "I love their honesty and their lack of pretence." The children had a rhyme which they enjoyed singing to him:

Master Ryokan, where's he been? Skinny as the year's first sardine.

When the weather was bad he stayed in his hut, cooking rice and miso, composing poetry or practising calligraphy.

My hut, located in a distant village, is little more than four bare walls.
Once I was a mendicant monk, wandering here and there,
Staying nowhere long.
Recalling the first day of my pilgrimage, years ago
How high my spirits were.

Ryokan

Ryokan loved the view from his porch down over the Shinano River valley. He spent many happy hours sitting there, soaking up the sunshine. Memories and thoughts drifted through his mind, like the river below drifting through the valley towards the East Sea. As they floated past, they reached out their hands to pull him towards them, but he was content to let them drift out to the ocean.

In Otogo Forest, beneath Mount Kugami
You'll find the tiny hut where I pass my days.
Still no temples or villas for me!
I'd rather live with the fresh breezes and the bright moon,
Playing with the village children or making poems.
If you ask about me, they'll probably say,
"What is that foolish monk doing now?"

Ryokan

Falling in Love

After Aiko's death, Taishin cleaned the tea room, stacked the cushions and tables inside and locked the door. She packed the crockery and other utensils, along with the framed piece of Ryokan's calligraphy, into a bamboo basket and took them down to the store room in the monastery. She packed her travelling bag: begging bowl, razor to shave her head, ink, bamboo flute, brush and paper, bag of tea, and cooking pot. She picked up her bokken, turned and had one last look at the tea house. She closed her eyes and remembered Aiko. A tear waved down her cheek. She was ready to return to the path of the Unsui and head north.

She looked up at the hanging sign and took a deep breath. She felt like she was standing on the edge of life again, joining the creatures of the forest, not knowing where she'd spend the night, what she'd eat next or when she'd eat it. One with nature.

> *Distant waves*
> *seem to come*
> *seem to go*
> *So I have lived my life*
> *leaving everything to the blowing wind.*

> *Taishin*

The days passed quickly as she made her way towards Nigata. Although she passed several monasteries, and stayed in some of them, her destination was at the bottom of Mount Kugami, where she hoped to find Master Ryoken. It wasn't that she wasn't interested in other teachers, rather she hadn't met any on her journey to Nigata. After a few days she found herself not far from the Kokujoji Temple. She was told Ryokan lived near the temple, in a hut at the bottom of the mountain.

As Taishin entered the local village, she noticed a sign by the side of the road. It displayed a poem:

> *On a short day*
> *There is no time*
> *to dry the rice stalks.*
> *Keep the hunting field*
> *in your heart.*

She stood reading the poem. A local farmer walked past, paused and said, "Our monk wrote that."

"Your monk. Who is that?"

"Ryokan. He's very well known around here. He lives in a hut nearby. Everybody loves him."

"How did his poem get here?"

"He put it there himself. One day our local Lord Naito planned to go hunting. He wanted the road cleaning. As you can see, the road is long and if everyone in the village works hard, we may just get it done in a day. This was not very convenient, because we were in the middle of a harvest. That's the busiest time of the year when the whole village must work from dawn till dusk. If it rains the whole crop may spoil. Well, when our monk arrived he could see everybody on their hands and knees, cleaning the road, and nobody in the fields. He asked what was going on. He told her that when Lord Naito was out hunting, he demanded that the road was immaculately clean before he rode on it. Ryokan looked up and down the road, then had an idea. He said, "Lord Naito has no idea what difficulties you farmers have. I'll try to stop him. Can you make me a signpost to put here by the road?" The farmer made the post and Ryoken came and fixed his poem to it. When Lord Naito came down the road with his entourage, he stopped and read the poem. Then he turned around and went back home."

The farmer looked at Taishin's nun's habit and asked, "Are you here to see our Monk?"

"Yes. Can you tell me where his hut is?"

"I can. But he's not there right now. "

"Where is he?"

"He's in the village, dancing. Today's the end of the Obon festival. But don't disturb him or let him know you recognize him."

"Why not?"

"Well, he's a monk and he's not supposed to dance. So let him get on with it and talk to him later."

Taishin was puzzled.

Ryoken would dance until he dropped. Given the slightest chance, he was up bopping away with everyone else. He wasn't in the least concerned what he looked like. As anyone who loves dancing knows, trying to imagine what you look like inhibits you. It's only when you cease being self-conscious and let the music and the rhythm take control that you begin to enjoy the dance. As with calligraphy and many other things, it works best if you let it happen by itself.

The village was busy. Lots of people were eating savoury pancakes and many of the children were tucking into sweet dumplings called *dango*. People were hanging paper lanterns outside their houses and putting offerings of tea, sake, rice and lotus-shaped sweets on the family altars outside their houses. Others were taking offerings to the graveyard to put on their family graves. The festival was to commemorate your ancestors and the lanterns were to guide their spirits home. When the lanterns had been lit and the offerings to the departed had been made the dancing began. This was an important part of the festival and what attracted Ryoken to the village at festival time.

As Taishin walked into the village, the drums became louder. It was as if she was a fish on a line that was being hauled in towards the boat. The women were dressed in beautiful brightly coloured costumes. Groups of them wore identical outfits and danced in unison. The men stood around munching pancakes and sipping small cups of sake, happy to watch and leave the dancing to the women. A variety of percussion instruments was beating out the dance rhythm, supported by flutes, lyres and harps. The dancers were losing their inhibitions and enjoying themselves. Taishin took out her flute and joined the impromptu orchestra.

174

Taishin looked around for Ryoken, but saw only the women of the village stepping up a storm. An old man next to Taishin was sliding octopus balls from a bamboo skewer and popping them into his mouth. Taishin asked, "Do you know where the monk Ryoken is?"

He replied, "Yes. He's dancing over there." He pointed with his skewer to group of dancers who was twirling faster than anyone else. Taishin looked hard, but she could only see women, "I can't see him."

"Look harder."

Suddenly, Taishin noticed one of the dancers who was much taller than those around her. She was dancing and singing with deep passion. She wore a summer kimono with long flowing sleeves that seemed too big for her, The women surrounding the tall dancer were complimenting her. "How beautiful she dances. See how sensitively her makeup is applied." (Her lipstick wasn't quite straight and her rouge was a little too dark and the flower in her headscarf was gigantic.) If you could have seen the tall dancer's legs you would have noticed how knobbly and skinny they were. This was because they belonged to the old hermit monk who lived at the bottom of the mountain.

"Miss Ryoken" disappeared into the crowd and Taishin looked for him, but the festival had swallowed him up.

Everybody knew that the mysterious dancer was Ryoken, but they played along with the disguise, complimenting "her" on her outfit, makeup and graceful dancing.

The next time Ryoken appeared in the village as himself, the women told him about the party at the Obon festival, particularly the mysterious tall dancer who captivated the audience. Ryoken was pleased that his cunning disguise had fooled everyone. In reality, the strange old woman with too much makeup, and a good head taller than the other women, had fooled no-one. They all loved him and didn't want to disappoint him and break the spell.

Taishin spent the night at the Kokugoji Temple, and the next day found the path through the forest to Ryokan's hut, When she arrived, he was on his knees on the veranda, cutting a hole in the floor. He raised his head and looked at Taishin. The happiness she felt in meeting him spread across her face, radiating warmth. Her beauty slapped him gently on his cheek. He was smitten. She glanced down at the hole he was cutting in the floor. Here was the eccentric monk she'd heard about, who did elegant calligraphy and wrote exquisite poetry. He was like a lovable feral dog, complete with fleas. She'd found him at last and she had him all to herself.

"Oh that hole's for the bamboo. It's growing underneath and has reached the underside of the floor. There's no room for it to go any higher and it's all cramped under there. I felt sorry for it and decided to cut a hole in the floor so it could grow properly." Taishin looked upwards. "When it hits the roof I'll cut a hole in that too. Would you like some tea Sister?"

At 69, Ryokan was old and weathered. Taishin was forty years younger, but if you mistook her piety for naivety you'd be making a mistake. She was cultured, intelligent, sensitive, strong in her Buddhist faith and carried a *bokken*. It wasn't long before Ryoken was completely in love with her. And, like most people who met him, it wasn't long before she was in love with Ryokan. They sat on the porch, discussing and exchanging poetry, talking about whatever topic appeared, making each other laugh with stories of their time as *Unsui*. Their love for each other grew as fast as the bamboo charging through the hole in the floor, and it wasn't long before Ryoken had to get up on the roof and cut another hole for it. Bamboo is the fastest growing plant in the world.

"From where does spring come?" I ask
The plum flowers do not reply
But in their midst
A warbler sings

Taishin

Spring announced its arrival with delicate pink plum blossoms. They arrived even before the cherry blossom. Taishin was pleased to see them. Ryoken was ill. The cold weather was lethal, and although the summer sun would bring mosquitos, vomiting and diarrhoea, it didn't have the vicious edge of winter which always seemed as if it was trying to kill him.

176

Ryoken was getting old. He became sick more often. There was something wrong with his stomach, probably connected to his erratic eating habits. He was skinny, and the older he became, the more he felt the cold. His draughty hut, the cold and damp eventually became too much for him, and he finally accepted an invitation from Kimura, one of his friends and followers, to live in a small house in the Kimura's family garden. He missed the solitude, peace and simplicity of his hut at the foot of the mountain, but he didn't miss the cold, snow, rain, coughing, shivering, snot, stomach ache, loose bowels and the accompanying stink. It occurred to him that somehow his life had almost gone the full circle. When he was a baby, he soiled himself and needed somebody to keep him clean. He needed feeding. His food needed to be easy to digest. He slept more, craved love and attention, cried easily, ate whenever he was hungry. If fact it was just like the good old days when he'd first arrived on Earth. The only thing missing was his mother's love, and he would find no better substitute than what Taishin provided.

On the Road Again

Meanwhile, on the small island of Amami Oshima, in the middle of the East China Sea, the school was going from strength to strength. Saigo loved teaching and the children were progressing well with reading, writing and arithmetic. Akari, the old woman who at the age of eighty had learned to read and write, had transformed from pupil to teacher, and taken responsibility for the youngest children. A carpenter from the nearby town had sent his two children for lessons, and to express his gratitude, he made an abacus for every child in the school and included a few spares. Regular bundles of paper arrived on the ferry from Okinawa. Mostly they had been used to wrap food or other objects. Sometimes they were printed on one side. Newspapers had recently begun to appear in Japan, but they hardly ever made it out to the island.

Yosu had made enough ink-blocks and bamboo brushes to keep the school calligraphy lessons going for decades. The samurai had given up looking for Saigo, the last Shogun. Everyone assumed he'd been shot and drowned when he went overboard while escaping in Kagoshima Bay.

Everyone on Amami was proud of their school, and happy that their children were being educated. Saigo couldn't have left the island, even if he'd wanted to, which he didn't. It was a beautiful place and for the first time in his life he was truly content.

Yosu, however, was getting itchy feet, and it wasn't athlete's foot or the bits of grass between his toes. With Saigo at the helm, the school was almost taking care of itself and Yosu was feeling redundant. He had enjoyed travelling with Saigo and got great satisfaction from starting the school, but it didn't need him anymore. Saigo was happy. He'd finally found his true vocation and was making a great success of it. He'd fallen in love with Aigana,, a local woman and they were married. Life had another surprise in store for him, and he fathered a son.

Yosu knew his days as a monk still had a long time to run. He missed the uncertainty of not knowing where his next meal was coming from and the pleasant surprise when it arrived, or where he was going to spend the night. He missed standing on the edge of life waiting to see what the next moment would bring. And he wanted to see Ryokan again. It was time to pick up his bowl, buy a bottle of sake and some tobacco for his old master, and walk to Mount Kugami and find his hut and see if they could borrow a Go set from somebody.

It had been nearly three years since Yosu and Saigo had escaped from the samurai, and he didn't even know if Ryokan was still alive. He wanted to find out. The years rolled by relentlessly, and while you weren't looking, time tinkered with stuff behind your back. Then one day you realized that the world had changed. Half the people you knew were no longer there. Somebody had been knocking buildings down and constructing new ones. What was going on?

Yosu told Saigo he was going to leave the island and see what had happened to Ryoken. Saigo was sorry to see him go, but he had plenty on his plate with the school and his new family.

"Do come back and see us again, Yosu. You've been a good friend and I've learned a lot from you."

"You too, Saigo. You're not bad for an ex-daimyo politician with too much money and not enough sense. You make a much better schoolteacher."

Yosu handed him a roll of paper.

"What's this?"

"It's a sketch with some calligraphy I did for you. Unroll it. Have a look."

Saigo untied the string and unrolled the paper. It displayed a poem and a sketch of a bird.

Loneliness: spring has already passed.
Silence: I close the gate.
From heaven, darkness; the wisteria is no longer visible.
The stairway is overgrown with herbs

179

And the rice bag hangs from the fence.
Deep stillness, long isolated from the world.
All night the hototogisu cries.

Ryokan

"The poem is by Ryokan."

"He's one of my favourites."

"Me too. The bird is a *hototogisu.*"

Saigo walked with Yosu down to the dock and waved him off as the boat to Kagoshima set sail. He went back to the classroom. The children had gone home. Only Akari was left. Since she'd first appeared in centre of the village and asked Yosu if she could join the children in class, she'd been absorbed into the school, and spent most of her time teaching the youngest children and helping in other ways. Today she was tidying up.

Saigo untied the thin strip of bamboo that was wrapped around the paper. He straightened the sheet. Along the top, in exquisite calligraphy, it read, "The Schoolteacher and his Pupils,". Below the script was a picture done in the same style as 'The Greedy Abbot" which had hung in Saigo's gallery in days of plenty and nearly cost Yosu his life. It was a scene set in the classroom, around the blocks of stone that had once formed the monastery. Akari sat on a block at the back, with four small children at her feet. She was reading to them. They sat there enthralled, oblivious to the mayhem around them. In the centre of the picture stood Saigo. He was covered in children. They hung from his clothes, swung from his hair, scrambled over him like lice. One was stabbing him with a bamboo brush. Behind him, a girl who had difficulty with arithmetic was building a bonfire from the abacuses. A boy who was a bit cheeky was swinging across the classroom on a vine, clasped tight to a monkey. A seven-year-old boy who fancied himself as a samurai warrior was about to launch a spear into the air. Tied to the end of the spear was the smallest child in the class. Three shrimpy boys sat behind a large stone, smoking pipes and drinking sake.

180

Saigo and Akari laughed until tears rolled down their cheeks, pointing out things to each other and recognizing different members of the class. Saigo would treasure the picture for the rest of his life. If there had been a wall in the school, he would have hung it there.

My Years Are Gone

Yosu's journey to see Ryoken was uneventful. He spent the night at monasteries in Kumamoto, Kitakyushu, Hiroshima, Osaka, Gifu, and in a few fields and on a couple of beaches. The weather was good: it didn't rain, it wasn't too cold and the wind was strong enough to move most of the muttering mosquitos along. He still missed his mattress and extra blanket. After a night in the open, his knees and back ached, and he had a slight cough.

"Bugger this. I must be getting old. I need a cup of tea," he muttered to himself. He arrived at Nagaoka, had his pot of tea, bought a bottle of sake for when he met Ryokan, and made his way to the local hot springs of Yomogihira, to the South of the town. Soaking in the hot water, looking at the mountains in the distance, watching the clouds crawl across the sky, he was perfectly at peace. His aching back and limbs were tamed. The life of the renunciate wasn't as bad as it had seemed when he woke up in a field that morning, soaked in dew with a beetle crawling up his nose.

He left the hot springs and set out for Ryokan's hut, at the foot of the mountain. The hot bath and pot of tea had restored his faith in the path of the *Unsui*.

He wound his way along the forest path and found himself outside Ryokan's hut. His heart leapt when he saw smoke coming through the thatch but sank when a teenage boy stepped out on the veranda. It was Hencho, a fourteen-year-old Shingo monk. Hencho had appeared at Ryoken's hut a few months ago and begged him to be allowed to serve him as his assistant. Although Ryokan preferred to live alone, and eschewed disciples, he was too old and frail to carry firewood and water up the mountain to the hut every day, so he agreed to let Hencho help him. It was also useful to have Hencho around when Ryokan left the hut. He could act as caretaker and take care of things while the master was absent, and chase away the monkeys.

Hencho made a pot of tea, then sat on the veranda with Yosu and brought him up to date with Ryokan's situation. "He is ill. There's something wrong with his stomach, he doesn't sleep very well, he gets tired very easily. Two doctors from the village visit regularly and bring him medicines, but he isn't getting any better. Winter is worse. The cold really gets to him. This year one of his disciples, Kimura Motoemon, could see he was struggling in the hut and invited him down to the village to stay with him. Kimura is a wealthy merchant with a large house He has a small, self-contained house in his garden that he has given Ryoken. The Master now lives down there. I don't think he has the strength to walk up to his hut anymore anyway. Although he constantly complains about the lack of space and privacy, I don't think I'll see him up here again. I'm going down to the village in a while. I'll take you to Kimura's home if you like."

"Thank you, Hencho. I haven't seen the Master for about five years."

"Just don't expect him to be as you remember him. His life is slowly fading away."

Life is like a dewdrop,
Empty and fleeting,
My years are gone
And now, quivering and frail,
I must fade away,

Ryokan

They walked down the mountain and into the village. Hencho knocked on Kimura's front door. It was a large, expensive house. A servant answered the door. "This is brother Yosu. He is an old friend and colleague of Ryokan. May I take him round to see him?"

"Of course."

They walked down the side of the house into the large garden at the back. To one side, in the shade of a cedar tree, stood a small cabin.

Hencho knocked on the door.

A voice came from inside, "Go away. He's not in."

"Master, it's me. Hencho. I've got a visitor for you."

"I don't do calligraphy or pictures any more. So the visitor can piss off."

"What about sake? And Go. Do you not drink sake or play Go any more, you miserable, bad-tempered old monk?"

Silence.

"That voice sounds familiar. It must be the thief who stole my mattress."

"I've brought you some new ink-blocks. But if you've given up calligraphy, you can make soup with them and eat them for lunch."

The door swung open and Ryokan stood there with a smile on his face. "It's the ink-maker who mistook his uncle for a Tengu."

"Ryokan! How good to see you after all this time. You've lost weight. What's your secret?

"Well, it's called 'the sickness and starvation diet'. Come in, you unholy filthy old monk, Hencho, put the kettle on and make us all some tea."

They sat down and Hencho served the tea.

"So what's been happening to you for the past few years? I've been hearing all sorts of things. You've become famous," said Ryoken.

"What did you hear?"

"Well I heard you had a disagreement with your abbot which ended with his head rolling on the floor."

Yosu looked embarrassed. "It wasn't me that chopped it off, Master."

"And I heard the shoguns wanted your head when you were on the run with Saigo Takamori. And you were both shot by samurai archers while trying to escape, and thrown into the Japan Sea where you drowned and became lunch for some sharks."

Yosu looked at his arms then clenched and unclenched his fists. "Clearly false news."

"Clearly you can swim. Or at least float. So, tell me all about it."

"Where should I start?"

"Well, you could start with Abbot Nami. I met him a couple of times. From what I remember he was a complete, obnoxious, lecherous little prick."

"That's the one. He nearly killed me."

Yosu told him the story of the one hundred works of calligraphy, of Abbot Nami's "Zen Face", his painting of the "Wise Abbot", how Saigo Takamori, the !"Last Samurai" had saved his life, and how they were reunited at the kite festival, their escape by boat to Amami Island, their discovery of the temple ruins and how they accidently started a school there.

Ryokan thoroughly enjoyed the story. He had the satisfied look of a young child, pleased with the end of a tale and happy that the evil Tengu got his just desserts.

Yosu noticed a Go board leaning against the wall, with a couple of bowls of stones in front of it.

He nodded towards the board. "Do you still play?"

"Just try and stop me."

Yosu reached into his bag, took out the bottle of sake and placed it on the table, "Well, this might slow you down a bit."

"Hencho, put the pan on. We need to warm some sake."

Hencho filled the kettle and pushed some more wood into the stove through the opening at the front, then placed the pan, half full of water, over the hole on top. Hencho took a sake jug and two small cups down from a shelf behind the stove. He wiped the cups with a cotton towel and placed them on the table. He removed the cork from the bottle of sake and carefully filled the sake jug. He then placed the jug standing upright in the middle of the pan on the stove, which was nearly boiling. As soon as the bubbles began to scramble upwards, he removed the pan and stood it on a bamboo mat on the table. Meanwhile, Yosu placed the Go board on the other side of the table, and placed the bowl of white stones in front of Ryoken and the black stones in front of

184

himself. He placed the lids of the bowls upside down next to the bowls. The upturned lids were the mortuaries, where the dead stones ended up.

"What did you have last time? Was it nine? That's probably what you need." Ryokan chuckled.

"I think it was six. And I nearly beat you."

"Nearly beat me? That's just a complicated way of saying you lost. Six it is then."

Yosu placed six of his black stones on six of the highlighted intersections on the board."

"You first," said Takamori.

Yosu clacked a stone down near one of his handicap stones in the corner, and the game commenced.

"So what's been happening to you Master?"

Ryokan slapped a white stone down. "The game is almost over,"

"What do you mean? We've only just started."

"I don't mean our game of Go, Yosu. I mean the Game of Life. My days are numbered. I'm almost out of firewood. It's nearly time to go and look behind the curtain, and see if Lord Buddha is home. As he said when he was down here on Earth, 'The world is afflicted by death and decay. But the wise do not grieve, having realized the nature of the world'."

Yosu looked at Ryokan. His skin was stretched tight over his bones. His eyes were sunken and his skull was prominent, as if it wanted to escape from his body. Somewhere at the centre of his being, something was silently coaxing him towards the void.

A tear formed in the corner of Yosu's eye.

Ryoken said, "'Dewdrop on a lotus leaf,'. Are you going to sit there and let that sake go cold?"

The click clack of the stones provided the soundtrack to their conversation as they sipped the warm sake. The lids of the bowls slowly filled up with dead stones, more black than white, and the sake flask was refilled.

Although Ryokan had deteriorated physically, the warmth and inspiration he had radiated when Yosu first met him at his Uncle Toshio's was just as potent as it was then. This invisible, indescribable atmosphere that he carried everywhere was just as strong as ever it was.

185

The atmosphere around him however was different.

When someone is dying, petty and irrelevant matters leave the room. Nobody needs to explain this. Life becomes too short to be taken up by meaningless trifles and nonsense. The love the people around them feel becomes so powerful it empties the room of trivia, just as lighting a candle empties a place of darkness.

They played in silence for a while. Then Ryokan said, "Do you want to know what I've learned in my sixty years living as a monk?"

"Yes Master."

"*Nashi. Nanimo*, Yosu. Nothing. There's nothing to learn. It's a trick. All we have to do is sit back and watch. When it's time to speak, the words come out of their own accord. When it's time to move on, your legs get moving. If you try to accumulate wisdom you get indigestion. I completed training under my master Tainin Kokusen. Kokusen gave me his *inka*, a certificate saying my study of Zen was complete. I was asked if I wanted to take Kokusen's place as abbot of Entasuji, a large Soto training school. I said, "No" and chose the life of an ensui instead. An *inka* is a bit of a joke. It's only a piece of paper. It means nothing. It's good for lighting the fire or mopping up spilled sake. It's like having a piece of paper with the word '**water**' and expecting it to quench your thirst. *Atari*. "('*Atari*' is the equivalent of saying 'check' in chess. It means 'I am about to take one or more of your stones unless you do something about it.')

Yosu realized a large group of his stones were doomed. He was cornered and couldn't get out.

"Damn, you've got me again. I'm trapped."

"How much did we bet on this game?"

"Er...I don't think we had a bet on it."

"Ah, that's a shame. Fancy another game?"

Yosu saw that Ryokan was enjoying himself.

"Of course, Master. You were lucky then."

"Lucky? Pah. Don't flatter yourself. I could beat you with my eyes closed. How about the loser buys another bottle? And seven stones? You might stand a chance with seven."

After losing the second game, Yosu emptied his purse and Hencho went down to the village to get another bottle. By the time he returned, Ryokan was fast asleep on his bed. Yosu's visit had cheered him up but exhausted him. Hencho slept on Ryokan's veranda, and suggested Yosu spent the night there too. The sake and the long day had made Yosu tired so he didn't need any more prompting to lay down and close his eyes.

Next morning he was rudely awakened by being prodded in the back with a stick. A female voice was addressing him, "You, wake up. What are you doing here on the Master's veranda? Who said you could sleep here? You look like a tramp. Does the Master know you are here?"

"Stop poking me with that bloody stick, will you? I'm awake." Yosu rolled onto his side to see who his tormentor was. He froze in surprise. "Taishin. The last time I saw you was years ago in Gisu monastery, when you were tormenting Abbot Nami."

"It's the famous Zen Face, the last time I saw you was in Gisu, when you also were tormenting Abbot Nami."

"Our old friend Nami." Yosu tugged the *bokken*. "He met his end when he was poking someone with a stick you know."

"Yes. I heard he'd lost his head. That was a weight off his shoulders."

"What are you doing here Taishin? I heard about a nun with a bokken who was running a tea-shop and wondered if it was you. I remember when the carpenter Raigen made the *bokken* for you at Gisu. When I learned that the nun had walloped a couple of horny young monks with it I thought, 'Who else but Taishin?' But how did you end up here with my old Master Ryokan?"

"I discovered the tea-shop on my travels. It was not far from a monastery and was run by a beautiful old lady called Aiko. Aiko was enlightened. She was kind, patient, gentle and wise. The abbot from down the road would sometimes send young monks down for tea, knowing they would get a good lesson in Zen. Those with the biggest egos usually ended up with tea in their laps. She was a wonder to behold. I loved her company and she was happy for me to help in the tea-shop, cleaning and looking after customers. She taught me Zen and she taught me how to make a decent cup of tea. Well, sadly, Aiko died a couple of months ago. She left the tea-shop in my hands, but I wanted a break. I hadn't finished my time as an *Ensui* and decided to take to the road again, although in my heart, I thought I'd eventually return to the tea business and continue Aiko's legacy. There was a poem by Ryokan on display at the front of the shop, and I always thought it would be good to meet him. And when you're a wandering nun, you never know what surprises are in store."

"Hence the *bokken*."

"Anyway Zen Face. What have you been up to since you left Gisu?"

"I don't really like being called Zen Face, Taishin."

"Why not?"

"That's what people who don't know me call me. I'm a monk and an artist. I make good ink and compose *haiku*. I've walked hundreds of miles, from one end of Japan to the other with a begging bowl and little else. I've composed dozens of poems. I've painted piles of pictures. I've made thousands of blocks of the best quality ink you can buy. I've drawn stacks of calligraphy. I've been the companion of Saigo Takamori, the last samurai, and helped him escape from the emperor's enemies. I've helped rebuild a ruined monastery and started a school. I splash one brushstroke of ink on the face of Abbot Nami and everywhere I go, forever afterwards, people say, "Oh look. There's Zen Face. It's all I be remembered for when I'm gone."

"Who cares what we'll be remembered for? We'll be gone. Anyway, it could be worse. If you'd painted a stripe on his backside, you'd be known forever more as 'Zen Arse'."

They both heard Ryoken laugh from behind the door.

Taishin said, "The Master's awake. I'll make him some tea."

Taishin lit the stove and boiled a pan of water. She made three pots of tea. She placed one pot and two cups on the table on the veranda, and another pot and cup next to Hencho, who was waking up on the other side of the veranda. The third pot she took into the hut for Ryokan.

She came out and sat down again opposite Yosu. "He's gone back to sleep."

"So what happened after you left the tea-shop?"

"I slowly made my way up here. The Obon Festival was in full swing when I arrived. Ryoken was having a good time, but I didn't meet him then."

"Why not?"

"He was dressed in drag, and didn't want anyone to know it was him. The whole village knew of course, but they didn't let him know his secret was out and continued the pretence. After the festival I made my way up to his hut, but he wasn't there. You know he loves playing with children." Yosu nodded. "His favourite game is 'Hide and Seek', but he always carries a small ball or two, so there's always something there to play with. I left him a poem:

You who play in the buddha way
bouncing a ball
endlessly
must be the one.
Is it your dharma?

Taishin

He sent me a poem in return:

Try bouncing a ball.
One, two, three, four, five,
six, seven, eight, nine, ten.
You end at ten
and start again.

Ryoken

"I met young Hencho at his hut." She nodded towards Hencho, still under his blanket. "He told me that Ryoken's health was failing, and he wouldn't survive another winter in the hut. Years of sleeping out in the rain and poor diet had taken their toll. He is too weak to collect firewood and too weak to carry water. This is why he allowed Hencho to help him. Kimura, one of Ryokan's followers in the village, invited

189

Ryoken to live with him in his house in Shimazaji. Although he hated giving up his independence, he realized he wouldn't last much longer in the hut. Hencho had been fetching wood and carrying water for him but his health wasn't getting any better. So he reluctantly accepted Kimura's offer and moved down here. He looked around and asked if he could live in the firewood shed. Kimura is sensitive to the Master's needs, so he had the shed cleaned out and made suitable for the new tenant.

"Hencho brought me down here and I met the master again. He changed my life in ways I couldn't have imagined.

"I wrote:

The joy of
meeting you
in this way-
I wonder if it is a dream
I have not awoken from.

Taishin

Kimura doesn't pester Ryokan. We get lots of visitors wanting his calligraphy and cartoons, but most of them just want to make some money from them, as his work is very valuable nowadays.

Shaving my head, becoming a monk
I spent years on the road
pushing aside wild grasses
peering hard into the wind
Now, everywhere I go
people just hand me paper and brush:
"Do some calligraphy!" "Write me a poem!"

Ryokan

"We tell them he had given up painting and *kanji* because his eyesight is so bad. Actually, he can see as well as he ever did, but if people knew that, the place would be like an overcrowded market."

"Yes, I understand. When I lived in the monastery at Gisu, Lord Saigo Takamuri visited and bought some of my pictures. Suddenly, my penmanship became valuable. It wasn't long before I'd get back from bathing in the morning to find a queue of people outside my bedroom. They were all holding sheets of paper. I thought they'd mistaken my room for the toilets and brought the paper to wipe their arses. They paid well for my work, but Abbot Nami kept all the money. He was always encouraging me to do lots of pictures, so he could get fat on the proceeds. I became sick of him and his greed."

"That was when he told you to do one hundred pictures, ripped one up and said he only had ninety-nine. And you asked him if he wanted his Zen Face painting. And you wiped the ink down his fat face and the front of his cashmere robe."

"And since that day, I've been known as Zen Face, the monk who painted Abbot Nami," Taishin laughed. "It's not funny."

Another laugh came from behind the door. Taishin opened it quietly and peeped inside then closed it again and said, "He's still asleep." They both knew Ryokan well enough to know he was awake and wanted to be left in peace.

"So what's been happening to you Taishin, since you embarrassed Nami when he was ' trying to take you on a pilgrimage' and you stood up in the main hall and told him if he really loved you he should say so there and then and he ran out faster than a rat with its tail on fire."

Taishin told him some snippets of her travels, the farmer who wanted his neighbour excluded from the prayers, and how she eventually met Aiko and became a 'tea lady'.

"Tea shops usually have a piece of calligraphy on display in a special place, like in an alcove or on a special shelf near the entrance. Aiko had a poem written by Ryokan, which I read every day.

The rain has stopped, the clouds have drifted away,
and the weather is clear again.

191

If your heart is pure, then all things in your world are pure.
Abandon your fleeting world, abandon yourself,
Then the moon and flowers will guide you along the Way.

Ryokan

His poem found its way into my heart and the desire to meet him grew. I was beginning fall in love with him and I hadn't met him." Yosu smiled. "He's someone who it's very easy to fall in love with."

The days passed peacefully, but Yosu felt uncomfortable living in Kamura's garden, sleeping on Ryokan's veranda. He hadn't been invited and didn't really have anything to do there. Taishin and Hencho were taking care of Ryokan's daily needs, and if he was honest with himself, he thought he'd be more use back in school on the island, teaching with Saigo, much as he loved the odd bottle of sake and game of Go with Ryokan. The desire to head back to Amami grew by the day. Finally, he made his mind up to surrender to what was tugging him back into the China Sea. He told Ryokan of his decision.

Ryokan said, "It's been wonderful to see you again. I'm sorry to see you go, but the wind blows us this way then that. I'm sure the children in your school will be glad to see you back. And I'm sure you'll be glad to be back too." Ryokan reached onto a shelf and removed a scroll of rice paper. He handed to to Yosu.
"Here this is for you. You can put it on the wall by your bed. We've spent many happy times together and I'm grateful Yosu."

Yosu was humbled. He took the paper and untied the string around it. He unrolled it. It contained a poem, written in Ryoken's unique skinny calligraphy that reflected the scrawny monk himself.

We meet only to part,
Coming and going like white clouds
Leaving traces so faint
Hardly a soul notices.

Ryokan

Neither of them mentioned that this would probably be the last time they were together, but in their hearts they both knew.

Yosu had so much to say. The unruly words blocked his throat like a rag ball. He put his hands together, bowed his head. He said, "Goodbye Master." He turned and began his journey back to Amami.

Back from the Dead

Saigo was happy with his life as a schoolteacher. He felt like he was on holiday. But in the back of his mind, he had a suspicion that one day the holiday would end and he'd have to go back to work. When he had been the daimyo, there was always pressure on him for one thing or another. He was entangled in politics. He was caught in a bramble patch. The more he struggled to escape, the more his clothes became caught on the thorns. He was an intelligent tactician, and his services were always valued by whoever he was working with. The emperor in Japan had always been viewed as divine and a command from him was as near as you could get to being asked to do something by a God. Saigo had been chased out of the mainland by the Shoguns who were purging supporters of the Emperor. As far as most people were concerned, Saigo had drowned when he left Kagoshima on the skiff. He'd changed his name and begun a new life on Amani Island. But he felt like a fish hiding in the reeds. He was worried that he'd be found and who knows what would happen then? He was immersed in his new life. It was comfortable and he didn't want it to change.

However, the nature of the world is that it is ever changing, and things were certainly changing on the mainland. Politics constantly involved swings in power and influence. The supporters of the Emperor were regaining some of their authority, thanks in part to the new army Saigo had formed a few years previously, when he was active in politics. Because of the birth of a baby in Kagoshima, Saigo was about to become involved again.

A sailor in Kagoshima was visiting his sister in the town to celebrate the birth of her first child. The guests were eating in the garden and drinking plum wine. The sailor got into conversation with a cousin whose wife worked in the palace of the local Satsuma daimyo. They were discussing politics and the name of Saigo Takamori came up.

"He's dead," said one of the group "He drowned escaping from the shogun's samurai, a couple of years ago."

The sailor said, "No. He's not dead. He didn't drown. He escaped."

"How do you know that?"

"Because I was one of the crew on the skiff who fished Takamori and his monk friend out of the sea. After rescuing them, we dropped them off on Amami Island, and as far as I know they're still there."

Two days later, the cousin's wife repeated what she'd heard from the sailor to one of her colleagues, who told her supervisor. The next thing she knew she was standing before one of the daimyo's samurai, recounting what she had heard about Saigo Takamori still being alive. The news reached the daimyo, and he decided to send someone to the island to verify the story. If the weather was favourable, they should be back in a couple of days.

Saigo was teaching a calligraphy class when two samurai arrived at the school. He handed the class over to his assistant, and walked outside (although everything was outside). The samurai told him that the daimyo had been very pleased to hear he was alive. The situation in the country was constantly changing. Like a farmyard in a storm, the chickens and animals were running around everywhere. The fight between the emperor and the shoguns was becoming more intense. Saigo was no longer secure hiding in the reeds. He saw the fisherman's hook slowly sinking into the water. He didn't want to bite. He told the samurai that he was happy being a schoolteacher and didn't want to return to the mayhem, wars and double-dealing that were part of life in the court. The samurai said that the daimyo and emperor missed his council. He was a voice of sanity in a madhouse and was needed on the mainland. Saigo told them that he was always happy to share his council. He was happy to communicate by letter or receive any visitors from the mainland. He wasn't going anywhere. Those loyal to the emperor took him up on his offer, and emissaries from court regularly appeared at the school on Anami, seeking his advice.

One afternoon, when school had finished for the day. Yosu and Saigo were sitting in the shade on the ancient stone blocks of the old temple, playing Go and sipping sake. Saigo said, "Yosu, you're a monk. You're not supposed to drink sake or waste your time playing board games. War games encourage violence. You should know better."

"Thank you for your spiritual wisdom Master. But how can a board game encourage violence? That's ridiculous, Saigo".

"Well you know that big hollow space beneath the board?"

"Yes. That's there to amplify the sound when you place a stone."

"There's another reason."

"Go on."

"Well that cavity is just big enough to conceal a human head."

"No. You're not trying to tell me…"

"In the days when our land was more dangerous, hundreds of years ago, Go was just as popular and important then as it is now. Sometimes a game between a couple of samurai would evolve into a dispute, or some know-it–all, meddling observer would constantly interfere with the game, interrupting by making comments or unwanted suggestions. Well, you know what samurai are like when they're pissed off. You saw them in action at Gisu monastery. The busybody was sometimes silenced and the argument settled with the removal of a head. The space beneath the board was created for such occasions. You could tuck the head under and finish the game, unless of course black or white had been decapitated before the score was worked out."

"How many points did you get for a head?"

"None. It wouldn't fit in the upturned lid with the other prisoners, so it didn't count. It was simply counted as an automatic victory."

"Well, you'd better be careful, because if you go back to court and get involved in one of their wars, you might end up looking at life from inside a Go board yourself."

Then Nariakira, the daimyo of Satsuma died. His brother, Hisamitsu became the new daimyo, and didn't respect Saigo's seclusion as his brother had. It wasn't long before he ended Saigo's life as a schoolteacher and called him back to court.

He was called back to Satsuma after a year. Hisamitsu appointed him commander of the Satsuma army and he became embroiled once more, in the life he'd tried to leave. Somehow the hook was through his lip and he was being hauled out of the reeds onto the shore.

The Emperor was returned to power. Saigo returned to Kagoshima, where he upset the emporer by organizing a military academy which mainly consisted of faithful samurai.

Conflict between the emporer and Satsuma increased, and things came to a head and another war began. and Saigo ended up fighting the government he had helped put in power. The Satsuma rebels, led by Saigo, marched on Tokyo and started the Satsuma rebellion. The imperial army, led by General Yamagatas, marched on the Satsuma forces at Kagomisha. It was ironic that Saigo faced the conscript army he himself had formed when he was supporting the emperor.

Saigo should have taken Yosu's advice. After a failed siege of Kumamoto castle, the Satsuma rebel army returned to Kagomisha pursued by the emperor's forces. They spent the night on Shiroyana Hill, where they were bombarded by artillery from the army and the imperial navy, who had warships in Kagoshima Bay. By sunrise the rebels had been whittled down to 300 men.

Saigo sat in the shade on the hill outside the town. His mind was racing, so he tried to calm it the only way he knew, by practising *zazen* mediation. His mind raced round like a horse attacked by a swarm of bees. Much as he longed for peace, it was just out of reach. It was like he'd been whisked away from his life on the island the whirlwind of politics and war. He was hooked and there was no escape.

From his vantage point on the hill, he could see Kagoshima below. Their army was almost out of ammunition. They had used most of their supplies in the failed siege of Kumamoto Castle. Saigo was with Beppu Shinsuke, his friend and confidant. "We made a big mistake trying to take the castle Beppu. Now we're out of ammunition. We'll have to resort to the old ways and use our swords."

"There's no more honourable way to die than holding a *katana* decorated with your enemy's blood. We're down to 300 men. The imperial army has 7000. This is the end of the rebellion."

"It's the end of us too, old friend."

"At least we can choose our ending. Not every character in a play can do that. What better way is there for a samurai to die than riding into battle with his comrades, and his sword in his hand?"

"There is no more honourable death than this. If we die this way, we are most fortunate."

"Fires and fights are the flowers of Edo."

"This is indeed the way of the warrior. Bushido has been the steel in the blade of Japan for a thousand years."

"And the stone on which our spirits are sharpened in readiness to meet death."

Saigo walked over to his horse, which was tied nearby. He looked upwards. "It's a perfect day to clash swords with death, comrade."

The remaining three hundred horsemen were ready and waiting. Saigo swung his horse round to face them, pulled his sword from the sheath and raised it above his head, "Brothers, fate is kind to us today. We are handed the greatest gift possible for a samurai: the chance to die in battle, with honour. The path of bushido has brought us to this place where we may fulfil our destiny, which is both pure and simple. This day, when brave warriors faced the guns of their enemy with only swords in their hands and courage in their hearts will be remembered for thousands of years. *Banzai!*"

He wheeled his horse around and set off at a gallop down the hill, followed by the 300 remaining samurai of the Satsuma army. They rode into 30,000 guns of the Imperial Army, which Saigo himself had assembled only a few years previously. .

The old world of bravery, chivalry and honour confronted the modern age of guns, artillery and the power of money. There could only be one outcome. Armed with rifles, the modern army had not been trained to fight with swords. At first they were in chaos. Skilled samurai swordsmen prevailed against an army that relied on guns. For a short time, Saigo's lines held, but in the end greater numbers prevailed.

The hill was cloaked in gunsmoke, the smell of sulphur, cries of courage and cries of fear. The synchronized cracks of gunfire announced swarms of round iron bullets flying through the air at the rebels. They responded with the vicious swish of the sword blades, and the dull thuds as they hacked into armour and bone. .A silent cloud of blood spattered over the grass.

Saigo's heroic charge came to end when an iron ball smashed into his thigh, shattered the bone and severed an artery. He slumped over his horse and his blood ran down the flank and joined the puddles on the grass.

Beppu had been fighting alongside Saigo. He saw what had happened and quickly took reins of his horse and led him out of the fighting and down the hill to a grove where the baggage, supplies and equipment had been stored. Beppu helped him dismount and sit with his back to a tree. The took off his silk scarf and bound Saigo's thigh tightly enough to slow the bleeding. "They must not take me alive Beppu. There is only one way for me to die."

Beppu understood immediately that Saigo was talking about *seppuku* (ritual suicide). "It will be an honour to assist you in any way I can, Lord."

Saigo put his hand into his robe and brought out a piece of rice paper, tied in a roll. He handed it to Beppu. "This is my death poem Beppu. I wrote it this morning."

Beppu unrolled the scroll:

> ***Unable to complete this heavy task for our country***
> ***Arrows and bullets all spent, so sad we fall.***
> ***But unless I smite the enemy,***
> ***My body cannot rot in the field.***
> ***Yea, I shall be born again seven times***
> ***And grasp the sword in my hand.***
> ***When ugly weeds cover this island,***
> ***My sole thought shall be the future of the Imperial Land***

Beppu felt a warm wave flow down through his body. He didn't need to speak. He prepared for the ritual. He placed the razor sharp dagger, called a *tanto*, on a piece of cloth. Saigo would use this dagger to make the deadly incision in his abdomen. He also placed a jug of sake and two small cups next to the *tanto*.

Saigo filled the cups and passed one to Beppu. They toasted each other and sipped the sake. Never had sake tasted so wonderful. They emptied their cups. Saigo nodded to Beppu. They put their cups down. Saigo opened his kimono and wrapped the cloth holding the *tanto* around the blade. Traditionally, the knife was picked up by the blade, not the handle. Wrapping the cloth around it preventing it from cutting his hand. Blood would make the blade slippery. He didn't want to lose his grip.

It was important that the second acting in a ritual suicide, in this case Beppu, should be a skilled swordsman. It was his job quickly, and neatly to decapitate the subject, after the fatal cut had been made. Saigo opened his kimono and raised his tanto. His mind was still. Things were happening automatically, just as when a calligrapher's brush moved itself. Saigo and Beppu were merely observers. Saigo plunged the tanto into his abdomen and cut from left to right. His head bent forwards, allowing Beppu to make the final cut. His blade swung down and Saigo's head was separated from his body. It rolled a short way down Shiroyana Hill, then stopped, staring out to the endless sea.

That night Saigo had said, "Don't let them have my head, Beppu. They don't understand the meaning of respect. If they got hold of his head, they would want to desecrate it in some way. It was important to protect it. Beppu looked around for somewhere to hide the head. Saiko's baggage cart was nearby. Beppu looked through the contents and discovered a wooden chest containing Saigo's Go set. He removed the board. It contained a cavity that looked large enough for his purpose. He wrapped Saigo's head in silk and placed it inside the board. The board was then placed back in the chest, along with two bowls of stones. After Saigo's death, Beppu, and the rest of the samurai drew their swords. Beppu addressed the remaining dozen or so warriors.

"Oh young folk, if you fear death, die now!
Having died once you won't die again."

They drew their swords and charged downhill to their deaths. This was the end of the Satsuma rebellion.

200

When Breath is All Out

Back at the Kimura mansion, the winter was taking its toll on Ryokan's health. His stomach was wrecked by decades of poor and erratic diet. He could no longer digest solid food. Like a filthy restaurant, whatever entered, sniffed the air and quickly departed. He could no longer get out of bed. He had been racked by insomnia for years, and during his final illness, it attacked every night. He was delirious at various times during the day, although in calm moments he continued writing poetry. He was lovingly tended by Taishin and Echigo
.He was as heavy as a bundle of firewood. On the sixth day of New Year, he asked Taishin to put a cushion on the floor by the wall, and Echigo to carry him over so he could sit on it and practice zazen. He sat with his legs crossed in the lotus position, closed his eyes and concentrated on his breathing.

His breath rose up from his navel to the space between his eyes, then descended back to his navel.

Wave comes up the beach. Wave goes back to the sea.
Wave comes up the beach. Wave goes back to the sea.

when breath is all out (up) and stopped of itself,
or all in (down) and stopped – in such universal pause,
one's small self vanishes. This is difficult only for the impure.

from the Malini Vijaya Tantra 3000 BC

He breathed out for the last time. The wave had gone back to the sea and would never return. When Taishin found him, she thought he had simply fallen asleep. When she realized he was dead, her warm safe world cracked open like an egg. All the trivia had flown away. It was replaced by an invisible cloud that prevented thoughts moving in the room. Death saw life as temporary trivia and banished anything connected to it from the space it had created removing a soul. It could sneak back into the room later.

Taishin looked lovingly at Ryoken. He was gone. Only the vessel that had carried him through life remained. The poet and artist had left quietly. The friend, lover, teacher and inspiration were no longer there. They had departed together. The glorious mystery that is a human being was gone.

There were many explanations for where a person went after death, but nobody really knew. Those remaining were simply aware of the invisible hole that existed after they had departed. The entourage of beauty, love, laughter, wisdom and warmth departed in the wake. A band of devoted courtiers following their master into the unknown.

Taishin remembered one summer's day coming across him sitting in the sun, picking lice from his clothes. He put them on a sheet of rice paper so they could sunbathe and jump around chatting with each other. At sunset, he put them back under his robe so they could have a meal before retiring

Ryoken's funeral was held at Kimura's house. It was attended by almost three hundred mourners. Many farmers and local villagers came, including the women he had danced with at the festival. Because transport to and from Amami island was erratic, Yosu didn't hear about the funeral until it was over. His Uncle Toshio, the ink-maker, did attend. Representatives from seventeen temples throughout Japan also attended. Many poets sent verses to the funeral service.

Mourning the Passing of Zen Master Ryoken

Year after Year
We frolicked together in the spring fields
But this year
With whom shall I pluck the young spring greens?

Tomitori Masanari

Having met you thus
For the first time in my life,
I still cannot help
Thinking it but a sweet dream
Lasting yet in my dark heart.

Taishin

After Ryokan's death, Taishin no longer felt comfortable hanging about in Kimura's house and she realized it was time to leave. She wasn't sure where to go, but she knew once she started walking her feet would show the way. She said, "Good-bye," to Kamura and thanked him prolifically for his kindness.

Before she left he said, "Wait. The Master asked me to give you this." He handed her a scroll of rice paper. She unrolled it. Written in Ryoken's skinny calligraphy was

Someday I'll be a weather-beaten skull resting on a grass pillow
Serenaded by a bird or two.
Kings and commoners end up the same,
No more enduring than last night's dream.

Ryoken

"He said it would sit well on the wall of your tea-shop."
She rolled the paper up, fastened it with the thin piece of bamboo string and slid it into her bag. She picked up her *bokken*, said "Good-bye." once more, dipped her head and walked out the door. She turned and headed south for tea.

After eight days walking with blisters on her feet, three nights sleeping in the rain, being eaten by mosquitoes, having her flute stolen by a vagabond and getting diarrhoea from some suspicious tofu, she realized that for this lifetime, following the path of the Ensui had come to an end.

She was happy and relieved when she reached the tea-shop. The sign had fallen into the grass and weeds had grown enthusiastically wherever they could get a grip.

She spent a couple of days putting the tea-shop back in order, cleaning the mess, removing the weeds, arranging the furniture outside, and collecting firewood. Before he left Kimura's house, Yosu had given Taishin a piece of calligraphy in the form of a haiku:

No, no, not even the cherry blossoms,
can equal the moon of tonight.

Yosu

She wove a small bamboo frame for the poem and placed it on the wall. Then she walked down to the monastery to retrieve the things she had left in storage before she left.

She arrived at the monastery and introduced herself to the abbot. He was pleased to see her again, and glad she would re-open the tea-shop. He enjoyed having a place where he could send arrogant novices to get a metaphorical slap from the tea lady.

The abbot sent a young monk down to the storage room, where Taishin's utensils had been patiently waiting for her to return for a cup of tea. He returned with the wooden box. Taishin opened it. The tea-bowls, tea-scoop and whisk lay undisturbed next to the iron stove. She took a small white linen cloth and wiped the bowl to clean it. She then took a small lidded tea-caddy down from a shelf, opened the caddy and sniffed the tea. It was stale. The abbot took the caddy and handed it to the young monk, "Go to the kitchen and fill this with fresh tea."

The young monk carried the box with iron stove and other bits and they walked back to the tea-shop. Taishin opened the box and took out the poem by Ryokan, that he'd given to Aiko.

What is the heart of this old monk like?
A gentle wind
Beneath the vast sky

Ryokan

She hung it in the alcove near the door above the cherry blossom and moon *haiku* from Yosu. She stepped back and looked at the poem.

204

A tear crept out onto her cheek. Despite all her understanding and realization, about the fleeting nature of life and the temporary state of existence, she felt something had been stolen from her. She had loved Ryoken completely, and now he was gone. The world was empty without him. All the scriptures, chants and prayers wouldn't change that. Something beautiful had grown in her life, and now it was empty.

She tidied up the furniture, then arranged the iron stove. There was still a pile of charcoal left in the corner of the hut, so she put enough in the stove to boil a kettle and lit it. It wasn't long before she was sitting in front of the tea-shop sipping a cup of green tea. It tasted good. The sun felt good. She was happy to be back. She felt like she belonged. She soon settled back into a life of infusion. She continued writing poetry and sat every morning in the lotus position for half an hour practising *zazen* meditation. When she had told Ryoken she had difficulty stilling her mind, he had said, "Stop stilling it. Just sit there and do nothing. Let somebody else do all the work for a change. Have a cup of tea and forget about it."

Meanwhile, after Ryokan's death, Yosu made his way back to the island, mixed some ink, picked up his calligraphy brush and joined Saigo teaching. Saigo's peaceful life didn't last much longer. The brambles were tugging him back towards the mainland. The conflict between the emperor and the shoguns was becoming more intense. It looked like all-out war was about to break out. Saigo was an excellent tactician and it became obvious in court that his political and military expertise were needed. There was a new daimyo in Satsuma and Saigo was recalled. Yosu advised him against going back. "You'll be entering a snake pit, Saigo. The place is full of jackals fighting for the biggest scrap of meat from the latest corpse. Nothing is what it seems out there. This world is a shithole of duality and illusion."

"You have such a lovely way with words, Yosu. But we all have our unique abilities and talents. Just as you know what to do with a brush, pot of ink and a sheet of rice paper, I see a tangled political mess and usually know how to untie the knots. Or if I see the formation of an army, I know the best way to attack it. It's my personal form of calligraphy."

"Yes, Saigo. But your brush paints a picture in blood, not in ink. And besides, who will I play Go and drink a cup of sake with after you're gone?"

One morning Taishin heard a noise coming from outside. She went to the door and looked to see where the sound was coming from. She was shocked. There was a column of troops, some on foot, some on horses, making their way slowly down the lane. The line of men stretched as far as she could see in both directions. There were donkeys and small carts carrying provisions, weapons and ammunition. The complete range of armaments from the dawn of time until the present day, was on display: swords, a variety of spears, polearms, pikes, bows and arrows, daggers, short swords, rope, chains, sickles and muskets. Behind each weapon was a highly developed art which involved long and thorough training in the eighteen martial skills. The most prized skills were horsemanship and archery. The most valued soldier was the mounted archer.

They all looked magnificent before the fighting started. Things changed drastically when they began decapitating each other, hacking off limbs, and firing arrows into each other's heads. Such is war. At least they possessed ardent martial spirit, fervent commitment to duty and a willingness to throw their lives away in battle. Everybody dies in the end anyway. It's better to burn out than to fade away. Better to go with a slice than a sliver. Such is the idiotic justification for war.

In the centre of the procession was a palanquin, an enclosed wooden seat, mounted on two long poles. The seat was contained in a beautifully decorated box, with a window on either side. It was decorated with inlaid floral designs, Buddhas and saints floating everywhere. Inside sat the daimyo. The palanquin contained Saigo Takamori. He was on his way to attack the Shogun's army in Edo (Tokyo).

Peering from the palanquin window he saw the sign outside the tea-shop. He was thirsty and thought this would be good place to stop. He called the porters to halt, climbed out and stretched his limbs. He noticed Taishin standing by the door. "Do you have some tea?"

"Yes Lord. This is a tea-shop. Will you take it inside or out?"

"Inside. Are you a nun?"

"Yes, sir"

A guard of a dozen samurai surrounded the palanquin. Riding with them mounted on a horse was Saigo's friend and comrade Beppu.

"Beppu. Shall we take some tea?"

"Yes Lord."

Taishin entered the shop, followed by Saigo and Beppu. Saigo stepped inside. He saw Ryoken's poem and stopped dead. "Ryoken."

"You know his work?" asked Taishin.

"Oh yes. He's my favourite. I've got three or four of his pieces of calligraphy back home. Such a wonderful character. Japan is a more miserable place without him. Did you know him?"

"Yes. I loved him very much. I nursed him until he died."

"Oh. You must be...?"

"Taishin."

"Yes. I've heard all about you. It's an honour to meet you." Saigo put her hands together and bowed. Taishin returned the gesture.

Saigo's eye caught the second piece of calligraphy on the wall. He studied it for a moment. "Yosu."

"You know calligraphy."

"I know Yosu. I got him out of a mess once and saved his head. Unfortunately Abbot Nami didn't keep his. He insulted one of my samurai and paid the price."

It suddenly dawned on Taishin who she was talking to.

"Saigo Takamori. Yosu told me all about you. Your fame precedes you Lord." Taishin bowed again. "I'll prepare some tea."

She boiled the kettle, made the tea, set out the cups and placed them on the table before Saigo and Beppu.

"Why don't you join us, Taishin? We've plenty to talk about, and we won't be here long."

A cloud drifted by and a shadow passed passed over the tea-shop. Taishin joined them and told them about Ryoken's final weeks.

She described his performance in drag at the Obon Festival, and how the village women humoured him and complimented "her" on "her" dress and make-up. She told him how he visited the village as himself next day, and devoured the stories of the "mysterious beautiful woman who was an amazing dancer". Beppu and Saigo found Taishin's stories hilarious and kept asking for more. Eventually, the well ran dry and they sat and watched the army flow past. Life itself marching along the road. She sat and watched it pass by.

The army was marching to battle. They were filled with anticipation, glad to have their comrades around them. Many were marching to their death. Their honour and duty were pushing them along to their appointment with the *shinigami*, sometimes called "Old Fart".

Old Fart sits waiting patiently in his boat, waiting to row souls across the river between Earth and the Kingdom of the Dead. He's exceptionally busy in times of war.

"Yosu told me how he salvaged a child's kite in the kite festival, and found you at the end of the string," said Taishin.

"Yes, I was lucky he was there, and lucky the kite became tangled in the bush where I was hiding. The shogun's samurai were out hunting my head. It never ceases to surprise me how the smallest most insignificant things, like a gust of wind blowing a kite off-course, can make the difference between a person's life and death. And that life can itself determine the fate of a battle, the result of a war and thousands of lives.

"And after the battle, everything turns to dust. Life rolls on and not a name is remembered."

The troops continued to march down the pathway. It seemed like they were going on forever. At first Taishin looked at the faces of the soldiers with sadness, particularly the young men. She became aware of the reality around everybody, like the light around a candle flame. We were all walking towards our appointment with the Old Fart. Dying bravely and honourably in battle gave you an opportunity make a glorious statement with your life, to turn your very existence into a piece of art, and end it with a glorious gesture. This was at the core of a soldier's being.

Saigo and Beppu finished their tea and bade farewell to Taishin. They left the tea-house. Saigo's baggage cart was waiting behind the palanquin. He walked over to it and removed a large folder. He opened the folder and removed a scroll fastened with a thin strip of bamboo tied in a bow. He climbed back up to Taishin, She was standing in the shop doorway listening to the hub-bub of the passing procession. He handed her the manuscript. She put it on the shelf holding the tea cups, intending to read it later when life was quiet again.

Saigo and Beppu rejoined the procession, back in line for their appointments with Death. Taishin felt sadness for such fine young men lining up to die. Then she realized, although she was observing the procession sitting outside her tea-shop, she herself was standing in the same queue. She wasn't marching to war, but she was also in the queue to meet the 'Old Fart' as was everyone else in the world.

She put the kettle on and made another pot of tea. Whatever anyone felt, believed, imagined or desired, there was no escaping the queue. We arrive empty handed, naked, crying and bloody, and leave in the same state.

A Hotogisu Sang

Yosu was happy to be back at school and enjoyed being with the children. The practical needs and problems of the children kept his feet on the ground and hauled them along from day to day. Yosu's philosophical enigmas were chased away like mice by the harsh realities of cut knees, spilt ink and wet pants. He loved the natural, unpretentious wisdom of the children. It was a pity that adults couldn't be as honest and open. Like his old master Ryoken, Yosu preferred the company of children to that of adults.

One afternoon, one of the villagers arrived at the school with a package for Yosu. It was on a small cart, in a wooden box. The box was well made and the lid was nailed shut. He assumed it was supplies for the school and put it aside, to wait until the day's lessons were over. Eventually the children left. He took a metal bar and prised the lid open. There was a letter laying on top. Yosu picked it up and read it.

My dear Yosu,

As usual you were right when you warned me that the world was a shithole of illusion and confusion. (I always suspected as much). Nothing is what it seems and things are constantly changing. Life on the mainland reminds me of when we were floating in the China Sea, tossed around at the mercy of the waves. It looks like another war is about to start, and this time the numbers are against us. The lines of the play are already written and we all know what to say. I'm sending you a couple of things I thought you'd appreciate. I have had a good life, Brother, and knowing you made it more meaningful and more beautiful. You have taught me what's truly of value. For that I thank you.

Saigo Takamori.

There was a flat package beneath the letter. Yosu removed the rice paper and discovered two pictures.

On top was a picture from a life, long ago. It was Yosu's cartoon of the The Wise Abbot. The picture was as outspoken and refreshing as the day Yosu first drew it. It portrayed the corruption of the abbot in no uncertain terms: his greed, his gluttony, his lust and his self-importance. "No wonder he locked me up and wanted me dead," Yosu thought. The picture had become part of Zen mythology. Yosu lifted the second parcel and removed the rice paper wrapping. It was Ryoken's poem about the song of *hototogisu*.

There was a large wooden box inside the case, wrapped in a silk sheet. Yosu lifted it out and removed the sheet. It was Saigo Takamori's Go board, beautifully crafted from kaya wood. It was even more elegantly made than the larger box containing it. Yosu lifted it out. The board had been hollowed out to amplify the sound of the stones. It was lighter than it looked. A smaller box contained two beautifully carved chestnut bowls, with lids for the prisoners. One bowl contained 181 black stones, made from slate. The other bowl held 180 white stones. They were made from Hyuga clam shells, gathered from Okuragahama Beach in Hyuga. These clams had much thicker shells and finer grains than any others. There were three grades of clam stones: *Jitsuyo* (Standard), *Tsuki* (Moon), and *Yuki* (Snow). The stones in Yosu's bowl were Yuki. These were the most highly prized because of their exceptional whiteness and the fine parallel lines running across the top.

The stones were why Hyuga had become the centre for making Go stones. The board contained an enhancement that originated in Korea: two small hooks were fixed on either side of the cavity beneath the board. A string from a musical instrument was stretched between the hooks. As well as a resonating click, when a stone was slapped down, the board also emitted a gentle hum.

When Yosu placed the board down the hum surprised him. He'd never seen a Korean board before. He picked the board up again and turned it over to see where the noise had come from. He noticed the musical string held tight across the inside and was pleasantly surprised. He'd thought the board was trying to tell him something. Before he put it down again, he noticed dark stains on two sides of the cavity.

Somebody had tried to scrub them clean, but whatever it was had soaked into the wood and refused to leave. He put it down and it hummed to him again.

At the foot of Mount Kugami, Ryoken's old hut, Gogo-an, was falling into disrepair. Hencho had long moved out and it was only inhabited by insects, rabbits and the odd fox. The forest was reclaiming it.

I took my staff and slowly made my way
Up to the hut where I spent so many years.
The walls had crumbled and it now sheltered foxes and rabbits.
The well by the bamboo grove was dry.
And thick cobwebs covered the window
where I once read by moonlight.
The steps were overrun with wild weeds,
and a lone cricket sang in the bitter cold.
I walked about fitfully, unable to tear myself away
As the sun set sadly.

Ryoken

On the island of Amami Oshyima, the ruined monastery, where Saigo and Yosu had started their school, was slowly being restored. Its new life was filled with the noise of children rather than the mumbling silence of monks. The ruin was slowly being rebuilt. There were swings and climbing frames where the children played. Parents had erected canopies and gazebos where the pupils could sit in the shade. A small hut contained the growing library and protected the books from mice and rats. The old stone Buddha now sat in the centre of an allotment, where the children grew vegetables.

Yosu sat on the old monastery wall beneath a gazebo and watched the sun set. The moon had already risen and shone brighter as the sun went down. He remembered Ryoken's poem,

Left behind by the thief
The moon
In the window.

A *hototogisu* sang from an azalea tree. On the wall of the gazebo, in a bamboo frame, was the gift from Saigo Takamori. Ryoken had painted a *hototogisu*, next to his poem.

Deep stillness, long isolated from the world.
All night the hototogisu cries.

Over on the mainland Taishin was also watching the moon rise. She had fitted comfortably into Aiko's old role running the tea-shop. Arrogant young monks still came occasionally to 'test her Zen' and sometimes ended up with hot tea in their lap.

She was tidying up ready to enjoy the last of the day. She'd washed the teacups and was replacing them on the shelf when she noticed the roll of paper had slipped down between the shelf and the wall. Saigo Takamori had given it to her before he went to war and she'd forgotten about it. She unrolled it. It was a poem written in Ryokan's familiar, spidery style.

Summer evening- the voice of a hototogisu
rises from the mountains
As I dream of the ancient poets.

Ryokan

Taishin was shocked. Ryoken was speaking from beyond the grave. As the sun sank behind the trees and the moon silently rose, a *hototogisu* sang 'Goodnight'. Taishin would treasure the poem for the rest of her life.

Books I looted and pillaged:
The Art of Zen. Stephen Addis
Zen Flesh Zen Bones. Compiled by Paul Reps.
The Way of Zen. Alan Watts.
Zen and the Beat Way. Alan Watts.
Three Japanese Buddhist Monks. Translated by Meredith McKinney.
The Last Samurai. Life and Battles of Saigo Takamori.Mark Ravina.
Kakurenbo Or the whereabouts of the Zen Priest Ryokan.
        Eido Frances Carney.
Great Fool. Zen Master Ryokan. Ryuichi Abe and Peter Haskel
Dewdrops on a Lotus Leaf. Zen Poems of Ryokan
        Translated by John Stevens.
Sky Above Great Wind. The life and poetry of Zen Master Ryokan
        Kazuaki Tanahashi
One Robe One Bowl. The Zen Poetry of Ryoken.
        Translated by John Stevens.
Shodo. Shozo Sato
Sengai The Zen of Ink and Paper D.T. Suzuki
Life in Medieval and Early Modern Japan. William E. Deal
The Classic Tradition of Haiku. Edited by Faubian Bowers.
Go for Beginners. Kaori Iwamoto

Thanks to:
Gerald Lopez bokken teacher on YouTube.

Pigment Lab Tokyo Ink-makers provided valuable background.

David Waddell for diligent proof reading for no wages.

Geoff Sutton.

My schoolteachers.

My Aunt Connie, who taught me to read and write before I went to school.

My parents, for keeping me alive and loving me.

My friends who encouraged me.

Zen Buddhists and their mums everywhere.

Dot, for unending loving care in the community.

Tim and Luke- two of the best.

You may like to know:
Although Zen Face is a work of fiction, Ryoken, Taishin, Hencho, Kamura and Saigo Takamuri, known as the last Samurai, really existed.

I've taken several liberties. Yosu, Abbot Nami and Polo are all products of my imagination. There is a time warp in the story.

Ryoken was born in 1758 and died in 1831.

Saigo Takamuri lived from 1828 to 1877.

Saigo did become embroiled in the Satsuma wars, and went on the run with a monk called Gesso. To escape capture they jumped from a skiff into Kagoshima Bay. They were pulled from the water but only Saigo Takamuri survived. He escaped to the island of Amami Oshyima, where he changed his name and started a school. He lived there for three years, married to a local girl and fathered a son. But in 1864 he became embroiled in politics again. He was called back to Satsuma, put in charge of the Satsuma army in Kyoto and fought in the Boshin war.

He retired a second time, but was once again drawn into another war- the Satsuma rebellion. He marched on Tokyo with an army of 12000, but faced a force almost four times as large. They were defeated at the Battle of Shiroyama where Saigo was badly wounded and beheaded.

Saigo's death poem was written by General Tadamichi Kuribayashi, the Japanese commander-in chief during the Battle of Iwo Jima in 1945.

Unable to complete this heavy task for our country
Arrows and bullets all spent, so sad we fall.
But unless I smite the enemy,
My body cannot rot in the field.
Yea, I shall be born again seven times
And grasp the sword in my hand.
When ugly weeds cover this island,
My sole thought shall be the future of the Imperial Land

Before the final charge in the Battle of Shiroyama Hill, Beppu quotes a poem by Zen monk and poet Hakuin,

Oh young folk
if you fear death,
die now!
Having died once
you won't die again.

The other poems in the story are written by Ryoken and Taishin.
The details of Ryoken's eccentric life are mainly taken fron 'Curious Accounts of the Zen Master Ryoken,' by Kera Yoshishiga.

Most of the incidents involving Taishin when she was an *ensui*, are found in Zen Flesh Zen Bones, adapted from '101 Zen Stories', and 'The Gateless Gate' by Ekai called Mumon. In the introduction Mumon wrote, 'Zen had no gates. The purpose of Buddha's words is to enlighten others. Therefore Zen should be gateless.'
I've also parodied a well known Zen story called '10 Bulls' written by a Chinese Master called Kakuan. In the preface to the translation of the first edition, it says, "The bull is the eternal principle of life, truth in action. The ten bulls represent sequent steps in the realization of one's true nature. '101 Zen Stories', 'The Gateless Gate,' and '10 Bulls' are all contained in 'Zen Flesh, Zen Bones' compiled by Paul Reps and translated by Nyogen Senzaki and Paul Reps

The poem Yosu wrote on the young girls' kite to help it fly,

Sky above
Great Wind.

was written by Ryoken on a child's kite for the same purpose.

The prayer for the dead, which Yosu he recited for the farmer's wife, came from Kadampa .org modern kadampa Buddhism.

Printed in Great Britain
by Amazon